Until I Find You

Anna Smith has been a journalist for over twenty years and is a former chief reporter for the *Daily Record* in Glasgow. She has covered wars across the world as well as major investigations and news stories from Dunblane to Kosovo to 9/11. Anna spends her time between Lanarkshire and Dingle in the west of Ireland, as well as in Spain to escape the British weather.

Also by Anna Smith:

Until I Find You

ANNA SMITH

A BILLIE CARLSON THRILLER

QUERCUS

First published in Great Britain in 2022 by Quercus
This paperback edition published in 2022 by

QUERCUS

Quercus Editions Ltd
Carmelite House
50 Victoria Embankment
London EC4Y 0DZ

An Hachette UK company

A CIP catalogue record for this book is available
from the British Library

PB 978 1 52941 583 4
EB 978 1 52941 581 0

10 9 8 7 6 5 4 3 2 1

Typeset by Jouve (UK), Milton Keynes

Printed and bound in Great Britain by Clays Ltd, Elcograf S.p.A.

Papers used by Quercus are from well-managed forests and other
responsible sources.

For all the Motherwell Smiths, and Mairi Timmons. For the memories, the laughter and the love.

We think we have time. We don't.

PROLOGUE

She can't feel the pain any more, but she can hear the scream of the sirens. She sees firemen cutting through the wreckage. There's a medic in green overalls kneeling down beside her, his voice gentle, telling her everything is fine, they'll get her out of here. *My baby. Where's my baby?* She's trying to say it, and she knows she's moving her lips, but there is no sound coming from her. She tries to move her head a little to see if she's in the back, strapped into her seat. But a pain shoots up her neck like an explosion. She can see raindrops on the side window, trickling down like tiny tears. *My baby.* From somewhere, she finds strength to grasp the medic's arm and tries to say it again. She sees the confusion in his eyes as he leans in to her and listens. *My baby,* she mouths again, but still she cannot hear her voice. His ear is at her lips. He pulls back, his grey eyes locking on hers for a second, then he looks away. Now there is the sound of metal being dragged and twisted, and she can see the grass verge through the space they've opened up. They are trying to move her, three of them. She can see her shin bone sticking through her skin, blood dripping from it, but she cannot feel her foot. She's dizzy now. Sick rises up her throat and she throws up onto her shoulder as they pull her out. Flashing blue lights, and a siren. She's on a stretcher, and she can hear people talking, radios crackling. But something is happening to her, because now she's icy cold and her whole body is jerking uncontrollably. She can hear her teeth chattering, as someone comes at her with a needle. She hears them saying she's going into shock. Then as they push her into the ambulance, a man's voice, but he's not talking to her.

'She keeps saying "My baby, where's my baby?" But there was no baby in the car.'

Everything goes black.

CHAPTER ONE

I'd read about Jackie Foster and her missing baby in the papers. It had sent shivers through me and gave me a sickening feeling in the pit of my stomach. Then I didn't see it any more. It disappeared. Like everything, life moves on.

In my line of business, you don't get much time for contemplation, which is probably just as well, given that some of what I do doesn't bear up to moral scrutiny. When something's done and dusted, I move on, whether or not it's a happy ending. I'm a private investigator, not a shrink or a counsellor. I find people who don't want to be found, and I find things out for people looking into buried secrets. Sometimes I even find people out, and *that* can be a real revelation. Stories like Jackie Foster's can bombard my head for a few days, and for good reason . . . Then they slip away. I hadn't thought about it for weeks – until the day she walked into my office unannounced.

I was on the phone to an insurance company who wanted me to look into a widow's claim on her missing, presumed dead, husband's wealthy estate. It was shaping up to be my next case. Insurance companies pay well and, unlike some clients, they don't need answers yesterday. But I could hear Millie out in the front office, telling some woman who'd turned up out of the blue that she needed an appointment to see me. The woman kept insisting, and I heard Millie tell her to take a seat. I wrapped up my call and replaced the receiver. I squinted through the space of my slightly ajar door and caught the woman's lean, tired face, the hollow cheeks beneath a shock of lush, jet-black shoulder-length hair. There had been no pictures of her in the news, but from where I was sitting, from the little snapshot I had of her, I could see she was haunted, desperate. I looked away from her and out of the window at the steady drizzle on the red-brick building across the street. I was dog tired. I'd had no more than four hours' sleep, and that was in my car, waiting and watching on an overnight stake-out – the kind of thing I seldom do these days, but sometimes it's the only way to get the picture. The last thing I needed was an unhinged client making demands before I'd even met them. I can be tetchy like that, which isn't always helpful in this business, but I'm not about public relations. I'm not selling anything here, except hope. Mostly to people who hope they'll find some justice or closure, or whatever it is they look for when they turn up at my office and walk through the half wood, half frosted-glass door. Most of the time I am, in fact, their last hope, their last resort. This makes me feel responsible as well as tetchy, if that makes sense. But then again, I also have this sympathetic streak that sometimes bubbles up to the surface. It's part of my historical make-up, part of who I am. And here it was, bubbling up again. There was something about Jackie Foster's face that morning, something about that look, that meant I found myself pushing my chair back and pressing the buzzer for Millie, knowing at that precise moment I might live to regret it.

'Just tell the lady to come in, will you, Millie,' I said with a sigh.

And so she did. The door opened and Millie came in ahead of her, wearing that kind of resentful bouncer look she sometimes has if she'd told someone I'm not available, and I overruled her. You had to get past Millie to get to me. She's what you might call my front-of-house lady in what passes for the office I occupy, three floors up in Mitchell Lane, right in the middle of the city centre. It's a good, discreet address for a private investigator, because of where it's tucked away. You wouldn't wander down Mitchell Lane unless you had some specific place to go.

'Jackie Foster,' Millie said, a perplexed look on her thirty-fags-a-day face.

I nodded and stood up. 'Thanks, Millie.'

When Millie closed the door, I took a long look at the

thirty-something woman before I said anything. She looked back at me, then around the room. Big, watery blue eyes. Something of the frightened rabbit about her. A strikingly beautiful frightened rabbit. She was wearing a powder-blue raincoat, a chic, big-collar, three-quarter-length job, the belt unbuckled. The shoulders were splashed with droplets of rain. And she was limping.

'Hi.' I stretched out a hand. 'Take a seat.' I motioned her towards the faux leather chair opposite my desk.

'Sorry for coming without an appointment.'

'That's all right.' I looked at her as she hobbled over and sat down. 'You could have phoned. I'm in the phone book.'

I said it not to be mean, but to demonstrate that though she'd got this far and inside my office, this was my domain. From here on in, I get to make the decisions whether she goes or stays. And I also just said it to see how she would react. Sometimes, the way someone reacts in a moment like that says a lot about them, and in turn how you will deal with them.

'I didn't know I was coming until I was almost here,' she replied, a rapid flush rising in her razor-sharp cheekbones. 'I mean, I was going to call yesterday, then I decided, no, leave it. You can't do this. And today. Well. I'm here now.'

Edgy. She might be on the verge of ranting. I was watchful. You never knew in this business. I was once sitting here and a man came rushing into the front office with a baseball bat – a case of mistaken identity. He was looking for Joey Balkan the debt collector on the floor above. And he got him. I heard Joey screaming for a full twenty seconds.

'Tell you what, Jackie,' I opened my hands, 'let's just start at the beginning. How about that? You tell me what you've come here for.'

'I don't know where to start.'

'Well, how about why you need a private eye.'

'I . . .' Her voice croaked.

She glanced around the room, up to the ceiling, then down at the floor, as though looking for a way out. I could see it coming with the lip trembling, then her face began to crumple.

'I want you to find my baby.'

Then the floodgates opened. Jesus! Heaving sobs like she'd been holding it in for ever. So much so that Millie came in the door again to check if I was okay. I waved her away. She came back a minute later with a box of hankies and a cup of tea. Good old Millie. A real softie at heart. I smiled at her as she backed out.

Jackie stopped crying and was now dabbing her eyes with a tissue.

'You all right?' I said eventually, but I could see she was far from all right.

'Yes. I'm . . . I'm okay now, I think. I just get so . . . I mean it's so difficult for me.'

I said nothing, just watched and waited. It had to come

from her. No prompting. But her words 'find my baby' had sent a jolt right through me.

'Okay,' she said. 'I'll tell you what happened. Well. Firstly, from the moment my baby disappeared. From the accident. The car crash. It was in the papers, on the television and stuff. Did you see it?'

I nodded. 'I did. I remember seeing it. A crash. But not for a while. There was no name and no pictures.'

'I know.' She drew a breath. 'Well, I was in a crash. My car was forced off the road, into the ditch. Overturned, and I was trapped. I keep trying to remember the moments before it, and sometimes things come back to me, little flashes and stuff, little images of what was going on. But then it's nothing, and I'm in the crash, and there's blood and pain, and sirens and all that chaos around me. My shin bone was sticking out of my leg. I remember that. And then I can see in the back seat that my baby isn't there. I . . . I . . .'

She stopped, and I hoped she wasn't going to break down again. I kept my patient face on.

I let it stay that way for a long moment, and then I said to her, 'What about your baby? How old? Boy or girl?' I wasn't taking notes yet. Notes were for later, once I'd established if I was in or out.

'She was two and a half. Elena. Beautiful, blonde. Like a little angel.'

'And she was in the back of the car as you drove – I mean, before the crash.' I raised my eyebrows, studying her face.

'Yes. Of course. We were singing nursery rhymes. "Miss Polly had a dolly . . ." That one. It was her favourite. She always finished every line for me and she was giggling.' She looked at me. 'I didn't imagine it. I'm not making this up. We were singing and laughing.'

While she was saying this, I was picturing the scene, almost hearing the sound of the little tinkling voice singing in the back seat. Just listening to her describe it gave me an ache in my chest. Because I know that sound too well. It comes to me in the night, haunts my dreams, follows me everywhere, reminding me of the gentle slap of tiny feet on a wooden floor, running towards me with outstretched arms. She paused talking, looking at me, puzzled. I snapped back to the moment.

'The police at the time reported a missing child,' I said. 'Then I saw something in the papers a couple of days later that they were no longer looking for it. What does that mean?'

She avoided my eyes.

'I told them I must have been in shock or something. That I had no baby.'

'Why did you do that?'

'Because whoever ran me off the road must have taken my baby. I've been scared to make any moves since this happened. And I don't think the cops can find her. I don't trust them. I don't trust anyone.'

I looked at her with a 'how do you know you can trust me' expression, which she seemed to read.

'Well, sorry. I don't mean you. I was told to think about talking to you.'

'By whom, if I might ask?'

Now *I* was curious. It's not as if I advertised all over the shop. Most of my clients were discreet, and few would admit to ever having hired me.

'Somebody told me that there was this woman private investigator – an ex-police detective. That you left the force after a shooting incident. Actually, I remember the shooting. It was in the papers . . .'

Her voice trailed off a little, and I stared at her, wondering why she would bring that up at a time like this. The newspaper headline flashed back: 'Left under a cloud . . .' I didn't need reminding of it.

I said nothing. The more I looked at her, and listened to her, I wondered what her background was. Her olive skin gave her a Mediterranean look. Italian or Spanish maybe, but the blue eyes told a different story. Her accent was Scottish, but with the edge off it that people sometimes have if they live in England or further away.

'Sorry. None of my business,' she added quickly. 'But I met a guy I know.' She shifted in her seat. 'He's not a cop.'

I waited, silent.

'And . . . well, not a criminal, not exactly. But he's connected. He said I should talk to you. But I still didn't know if I was doing the right thing.'

I let out a sigh, ran a hand through my hair, pushing it back from my face.

'Jackie. Let me just recap all this. You tell me you have a missing child. You've already told the police at the time and had your story in the papers. That's how people normally go about finding a missing child. But no. You change your story and apparently tell police that you imagined it or something.' I paused, leaned forward. 'I have to say, you're not endearing me to your case and that's the truth. Look, I know you're upset. But if you really do have a missing child, then you need the massive resources the police have to help find her. Okay, they might be wary of you after what you've done – changing your story. But it's the police you need, not me. You must have birth certificates, documents and stuff. You can prove to them you have a child. There must be hospital records – where she was born?'

'That's the problem. I can't prove it. That's why I can't do this in the normal way.' Her voice went up an octave. 'But please, listen to me. I do have a baby. I did have a little girl with blue eyes singing in the back of my car that morning. And she's gone. I think I know who took her, or something of what happened.'

Christ! This woman was either mixed up in something dangerous, or just a nutcase. There were alarm bells ringing all over the place. Yet I couldn't just send her away because I know what it feels like to know that you haven't tried hard enough. That somebody died, because you looked the other way.

'Okay,' I said. 'I'll help you, Jackie. I'll take your case. But you have to be completely honest with me. I'm telling you right now, and watch my lips: if I find one time that you lie or leave things out anywhere in your story or background you give me, that's it. I'm out. I walk away.' I paused. She nodded in agreement.

I explained my fee and upfront payment.

'Do you have money?' I asked.

'I do.'

'Okay. Then let's get started.'

She went into her black leather bulky handbag and pulled out a brown envelope. It was unsealed, and she pushed her hand inside it. I was waiting for her to fish something out, but she didn't. She simply slid the envelope across my desk towards me.

'There's a thousand pounds in there. Cash. That's more than you asked for upfront. But I'd like you to have it.'

I looked at the envelope and placed my hand over it.

'Hold on, Jackie. You don't have to give me cash right now. It's not necessary. That's not what I meant. You can do a bank transfer or something.' I pushed it back towards her. 'And I don't need that much upfront. We haven't even gone through your case yet.'

She reached across and pushed it back towards me. 'But you said you'd take my case. You said you'd help me.'

She looked crestfallen, and there was a twinge of desperation in her voice.

'I will. Of course. I said I'd take your case and I will.' I glanced at the envelope but left it where it was. 'But please, can we have a conversation first? Just take it easy, Jackie. Let's start at the beginning. I need to know all about you. So don't start thinking about how much money this will cost or anything else right now. I need you to tell me your story, as calmly and with as much detail as you can. Every detail counts. You understand what I mean?'

She nodded. 'Yes. Okay. Sorry. I will. I'll start at the beginning.'

She took a deep breath, and I sat forward, with my hands clasped together on the desk. She was about to start talking when her mobile phone jangled in her bag. Without a word, she reached in and pulled it out. Her face froze, and she seemed to be reading a text. Then, suddenly, she jumped to her feet, wincing in pain at the movement.

'I'm sorry. I have to go now. I . . . I need to get out of here.'

'What?' I looked up at her. 'What's the matter?'

But she was already on her way to the door.

'Please,' she said, her voice shaking. 'Please. I'll be back. Just take the money. Hold onto it. I have to go.'

Now I was on my feet and out from behind my desk.

'But, Jackie, I have no details about you. I need more information. A contact number.'

She grasped the door handle. 'I'll be back. Please. I promise. But I have to go now.'

She yanked open the door and fled out, limping as fast as she could past Millie, who looked up from her desk as puzzled as me.

'Nutcase.' Millie shook her head.

From what I'd known of Jackie Foster so far, I should have agreed. But I didn't.

CHAPTER TWO

My dad played jazz piano, and he named me Billie on account of his obsession with the jazz singer, Billie Holiday. It's not a name you want to grow up with in Glasgow – especially if you're a girl. If you were a boy called Billy in this city of bitter religious divide, you're most likely a Protestant. The other side, mostly Catholic of Irish descent, would never call their boy Billy. And nobody, but nobody would ever call their daughter Billie.

I learned how to punch early on in life. Because not only was I called Billie, I also looked different from the other kids. My primary school was a sea of pale, ginger-haired kids, or black-mopped kids with dark brown freckles. I was platinum blonde, pale faced with icy blue eyes, thanks to my Swedish father. So kids thought I was some kind of freak show when I showed up. I got laughed at, and pushed around a lot, until they realised I could scrap like a tiger. Billie Carlson was a tough little duker, the teachers said.

And I was. Unbreakable. Until my father threw himself off the Jamaica Bridge one icy December night and froze to death in the River Clyde. My world stopped turning. My childhood ended there and then. My mother fell apart like the delicate, beautiful flower she was, and she died six months later. I was twelve years old, shipped off to my father's sister in Sweden, where I grew up fast and angry and confused. Some of it stayed with me. Billie Carlson was unbreakable, they said. And she is.

If I was going to help Jackie Foster find her daughter, I'd have to rely on some old pals. I haven't been a cop for the best part of two years now, but I still have lots of contacts. Lots of goodwill among the guys on the front line. Plenty of them would have bought me a drink if they could to congratulate me for putting two bullets in the chest of child killer Charlie Provan. It cost me my job, my career, and always the cloud would hang over me, even though I was cleared by the official inquiry. Only I knew the truth of what had happened that afternoon. And my conscience was clear. But then I have a different threshold when it comes to guilt.

I hadn't clapped eyes on Jackie Foster since she ran out of my office like the place was on fire. That was two days ago. No phone call. No visit. Nothing. She hadn't even stayed long enough to give me a contact number. I stuck her money in my safe and left it there, while Millie nagged me to not even think about wasting my time on her. There were other, easier cases on the list I could be handling, she moaned, and she was right. But I couldn't let it go. In my brief encounter with Jackie Foster, she had got under my skin.

I knew it would involve me digging around in certain areas that would require the help of old mates in the force. But in the Glasgow police they weren't all mates, especially the ones who'd seen me as a fast-track hotshot destined for the top whose fall from grace had been swift and emphatic. But I could still rely on some guys. And Danny Scanlon was one of them – the salt of the earth. We were partners in uniform for the best part of two years as rookies, and detectives together for the next eighteen months in a stint on the drugs squad. It was during that time that I was approached by some shadowy figures from MI5 telling me that I was being earmarked for great things. In fact, I'd been approached before, in my last year at university where I got a first class honours degree, knowing that I'd probably never use it. But if I had any ambitions to enter the world of spooks, the mockers were put on it after the shooting. Maybe it's just as well, because I'm not sure I could have coped with all those clipped accents in the world of Her Majesty's Secret Service.

Danny was already waiting for me in the sandwich shop at the top of the city centre at Port Dundas, far enough away from Stewart Street police station where he worked as a detective. As I said, it's not every cop who would want to be seen openly associating with me, far less helping me on a case. But Danny was too much of a loyal friend, bullish enough by nature, and wouldn't kowtow to the bosses. When I'd called him about Jackie Foster's story, he'd told me no problem, he'd find out everything from the police reports that he could without leaving his fingerprints on the police computer.

'Hey, Billie. How's it going?'

He looked up from his mobile as I walked in, a smile spreading on his handsome face.

'I'm good, Danny. All good.'

It was a bit of an exaggeration, but I'm a great believer that if you say it often enough, you can make it happen. I sat down opposite him, my eyes drawn to the way his neat, pale blue polo shirt strained a little around the biceps on his suntanned arms.

'Look at you, Danny boy. All bronzed and gorgeous. And still working out, I see.'

He shrugged. 'I have to. You know what it's like. This job can kill you by the time you're forty if you don't get out and keep fit. I'd go nuts if I didn't work out.'

I caught him glancing me up and down, in my tight black jeans and jade green T-shirt.

'And you're no slouch yourself.' He grinned.

We'd been flirting like this since we were in police

college, where we formed an instant bond. But that's as far as it went. Danny would never get mixed up with a mixed-up girl like me, and I would never have wanted to jeopardise our friendship for a fling – even if the idea had always kind of appealed to me.

'Well, one of the perks of being self-employed is that I make my own hours.' I sat back and shrugged. 'However, the drawback is that I don't have access to all the information I used to have.'

'Which brings us to Jackie Foster.'

'Exactly.'

The waitress came up and I ordered a coffee. White, no sugar.

'I had a good look through the files on the computer,' Danny said, reaching for his jacket over the back of his chair. He pulled out a white envelope from the zipped bomber. 'I printed some off, but I'll email you more later when I get the chance to go back on. But the gist of it is in there. The accident happened out towards Milngavie, as you know, so they were the ones dealing with it first off. In the ambulance, she kept talking about her baby, but she didn't give a name. So when they thought there was a missing baby, HQ was brought in. Then when she came round a day or so later, this woman suddenly says she must have been in shock – that there was no missing baby.' He looked at me, puzzled. 'So now she's telling you there was?' He screwed his eyes up. 'Is she a headcase? How does she come across?'

I sighed, partly because I didn't even know the answer to that myself, and partly because I knew I was only at the foot of whatever mountain I was going to have to climb on this case.

'I honestly don't know, Danny. But I took her on, well, because my gut tells me that she's telling the truth.' The waitress arrived with the coffee and set it down. 'I get the impression though that there is something wrong with her. I have to say, it sounds like she's telling the truth. But what bothers me is that it might be that she believes this actually happened, you know, that there *was* a baby.'

I didn't want to tell him that I'd run a cursory check with the births register for a child named Elena Foster who would fit the age profile of Jackie's kid, but there was nothing. I was glad when he didn't ask.

He nodded. 'That's kind of the impression we got, from what I can see from the reports. And she actually didn't tell our guys too much about herself at the time – only that in her mind there was a baby. But we have nothing else. Maybe she was just in shock.'

'She did say that's what she told police – that she was in shock.'

'But why do that?' He shrugged. 'Then, of course, she disappeared. Nothing.'

I'd decided not to tell him about her vanishing act from my office, seconds after asking for my help. I didn't want to look stupid.

'She says she doesn't trust the police to find her baby.' I shook my head, frustrated. 'I know it's screwed up, but that's what she said. I just need to look into every aspect of this to see what I can find. I don't imagine, once she told police that there was no baby, that they did much more to find out. Why would they, I suppose, if she's not making an official complaint about a missing baby?'

'I know. I think that's what's happened.'

'What about forensics? Did Forensics take a look at the car after the crash?'

He shook his head. 'Not much, really, from what I see here. They removed anything that was in the car, her belongings and stuff. But there were no kids' toys or clothes or anything like that in the car. No signs of a kid. No car seat.'

I pondered, sipping my coffee. 'But they didn't exactly comb every inch of the car, the way they would if a crime had been committed,' I said.

'Nope. Because within forty-eight hours, this woman tells us there was no crime. That she must have just lost control of the car. Then she disappeared into thin air.'

'What about her belongings? The stuff from the car? Where is it?'

'We'll still have it somewhere, I suppose. Unless it's been chucked. I can find out.'

'Would you do that for me? How about Jimmy? Does he still work in Property? I loved old Jimmy.'

'He does. He's retiring next year. Why don't you give him a call?'

'I will. I need to take this as far as I can, Danny, find out everything and everyone involved in those hours before and after the crash.'

'Up to you.'

I nodded and we sat in silence for a moment. I was conscious of Danny watching me. More than just about anyone in the world, he knew why a case like this would get under my skin.

'Billie,' he said, reaching his hand across the table so that our fingertips touched, 'listen. I know how something like this would get to you – why you would take it kind of personal.'

I wanted to tell him to shut it, it wasn't personal. It was business. It was work. But I knew deep down I'd be lying to him as much as to myself. This *was* personal. I've been there, where Jackie's been – in that dark pit, that primal empty blackness when your child is taken.

CHAPTER THREE

I'd been waiting since eight in the morning in my car around the corner from the cop shop on London Road, and I was starting to look suspicious. This was not the kind of area of Glasgow you read about on TripAdvisor. If you're cruising in this neck of the woods, chances are you're some sleazebag looking to pick up an underage hooker dodging school, working the cheap streets to feed her heroin habit. Or, you're casing some of the shopfronts to pick the easiest one to rob. I watched as the shops strung along the gloomy street pulled up their steel shutters revealing grubby windows, ready for business. I was beginning to think about calling it a day when my mobile rang, and Jimmy Wray's name came up.

'Hey, Jimmy. I was just working out the best greasy spoon to have breakfast,' I said, more breezily than I actually felt.

'Make mine a fried egg roll with a twist of black pudding,

Billie. And hurry up, before anyone comes in. You'll get me hung one of these days.'

'Coming right up, sir. I'll be there in five.'

I've known Jimmy Wray since he was a uniform desk sergeant in Stewart Street, and he'd taken a shine to me as soon as I arrived there as a rookie. He was the go-to guy who always had his ear to the ground. If Jimmy didn't know about it, then it wasn't going on, despite how close to their chests the CID thought they held their cards. Poor Jimmy got shot in the leg and almost bled out one mad Friday night after some Turkish heroin dealer was brought in by detectives from a drugs bust in a city centre dive. Nobody had been prepared for the kamikaze attack which followed, as one of the dealer's cohorts burst in the front door of the police station with an AK47, spraying bullets everywhere. The siege lasted for three hours until the armed response team finally lost patience with negotiations and shot him dead from the top of a tenement building across the street. Jimmy lost a lot of the power of his leg but, still in his forties, he refused to retire on health grounds. So they put him in charge of the evidence room, where property was bagged, tagged and stored awaiting trial. They used to say the evidence room had the best quality drugs anywhere in Europe, and it was probably true. Now and again, Jimmy helped me out with information I'd otherwise not be able to find if I was tracking down something for a client. He told me he would be in deep shit if anyone ever found out what he was doing, and I was careful not to abuse the privilege. I hadn't spoken to him in a while. When I called him on the Jackie Foster case, like everyone else he declared she was the nutter who claimed her baby had gone missing. But he agreed to help me, and said he would dig out the contents from her car that had been brought in from the crash scene.

I went in the main door of the police station and was glad there was no sign of any officers at the front desk. I slipped down to the basement by the stairs and Jimmy opened the door when I buzzed. I placed a paper bag with his breakfast on the counter.

'I got you a black tea, to help burn through the grease, Jimmy. Always look after your heart in this game.'

He gave me a hug. 'Well done, kid.' He opened the paper bag and sniffed. 'Food of the gods.' Then sank his teeth into the roll. With his mouth half full, he indicated to me to take a seat on one of the plastic tubular chairs against the wall.

'Keep your head down while I go in and get this stuff.' He looked at his watch. 'With a bit of luck we'll not see anyone in here much before half nine.'

He disappeared behind a tall row of steel shelving, clutching his breakfast roll.

'So what's this bird like? Is she a headcase?' he shouted over his shoulder out of sight.

'I don't know. To be honest, there's something about her, Jimmy. I'm still trying to find out more.'

There was a few moments' silence, then he emerged, holding a cardboard box.

'What do you mean? Did she not give you the lowdown on everything in her life? Tell you what happened?'

I'd have felt stupid admitting that Jackie had done a runner before I even had her phone number, so I shrugged.

'Yeah. Well. A bit. But not enough.'

Jimmy looked at me as though he could tell I was bullshitting.

'Okay, darlin'.' He pushed the box across the counter as I stood up. 'Have a good look in here and see what you can find. I made a list of the stuff – it's on a tag inside the box. But it's all very run-of-the-mill.'

I looked through it carefully, picking up each plastic bag with a tag of contents. Mints, paper clip, small battery. Receipts from petrol stations, shops. I studied each one of them – nothing for baby food or stuff like that. One of the petrol station receipts was from somewhere on the A74, and I wondered what she was doing down there. I took pictures with my phone of each item, examined them carefully. Drinks bottle, nothing unusual there.

'Where's the car?' I asked.

'Her car?' Jimmy looked surprised.

'Yeah. I wondered if I could have a look in it. I don't expect Forensics swept absolutely everything once they'd been told there had been no crime.'

Jimmy shrugged. 'Suppose not.' He went below the desk

and pulled out a big ledger-type book. 'Let me see. What was the date again?'

I read out the date from the box, and he ran his finger down a list in the book, then stopped.

'The car is down at the pound somewhere, according to this. They'll keep it for a couple of months, then they'll scrap it if she doesn't come back.'

'I'd like to see it.' I held up the keys. 'Keys are right here.' I gave him the most endearing smile I could muster.

He puffed, and shook his head. Then he took a slurp from his tea and sat back behind his desk.

'Tell you what, Billie. I'm going to look away here at my computer and if those keys are not in that box when you give me it back, then I didn't see what happened. But if you get caught, you're in the shit, and so am I. You know I'm retiring next year, so I don't want to bugger things up.' He looked at his watch. 'If you're going down there, go soon before it gets busy with all the angry people whose cars have been lifted from the street last night. Then meet me somewhere and give me the keys back.' He clicked on his computer keys and looked at the screen. 'I must be off my fucking head.'

'You're not, Jimmy. You're not,' I said, stuffing the keys in my handbag. 'I've got a feeling about this. I'll give you a bell.'

He didn't answer and I was out of there and through the front door in less than a minute.

*

The car pound was in a yard behind a high fence two streets away, where a dozen or so cars or trucks were parked up in various states of wreckage. One or two, though – four-by-fours – were brand new, and probably had been seized in a drugs bust and kept while Forensics swept them for evidence. I'd stuck my head in quickly and told the woman at the front desk that I was from Forensics and held up the keys to the car, saying I needed a look at it. She nodded and I saw her giving me a cursory glance as she buzzed open the gate. If you walk the walk, you get away with a lot of things. As long as nobody else came on the scene I was good to have a rummage around for a few minutes. Jackie's car was an old burgundy Hyundai, and I could see immediately where the impact of the crash had been, and the door ripped off where the firemen must have pulled her out. I stood for a few moments, staring at it, imagining the scene that afternoon, the sirens, the urgency, and the panic she must have felt, just before she got run off the road. The image she'd painted of the little girl singing in the back seat burned in my head. But I could see from here there was no baby seat, none of those strapped-in jobs that you have to have by law. Damn. I should have asked her about that when she was in my office, just to see how she'd account for the fact she was driving with a child illegally. Placing her in danger. But she was in and out so fast I hadn't even begun a proper interview with her. I yanked at the back door, which was stiff and out of sync with the body of the car because everything must have been pushed a little by the impact of the crash. It opened after a moment and I knelt in the back seat to look for any signs of straps or a seat having been there at some stage. Nothing. Then I scanned the seat again, and shone my torch around, peering in as I pulled the seat back a little. I saw the loop and froze in my tracks. I could see a mark, as though it had rubbed at the metal clip which attaches the baby seat. Then my heart stopped as I saw further down the seat belt that it had been cut. I looked closer, then across to the belt on the other side of the back seat, which was intact. I know from experience that you don't have to cut any belt to remove a baby seat, though it's always a bit fiddly if you don't know what you're doing. But you definitely don't just slice it – unless you're in a helluva hurry to remove it. But then again, this proved nothing. It could have been there before Jackie even bought the car – if she was actually the owner of the car. I scoured the floor and greying carpet. Nothing. Couple of crisp bags and scraps of paper. Just a messy car. Not even as messy as my own beat-up old Saab convertible that served me well, despite its age. I went to the front passenger seat and sat there in the quiet, just staring. Again, I pictured the scene. Then I opened the glove compartment, but there were only a few handbooks inside. I flicked through one book and could see the last owner. It was bought new from some garage in the Borders, and the next owner was also from there. In the side pocket of the door there were some more mints, and I fished out a piece of paper. It was another petrol receipt, from a garage off the A74, and the date was two months ago. How did Forensics miss this? I stuck it in my pocket. Then I got out and popped the boot open, where a few spanners were scattered among old supermarket shopping bags, and a half-empty bottle of mineral water. I pulled up the compartment where the spare wheel was kept but it was only a wheel. I went to the back seat and took a couple of pictures with my mobile of the seat belt that had been cut, wondering why Forensics hadn't seen this either. Then I closed the door and left, catching the eye of the front-desk woman who buzzed the gate to let me out.

CHAPTER FOUR

It was already dark, even though it was only five thirty in the evening, by the time I pulled up outside my office. Those dark, dreary, long winter days, those bleak afternoons without sunlight and an ever-threatening sky. I hate winters. I spent plenty of them in Sweden where I swear to God there were entire months when the sky was as gloomy and desolate as me. An icy December wind whipped across my face as I stepped out of the car, grateful that at this time of the day the traffic wardens would be at home stoking up their bitterness for tomorrow's victims. I glanced up at the ancient red sandstone building, a stark silhouette against the sky, and the street lamps, and could see that all the offices were in darkness, except for Joey Balkan's, the debt collector. Joey seldom left the office before seven in the evening, and from my window I sometimes watched him scurry up towards Gordon Street and into the biz of the city, as though he was in fear of someone waiting in the shadows to clobber him like before. That kind of shit went with the territory, he told me the day after the baseball psycho left him with a broken nose and smashed cheekbone. I could never figure out why Joey didn't just jack in the debt collecting, but he told me it was a dirty job and that his family had been doing it for generations, working for a big city warehouse collecting debts from door to door. So he kept on going, bringing in the debt, and watching his back.

I let myself in the main door, slapping my fist on the timed light switch on the cold stone walls, hoping it didn't time out until I got off the lift at the third floor. The lift was one of those old-fashioned jobs, the kind with the iron gate you had to pull shut, and which in a bygone era would have had a guy working as a lift attendant, ferrying you up and down. As it shuddered its way up, I could see the shaft getting deeper and deeper, adding to the general eeriness of this grim building in the gloomy light. I made it out of the lift just as the ground floor switch went off and I was plunged into darkness. Shit. But at least I knew exactly where the switch was, just out of the lift door. I dragged the cage open and stepped out into the blackness. As I automatically reached for the timer switch on the wall, I froze. There was a cold hand where the switch should be. And now my hand was over it. Then I felt the heat of a face next to mine, and I held my breath.

'Wh-what's going on?' Stupid question.

Nothing. Just breathing. In the pitch black I couldn't even make out a face. Only the shadow of a hoodie. We both stood there, silent. Then a voice came from the hoodie.

'Jackie Foster. Keep the fuck away from her. Or you're dead.'

'Says who?' I said, standing my ground. So far I couldn't feel a knife or a gun poking into my ribs. And unless this hoodie could really fight, I could take him on. I stood braced, with my legs apart, ready to go.

'Stay away from her. Or you're dead.'

From the level of the breath on my face, I guessed the hoodie was about my height. If he was armed, he'd have done something by now. So whoever it was, I'd take my chances. Before I could stop myself, I lashed my fist back and punched him as hard as I could down where I thought would be between his legs. Bullseye. He buckled over and his hand slipped from mine. I banged on the light as he slid down the wall, groaning, and I was on him instantly, all my old self-defence and police college training kicking in. I'd brought down bigger guys than him plenty of times. I had my foot across his neck and his hoodie had come down. From what I could see he was a skinny guy who couldn't have been much more than twenty, but with a kind of wizened look.

'You move a muscle, son, and I'll choke you,' I warned. 'I won't say it again. You got that?'

He nodded as well as he could with my foot firmly on his throat.

I eased my foot off a little.

'So, speak. Who sent you? Who the hell are you?'

'I'm sorry,' he spluttered. 'Please. Let me go. I . . . I was just sent here. The guy gave me twenty quid. I don't even know him.'

'What guy?'

'A guy that knows my dealer. He said he wanted someone to go in here and wait for somebody called Billie Carlson. I thought it was a bloke.'

I took my foot off his neck. I could see he was no threat, just a skinny bag of bones in a thin bomber jacket and jeans that may have fitted him before the heroin had wrapped its deadly grasp around him. I felt a little sorry for him.

'Sit up,' I said.

He did, watching me, his hands trembling.

'Look,' he croaked, rubbing his throat, 'I'm sorry. I didn't want to do it. But Jimba said I had to. It was stupid. I mean you could have pulled a knife on me or something. Now it's a total rid neck that a bird slapped me down like this.'

I sighed. 'So don't tell him that. Tell him you scared the shit out of me, and that I said, okay, I'll stay away from Jackie Foster. That I only saw her once and I thought she was a nutter. Okay? Got that?' I poked him with my toe. 'Now stand up.'

He got to his feet. I reached out to bang the light switch again before it timed out, and he dodged my hand like a boxer about to be caught with a right hook.

'Relax.' I half smiled. 'I'm not going to hurt you. But, hey, listen. If you want to make some money, then maybe you can help me.'

He shook his head. 'No. I'm scared. I just did it this one time to get money to score. I need to get sorted, man. I have to go. I'm no good at this. I don't want to get involved.'

He was about to go, when I grabbed him firmly by his emaciated upper arm.

'Listen to me,' I said. 'What's your name?'

'Johnny.'

'Right, Johnny. You do this one thing for me, and I'll sort you with a good bung. You go back to your guy and tell him you scared me shitless and that I'll do as you told me – got it? Then try and find out a bit more about who she is – this Jackie woman. If you can find out what the connection is between this guy and her, and why they want me to butt out, then it's worth some readies for you. Understand? Let's see how smart you can be.'

He nodded. 'But I don't know if I can. I mean, I might not find out anything. Maybe even he doesn't know.'

'Well you can try. That's all. Okay?'

He nodded. 'Can I go now?'

I almost smiled at him. Whoever sent him must be pretty stupid to send a shivering junkie on an errand like this. But it was the fact that he'd been sent that was important. Somebody was after Jackie Foster. She'd said as much in my brief encounter with her in my office, then she'd bolted like a frightened deer when she got a text on her mobile. Whatever was going on with her, it was leaving more questions unanswered every day, and the fact that someone wanted to get to her before me began to worry me.

'Sure. You can go. Take the stairs, and go down as fast as you can. I'll keep the light on. But don't go ratting me out, Johnny. Because I'll find out. I'm one of the good guys, I promise. But you don't want to cross me.'

I took one of my cards out of my pocket and handed it to him. He glanced at it and put it in his jeans.

'Aye. All right.'

I watched through the iron walls of the lift at the stairwell as he rushed down on shaky legs to the front door. Then I unlocked the door to my office and went inside, switching on the light. I walked behind my desk and sat down heavily. I should go home now, go to bed, grab some sleep, but I needed to pick up my laptop in case Danny Scanlon had sent me any emails with background he'd dug up on Jackie Foster. I saw from my desktop screen that he had so I opened it and read, engrossed. Three paragraphs into the initial police report, it said that a witness had come forward and told police that he had seen the crashed car on the road that day, as he was a couple of minutes behind it. He said he saw the car overturned and in the ditch, and his instinct was to stop and help. But there was a four-by-four up alongside it, and someone was climbing into the back seat of the crashed car. The witness said he slowed down, and was about to pull over, but a big guy in the driver's seat of the four-by-four got out and waved him on. He said he had felt a little uneasy about it, about not stopping, but from the look on the guy's face he didn't think he should ask any questions. He drove on. But slowly. And a dozen or so yards down the road, he saw in his rear-view mirror someone coming out of the crashed car carrying a screaming baby in a car seat. From what he could see, the kid didn't look hurt. But the guy was taking the baby into the back of the four-by-four. The witness didn't stop. He wishes he had, but he said he felt a little scared. You never know what's going on with people these days, he'd told cops. He didn't want to get involved. I scrolled down to see his name – William McPhee – and address and scribbled it on my book. I scrolled back up and reread Danny's first couple of lines of the email – he said he was surprised this information had not been passed on to HQ by the local police in Milngavie at the time.

CHAPTER FIVE

I didn't want to go home. My encounter with the junkie in the dark had given me a jag of adrenalin. Between that and the information about the witness to Jackie Foster's crash, I knew I wouldn't sleep. But most of all, I couldn't go back to the empty flat. Not tonight. Not with the picture in my head of a child being taken, screaming, from its mother. Because every time the picture came, it was *my* child screaming, *my* baby, my Lucas, somewhere out there sobbing for me. It was almost eighteen months now since I'd lost him, and the grief walks beside me sometimes, crippling me with an ache I can't even begin to explain. I still look for him every single day, refusing to believe that I may never see him again. I hardly ever talk about it, but those closest to me know my pain. His fourth birthday is coming up in a couple of months. Four. My baby boy is four and I don't even know where he is. But finding him is the only real reason I want to stay alive, and that's the truth.

Right now, I needed someone to talk to. I needed a drink – more than one drink. But if the darkness was creeping up on me, then alcohol wasn't going to stop it. Even so, I found myself driving up Charing Cross, towards the bar where I knew I could find Tom Brodie. He would listen to me. He wouldn't judge me – even if I did have a drink.

Tom looked up when I came through the half stained-glass swing doors, almost as though he'd been expecting me. He was sitting at a small round table in the corner, a pint of Guinness and his usual whisky chaser on the side.

'And here she is, a vision of loveliness on a cold winter's night.' Tom raised his almost empty whisky glass as I walked towards him.

'Just what I need,' I said. 'A drink and a bit of flattery.'

He glanced up at me, a flash of concern as though he could see something in my face that I'd hoped I was managing to hide. He raised his eyebrows a little, then cocked his head to the side.

'You're kidding me, aren't you, Carlson? You having a drink?'

I smiled. 'Yeah. Course I'm kidding,' I replied. 'I'm not drinking. I feel like one, but I'd rather have six, and that's not a good idea. But let me get you something.'

He stood up. 'No. You sit down, pet. Take the weight off your little feet. What you having?'

I knew he was opting to go to the bar to save me the strain of standing in front of the array of drinks I might be craving. Tom was saving me from myself, and not for the first time. But he needn't have. I was strong enough to not fall back off the wagon. Sure, I wanted a drink. But not so much that I'd throw myself into oblivion. I trusted myself these days to have the odd one, but only if I was feeling good. Getting drunk was no longer an option for me. Not these days. But I sat down just the same and let him protect me – part of me felt glad that he was, because I don't have anyone older like that, like a father figure, to look out for me.

'I'd like some tea. Black tea.'

'Coming right up.' He went to the bar with his glass, draining it on the way, ready for another.

Tom Brodie was a hotshot criminal lawyer, the best in the business, or he had been. He used to mesmerise juries and lawyers alike when he got to his feet in a courtroom. Whether he was defending a murderer or a jewel thief, the theatre he created was compelling to watch. Young trainee lawyers and seasoned QCs used to come into court to watch him perform. But not any more. Not for the last couple of years. The drink, his wife dying, the loss of his teenage son to heroin, all took its toll. In recent years he'd lost his partnership in the biggest criminal law firm in Glasgow, and these days, with his drinking problem, nobody wanted to hire him any more. Now in his late fifties, he didn't have the nerve any more for court, so he was just about on his uppers. But he worked for me when I needed him, and I didn't do it out of sympathy, because Tom would read and nitpick through complex information for me, give me the benefit of his brilliant mind. I loved him, like a friend, or an uncle, or a mentor who would always look out for me. He knew my story because it was like his, perhaps worse because I have no closure. He knew he would never see his child again. I couldn't accept that I wouldn't see mine. Even though maybe I should.

He came back with a steaming mug of tea and set it on the table with a small straight whisky for himself. He swirled it in the glass, as though relishing its rich, golden colour as a thing of beauty.

'This is my last one, then I'm up the road. I'm honestly trying to cut down.'

I smiled at him. 'I know, Tom.'

'So, what's the craic? What's happening?'

I sighed. Then I told him what had happened today, from the moment Jackie Foster came to my office. He remembered the story from a few weeks back. He listened, taking it in, asking questions, then sat back and took a deep breath, letting it out slowly.

'So, do you think she's telling the truth?'

I waited a moment; he was watching me, studying me.

'I do. I think she is. I mean, she comes to my office, pushes a wedge of money at me. She looks frightened, then runs before I can even get her story. I'm intrigued. And if she is telling the truth, then I need to help her. I felt that way as soon as she left. I got an email just now from Danny telling me that a witness saw the kid being taken. I can tell you, Tom, it really made my blood run cold. Something doesn't ring true.'

He nodded. 'I think you might be right, by the sounds of it. So, what you going to do?'

'I don't know. I wondered if you might have some thoughts. Well, apart from going to see the witness, which I'm doing in the morning.'

'You have to be careful. If this is true, then you need to watch whose cages you rattle.'

'I know. But someone's cage is already rattled, hence the gypsy warning from the junkie.'

'Well whoever sent it isn't smart, that's for sure. But that doesn't make them any less dangerous.'

I nodded. 'I know.'

We sat in silence for a few moments and I sipped my tea, knowing that Tom was watching me and knowing what was going through his mind.

'You know, Carlson, it wouldn't be good if you got all hung up on this Foster woman. I know it's more important to you because of your own situation.'

I looked away from him. My situation. It was a funny way to put it, like it was just an everyday occurrence. I knew he wasn't trying to belittle what was killing me, but he was trying to spare me the mention of my child, my little boy, my heart. People seldom alluded to it, thinking it would be easier. My situation. All of a sudden I felt choked. He could see it, and he leaned over and took my hand.

'You know what I mean, Carlson. If you're going to take this on, you have to try to do it kind of detached – if you can.'

I swallowed. 'Yeah. But if I was detached it wouldn't be important to me. It would be just another case. I can't be detached. Because I can't help but feel our stories are similar. Except that she has someone who saw her baby. I have nobody. Or nobody who has told me anything yet. And if she hadn't come to my office, and if I hadn't asked Danny for help, then Jackie Foster's story would be dead and buried. Like the way I feel about mine sometimes. But now I know about the witness, that changes the game. Maybe there's a witness out there who knows something about my story. I mean, I know that sounds stupid, that I may not ever have that. But all I'm saying is, never say never. That's all. I want to help her, Tom. Because nobody can help me. And if I can help her, then I'll have done something good, for somebody who's feeling what I'm feeling.' I stopped abruptly, feeling my throat tighten.

'I know, sweetheart,' he said, looking across at me with whisky-clouded eyes.

'Do you think I'll hear from her again, Tom?' I asked.

He pushed out a sigh and shrugged as he put the last of his whisky to his lips.

'I don't think you've seen the last of her, that's what I think. Whether that's a good thing or a bad thing, I just don't know. But, be careful, Billie. Promise me that.'

'Of course,' I said, managing a tight smile.

We sat again for a while saying nothing, then he drained the last of his Guinness. I told him that I had a few other cases I might be looking at that I would want him to do a bit of digging for me, and he said he would be glad to. He said he'd been spending too much time in the pub lately, and was really trying to get a hold of things. I listened to him, nodding at all the right bits, but wondering inside if this was just the same old story that alcoholics always told themselves. I offered to drive him up the road to his flat, and he stood up, a little unsteady on his feet, and walked behind me out of the pub door. I dropped him off at his flat in Finnieston and watched him go up the tenement close. His shoulders were drooped and he cut a lonely figure as he disappeared into the entrance.

CHAPTER SIX

I watched the snow falling softly as I sat in my car. From the satnav on my mobile, the address of the witness, William McPhee, looked like a farmhouse off the beaten track, at least two or three miles up the backroads from Milngavie. Just my luck in this weather. It had been snowing steadily all night, and when I woke early this morning the streets were under a blanket of fresh snow. Somehow everything looks silent and calm in the snow, but the reality would be cars stranded everywhere, because Scotland is always, always unprepared for bad weather, for some inexplicable reason.

Nearly an hour later, I finally found myself on a farm road that hopefully would lead to McPhee's house. There were no tyre tracks on the path, so whoever lived here hadn't been out this morning. I made my way up the pathway, my tyres scrunching on the snow. When I got to the farmyard it was a complete whiteout, not a single track or footprint anywhere. A tractor stood abandoned next to a barn, and an old Land Rover Defender was parked a few yards away from the front door. The small windows had grubby net curtains and the place looked creepy and lifeless. I sat for a moment in the eerie silence, then I pulled up my coat collar and stepped out of the car, trudging across the fresh, untrodden path and up to the door. It was one of those big stable-door jobs and I could see it was slightly open at the top. I gave it three hard knocks. Nothing. Then I banged it harder a couple of times, and it opened a little more, as though it had been stiff. I peered inside and saw it was dark. But then my nostrils twitched to the recognisable smell of blood. As a cop I'd been on a blood-soaked murder scene plenty of times, so I knew what that smelled like. I pulled on a pair of surgical gloves, then put my hand inside and slid the bolt across. I pushed open the door, knowing I shouldn't be doing this, that there could be someone in there with a loaded shotgun to blast away any intruder. But I was in, and as I stepped into the room, I felt an icy blast as cold as outside, as though somewhere in the house a window had been left open. The place was freezing, and it was obvious there had been no heat in there for at least a couple of days. I walked carefully across the floor to where a jar of jam lay on the kitchen table next to an unsliced, unwrapped loaf. I touched the bread. It was rock hard. I knew I should leave right now, but I stood there, smelling the blood, curious as to where it was coming from. Then, keeping close to the wall, I gingerly picked my way across to the half-open door of the other room and stepped inside. And there it was. The body of a man, on the armchair by an unlit fire, his mouth gaping open, eyes wide and staring, a hunting rifle pushed into his hand in what looked like suicide, or was meant to look like suicide. Shit. If it wasn't a suicide, then I'd stepped onto a murder scene and now my footprints were all over it. I took out my mobile to phone the cops, then I stopped. As soon as they got here, I'd be thrown out and would learn nothing. After all, they were the ones who hadn't passed this witness's name on to HQ, or had they? And if they had, why wasn't it followed up? Was there any point in even going into that with whatever detective team they sent here to investigate? Firstly, they would see it was me, and once they found out who I was, and my background, they would either be ready to charge me, or be on my side – depending on who turned up. I had no idea which, so I stood, gazing around the room to see what I could find out. I didn't even know what I was looking for, but maybe I would see something. Then I told myself not to be so reckless. They'd find out sooner or later, and if I didn't declare myself now, then they'd be looking for tyre tracks and footprints in the snow whenever they did get here, which could be any time today, tomorrow or next week. The cop in me suddenly had me dialling 999. I went back out to my car, put the heater on at full blast, and waited for the fireworks that might ensue.

*

It didn't take long. Within fifteen minutes the first squad car arrived with two uniformed officers jumping out and approaching my car. I opened the door and stepped out, pulling my scarf up around my neck.

'Morning, officers,' I said, blowing on my hands. 'Billie Carlson. It was me who phoned in.'

The tall fat one introduced himself and nodded as he named his colleague.

'We're just here as back-up until the CID arrive. Can I ask you what you're doing here?'

I looked at him. No way was I going to answer this straight up, because I'd have to repeat myself again and again when detective squad officers arrived in the next few minutes.

'I'm a private investigator. I'm working on a case. I came to talk to Mr McPhee.' I paused. 'But it appears I was a bit late.'

The big cop nodded, the small squat one eyed me suspiciously.

'Billie Carlson, private eye. I've heard of you. Were you not a cop at one time?' the small one said.

'Yep.' Let's not do a this-is-your-life story here, I thought.

'Not that long ago,' he pressed. 'My older cousin is also a cop and he told me about a Billie Carlson.'

'Is that right?' I gave him a disinterested look and turned my eyes to my car. 'It's cold out here. I'm going back inside my car to make some phone calls.' I looked out along the road. 'I'd say the whole squad will be here shortly – detectives, Forensics, et cetera.'

'Did the guy shoot himself?' the big guy asked.

'That's for the detectives to work out,' I said. 'Hard to say from what I saw.'

'Is it a mess in there? Blood everywhere?' he asked, as though he was dying to go in and have a look. Working out of Milngavie, a wealthy suburb on the outskirts of Glasgow, it was mostly rich teenagers getting drunk at weekends. You didn't get to see a shooting victim very often, if ever.

'It's not pretty.'

'But you'll have seen plenty of that kind of thing.' The little smart-arse guy said it pointedly, given my background, and I glared back at him.

'Yeah. I have. Plenty. Most of it when you were in high school smoking behind the bike sheds.' I turned and went to the car, closing the door, quietly seething. Cocky little bastard, who did he think he was, throwing stuff like that at me?

A few minutes later I saw in my rear-view mirror the flashing lights of at least another two police cars, followed by a van, and a couple of unmarked cars. I sat, scrolling on my phone, one eye on the mirror. I watched as the big white van pulled up, the side door opened and a couple of Forensics boys got out and stepped into white zoot suits. I recognised the pathologist, Marion Johnson, from years ago, older and just as po-faced. Behind them, in an unmarked car, I could see trouble on its way. I braced myself as DCI Harry Wilson pulled his big six-foot frame out of the car, lit up a cigarette and stood for a moment as though sniffing the wind like some predatory animal. Then he looked over and turned to say something to his sidekick, and marched across to me. Another CID car pulled up, and I could see Steve – DS McCartney – get out. At least he wouldn't be hostile. There's a bit of history between Steve and me, on and off for a couple of years, and sometimes it ends up in my bed, both of us throwing ourselves into sex more out of need than affection, both of us knowing that's as far as it would ever go.

Because of the contempt I felt for Wilson I didn't get out of the car, but sat there waiting for him. He noticed and rapped the window impatiently.

'Come on, Carlson. Get out of the car and talk to me.'

I opened the door and got out, pulling my coat tight around me. I stood tall, almost as tall as him, and tried to look him in the eye. Not that it had any effect on him. His mind was already made up. He was looking for trouble.

'What the fuck are you doing here, Carlson?'

I gave him my best Who me? innocent look.

'I'm a private eye. I'm on an investigation.'

'And so you walk into a remote farmhouse in a snowstorm and a guy is lying stiff from a gunshot wound. What is it with you?'

'What do you mean? It's a routine call for me, interviewing a witness.'

'A witness to what?'

I said nothing, wondering if he actually knew anything about McPhee, the fact that he had been a witness to the aftermath of a road crash that was still a mystery. But then he was a witness whose name had not been passed on to HQ, so perhaps he didn't know. And if he didn't, then I wasn't about to tell him.

'Sorry, I can't share my investigation with you. It's a client confidentiality thing. You know how it is.'

'Aye. I know how it is, Carlson. And if our forensic boys go in there and find this guy has been bumped off, then you'd better start talking to us.'

I said nothing and stood my ground. I glanced over his shoulder and saw Steve give me a sympathetic shrug.

'Did you go in there?'

'Well I phoned it in, didn't I? So I must have gone in the house.'

'Carlson, if you've been walking all over my murder scene and contaminating it with your boots, then you'll be in trouble.' He glared at me.

I waited for a moment then I answered. 'I didn't traipse about dancing all over the evidence, for Christ's sake. I'm not stupid. I went in. Smelled the blood. Thought, this is a bit odd. Then I was careful where I walked and went into the other room, where I saw him lying on the chair.'

'Did you touch him?'

'No. For Christ's sake. What do you take me for?'

'Did you poke around the house, in drawers or anything? I know what you're like.'

I almost smiled. He knew what I was like because he was my first DI as a young cop and he told me the things to look out for when I went with him on a couple of death calls. But I knew what he was like too. I once saw him planting cocaine as evidence in the drawer of a notorious drug dealer who had murdered his partner in crime. To this day he doesn't know that I saw him do that, but I did, and I kept my mouth shut, even when the guy went down for seven years on planted evidence. He deserved it anyway. But I kept schtum about the fit-up. You never know when you might need a bit of leverage.

'I didn't touch anything,' I said. 'So, are you going to go in and have a look? Who is the guy, anyway? I don't know much about him.'

'No idea. He's not on any radar of ours. He's just a farmer, retired, as far as we can gather. No livestock, but a couple of fields rented out to people for silage and grazing. Lives on his own. That's his Defender there.'

'So you don't know anything about him at all? His name never came up?' I fished.

He looked at me suspiciously. 'No. Should it have?'

I shrugged. 'I don't know.'

'So why were you here?'

'I was here for a client. As I said, I can't tell you.' I turned to my car. 'Look, if you've no further need for me, I've got work to do. One of my lines of enquiry has just bitten the dust, so I have to break that news to my client.'

'Aye, fine. We'll need a statement. Go and tell it to the young detective with McCartney over there, then piss off out of here. But don't be leaving the country.'

'Yeah right!' I said, sarcastic, walking across the yard with a swagger, knowing Wilson was watching me. He always brought that side out in me.

Steve said something to his partner, then took a few steps towards me.

'That's you told,' he chuckled. 'He'll be bitching all morning now.'

I snorted. 'No change there then. I think the big bastard thinks I'm still working for him – ordering me around.' I smiled. 'But we all know what a pussycat he can be.'

'Aye right,' Steve said, nodding me away from the police activity. 'Come over here and talk to me a minute.'

I followed him.

'Don't be giving me your good cop, bad cop routine, Steve. I've seen it all before.'

He glanced over his shoulder, a half smile on his handsome, if slightly lived-in face. We walked a little more and then stopped. He looked at me, his eyes wandering over my hair and my face. Steve was a friend and my occasional lover, but he'd never been a proper-relationship kind of guy. He cared about me, he'd picked me up from some of the dark places I had gone to, but he would never have taken it any further and I wouldn't want him to. He was on the way up the greasy pole of Glasgow Police, and being tied to Billie Carlson with the shadow that hung over her was not good for your CV. I knew it, and that was fine by me, as the one thing I wanted less than a steady relationship these days, was a steady relationship with a cop.

'What you up to, Billie? Are you all right? I haven't talked to you in a while.'

I held his gaze.

'Yeah. I'm okay. Getting on with stuff. I'm busy with a lot of things.'

'What are you doing here?'

'Christ, Steve!' I said, a little irritated. I sensed what he was up to, using our liaison to try and wheedle information out of me. 'Wilson was just asking that. I'm a private investigator. What the hell else would I be doing in the middle of nowhere in the snow? I sure as hell wasn't out for a jog. I came to see this guy McPhee for a client. That's all. But somebody got there before me.'

'How do you know it isn't a suicide?'

'I used to be a cop, you know – and I watch all these TV crime shows!' I made a give-me-a-break face. 'Come on, Steve. For someone like me or you, it's fairly easy to spot the suicide, or the murder made to look like suicide. Somebody shot this guy with his own rifle and took the trouble to put it in his hand and make it look like he took his own life. Your forensics will confirm that before the day's out. But who the hell is William McPhee? Why shoot him?'

He shrugged. 'Who knows? Robbery? A fall-out with other farmers. It could be anything. The troops are all here now, so we'll be doing the usual routine. But why did you want to talk to him?'

As much as I knew I could trust Steve to help me in a crisis, something as sensitive as the police not passing on a crucial witness to HQ was another matter. If that got out, the papers would have a field day. So either he knew, and wondered what I knew, or he didn't. Either way, I wasn't going to tell him. I couldn't trust him that much. But my instinct told me he knew something. I also didn't like the way he was trying to grill me. We may have slept together a handful of times, but that didn't mean he had any rights to my life.

'Come on, Steve. You know I can't do that. But I wasn't here on anything other than routine business. I could have done this last week or yesterday, but I just happened to walk in here today. Though, by the looks of things, he's been sitting there like that for some time.'

Steve glanced across at the big DCI glaring over to him, then he turned to me.

'The boss is waving me over. You going to give a statement to my mate?'

'Yeah. I'll do that, then I'm off.'

We were walking back when he turned and said quietly,

'You fancy meeting for some dinner later? Or a drink. Well, I know you don't drink but, you know, go out?'

I didn't look at him. I knew what he meant. And the thought of losing myself in a few hours of passion with Steve-no-strings had a certain appeal that could make me forget everything for a while.

'I don't know. I'll have to see what's on. I've got some work to do. I'll let you know.'

'Yeah,' he said. 'Sure you will, Carlson.'

He knew I wouldn't.

CHAPTER SEVEN

I was getting close to the city centre, snaking along the Clydeside Expressway behind a line of traffic, when my mobile rang. I could see it was my office, and Millie's voice came on as I hit the hands-free key on my steering wheel.

'Millie. You made it into work in this white hell.'

'Yeah. That's devotion for you. Might as well be working as holed up watching movies and eating crisps. Where are you, Billie?'

'On my way back. I was over in Milngavie. I'll tell you about it when I get in. What's up?'

'Guess who phoned looking for you?'

'Who?'

'That girl. That Jackie Foster.'

My gut did a little twitch.

'Really? She phoned in? When? What time? Did you get a number from her?'

'Hold your horses, lady. She phoned about ten minutes

ago. Very short call. She sounded shifty, but kind of desperate too. I'm beginning to feel sorry for the kid.'

'So what did she say?'

'Only that she needs to talk to you. Now. She wants to meet you.' There was a pause, and the sound of papers being shuffled. 'Here's where she'll be. A place called Bar Gonzalez. I looked it up. It's at Bath Street on the corner of St Vincent. A basement place.'

'I know it. Studenty place, mostly. Bit of a dive though.'

'She says she'll be downstairs there. If you can meet her in ...' She paused again. 'Well, about fifteen minutes because she called ten minutes ago.'

I was at the back of a long line of traffic, and automatically wheeled into the inside lane that would take me off the Expressway so I could swing up to the city centre. Horns were honking as I slipped out in front of a couple of cars.

'I'm on my way. If she phones again, tell her I'll be there pronto.'

'Okay, Billie. Good luck.'

The stairs to the basement were slippery from the snow and I had to hold onto the iron rail as I picked my way down. Pushing the door open, I scanned the gloom of the deserted bar, and caught a whiff of last night's stale booze and spillages from the sticky carpet. The only customers, a young couple, glanced up at me, then went back to wolfing down what looked like a bowl of hangover-curing stew. The barman pushed himself off the counter he was leaning on and looked in my direction. I couldn't see Jackie anywhere. I stood by the door thinking of going out and waiting for her in the street. Given her track record, she'd probably got as far as the door and done a runner. Then I saw her. She leaned out from behind a wooden snug, at the far end of the bar. In the few times I'd been here in the past, I hadn't even realised the snug existed. It was one of those fake wooden small-door jobs to give the place the look of an old-style Glasgow bar where you could hide from crowd. It worked, because if she hadn't been looking for me, she could have stayed hidden. I didn't nod or acknowledge her, but went straight to the bar and ordered a tea.

'Still snowing?' the barman asked as he placed a mug below the font on the water machine.

'Yeah,' I said, because I didn't know what else to say and I didn't want to make idle chat.

I turned and walked across the room, and I could see Jackie straighten herself up, a glass of what I hoped was soda water on the table, and the same edgy, tired look she had on her face when she ran out on me three days ago.

'Thanks for coming,' she said, just louder than a whisper, her voice a little husky. 'I'm sorry for running away.'

I didn't answer, just searched her face for an explanation which didn't come.

'You want a drink?' I asked, blowing on my hands. 'I'm having tea. Bloody freezing out there.'

She shook her head.

I went back to the bar where the guy had placed a black mug of tea on the counter and a small jug of milk. He gave me a look that made me think he was curious whether I was the woman in the snug's drug dealer or her social worker. Jackie didn't hide her desperate look very well, which was not a good thing for someone who is apparently hiding from whoever the hell was after her. I gave him a blank look back and put three pound coins on the counter, took my tea and went back to the snug. I closed the door behind me and sat down.

'So,' I said, taking a sip of tea and warming my cold hands on the mug. I can never seem to get my hands warm in winter, no matter what I'm wearing. 'You want to tell me what's going on?'

She swallowed and nibbled her lip nervously, and I hoped she wasn't about to dissolve like the last time we'd met. But she managed to keep it together – just.

'I . . . I don't know what to do. I've been hiding in a hotel for the last couple nights. I've nowhere to go.'

I said nothing, hoping she would continue. She did.

'They're after me. They won't stop till they find me. They've got my baby. I . . . I need your help.'

I put my hand up to stop her.

'Jackie,' I said, 'we've been here before. You told me

someone took your baby, you said they were after you. But who? You need to take your time and tell me. Who has your baby? Tell me what happened. I can't help you unless you spill it all out. Come on now. Just take it easy.'

I could see she was on the verge of tears and her hand trembled as she sipped her drink.

'What's that you're drinking, by the way?' I asked.

'Just mineral water,' she said. 'I don't drink.'

I shrugged as though it didn't matter, but I was glad she was sober.

'Okay. Just curious,' I said. 'Go on. Talk to me.' I glanced over my shoulder. 'Are you sure you're comfortable here? Do you want to leave, we can get in my car and I'll take you some place else?'

'Maybe,' she said. 'In a minute. But I want to talk to you a bit first.'

I spread my hands in a let's hear it gesture and waited.

'I have something they want – these people who took my baby,' she began. 'That's why they took her. The guys who forced me off the road that day. They were following me. They caused the crash. I panicked and it just happened. I lost control of my car. Next thing, I was in the ditch. If I hadn't been in such a bad way with the crash – trapped and with my leg ripped apart – they would have kidnapped me too. But there was no time for that. They couldn't have got me out of the car, so they just went in and took the baby from the back – to bargain with. They know I'll come looking for my baby. They know they can get to me through her.'

'Okay, slow down a bit. For a start, who are "they"? Are they criminals?'

'Yes.'

'British? Glasgow guys? You know them?'

'No. I don't know them. I know a couple are Scottish, but they're all connected, and there are some Turkish guys too. I didn't know that in the beginning, but I heard later.'

'What have you got that they want?'

Silence. I watched her staring into the middle distance as though she was picturing an image or a scene, her expression a mask of fear.

'The tapes, the discs. I've got the recordings. The evidence. Except that, well, I don't have it now.'

I let it hang for a moment, hoping she would elaborate, and wishing that I didn't have to tease this out of her.

'Tapes of what?' I said, trying my best not to sound frustrated. 'Evidence of what? Come on, Jackie. You need to help me out a little here.'

'I was there,' she said, her voice dropping to a whisper.

I could see the fear in her eyes as though she was remembering something she saw, something that terrified her so much she was scared of even talking about it.

'Where?' I leaned across, closer to her, locked my eyes on her. I found myself reaching out and touching her wrist, feeling her flinch. 'Where were you, Jackie? You need to tell me.'

She was either trying to find the words, or didn't know where to start, but we sat that way for a long moment. Then she swallowed and spoke.

'I was in the room,' she said softly, her eyes dropping to the table. 'In the basement room. Where they made the films. Porn films.'

She brought her eyes up to mine as she said porn films, as though she expected me to show disgust or contempt, but I showed nothing, said nothing. So she made porn films. I wondered what had happened in this girl's short life that brought her to a dingy basement to film sex scenes. She shook her head as though she was looking back, remembering, and suddenly embarrassed and ashamed. I wanted to tell her she had no need to be, but I was more anxious to let her tell the story.

'I worked for the escort agency, you know, meeting clients, spending time. Sex. Most of the time.'

Again her eyes dropped. She picked at her chewed fingernails. I said nothing.

'I'm not ashamed of that,' she said quickly.

I shrugged. 'Nor should you be,' I said. 'But you don't have to tell me that. It doesn't matter to me if you made porn films, Jackie. What matters is why you are here, where is your baby. That's why I'm here. To help you.'

She nodded and blinked a kind of thanks that I wasn't judging her.

'So, go on,' I urged.

'It was through the agency that I got asked if I wanted to earn some real money making porn films. I didn't know anything about it, obviously, except what I'd seen on the telly. But they were offering me two thousand quid for each film. That's a lot of money to me. So I agreed. I didn't even know anyone who did it – except for one young girl I saw there the third time I went. She was very young and that surprised me. We didn't talk much, but she said her name was Hannah.'

'Have you ever seen this girl again?' I asked. 'I don't suppose you had a contact number or anything, in case you wanted to keep in touch?'

'No. It wasn't like that. We barely talked. You don't make friends in that kind of shit. You just do your bit and get out. I just saw her that once and that was it.'

Already my mind was working overtime on who makes porn films – anything I might have picked up back in my days as a cop. But nothing came to mind, except a Glasgow guy who was busted years ago for a haul of imported porn movies. It wasn't my case, but from what I heard they were gruesome, murder movies of victims hacked to death in some far-flung hellhole. For all anyone knew it might have been staged well with special effects; it could have been all theatre and nothing else. The guy got jailed but

I had no idea what his name was or what happened to him. Or even if it was relevant to what she was talking about. But I made a mental note to have a look at the background on it.

'And did you make many films?' I felt it was better to lead a bit of the conversation because right now it was like pulling teeth.

'Yes. I made three. They paid me the money. Six thousand pounds. And that was it. It was enough money to get me and my baby a rental deposit and furniture for the flat. I had just moved in. I was happy. I was getting another job in a hotel as a receptionist, and my life was going to be different.' She paused, sniffed. 'Then I got another call from them and they asked if I would take part in another film. This time they said it would be five grand.'

'Five grand?' I said. 'That's a helluva lot of money.'

'That's what I thought. But I wasn't going to argue with that. I mean, the other movies involved me getting naked and apparently having sex with this guy – but I wasn't actually having sex. The film didn't show the actual sex, because that didn't happen.' She stopped, looked away. 'Though I did have to perform oral sex on screen for the movies I already made.'

Out of curiosity I wanted to ask her if she had any idea where these films were marketed, in what country, to what audience. But it wasn't the time, so I kept my mouth shut, and raised my eyebrows for her to go on.

'So I agreed to the next movie for five grand. I turned up to the place – the same place, the basement. I can show you where it is. Outside of the city. It's in a kind of industrial estate – you know, different units and stuff.'

I nodded, hoping she would stick with this now, but half expecting her phone to ring again and for her to do a runner.

'When I got to the place this time though, there was a minibus there, an old battered thing, parked outside the building. And I could see through the windows there were about five or six people in it. Women. Foreign-looking women, and also men.'

'Foreign-looking?' I asked. People always said foreign if someone didn't look exactly like the way they did or the people they were used to. 'What do you mean, like from what country?'

'Two or three looked like they were from Eastern Europe. But I don't know for sure. And two were Asian. They looked very young. Later, I overheard someone saying they were from Vietnam.'

'Refugees, you think? People trafficked?'

She nodded. 'Exactly. I'm sure of that. People trafficked. But Christ! I didn't know that, or anything about them. I only went there to make a movie. There wasn't anything like this before. The only people were the film makers and the men I was acting with.'

I was glad I didn't say 'acting?' out loud, because whatever she was doing as the cameras rolled in that creepy basement, it wasn't acting. I managed to keep my face straight as she tried to go on. But I could see she was beginning to fidget and get stressed, her face becoming flushed.

'You all right? You want some more to drink? Tea or something? You seem upset.'

She nodded. 'I am. Because the next part still scares the shit out of me just to think about, never mind tell a stranger.'

I said nothing, watched and waited.

'It seemed to take for ever for the film to get started. I was standing around in the little back room off the studio, and the guy who was the director, or whatever he was, told me that there would be a bigger story to this film, that it was about punishment for people who had done something terrible. He said it would be violent, and asked if I was okay with that. I was beginning to get a bit scared. I asked him what he meant, and he said not violent to me, but something might happen briefly at the end, after I had done my bit. He said I had to turn away, and just forget I ever saw it. He was clear about that. I was freaked out. I told him I didn't want to do it, but he said I was the only actress there who spoke English and it was necessary for the film. I asked him who the people were in the minibus, and he gave me a look and said they were actors too. Then he reminded me that I had agreed to it, and it was too late now to back away.'

'What?' I asked, confused. I was beginning to get the drift of what kind of film this was, and my stomach was starting to knot. 'Why didn't you get the hell out of there at that point?'

She looked at me, a little startled.

'You don't think I tried? That's exactly what I did, Billie. I told the guy no way, I want out of here, I'm finished right now. Keep your money, I said. I want no part of this. Then another guy came in, who I didn't know. A big hefty guy, and he came over and put his hands on my shoulders and pushed me onto a chair. Then the boss man – I didn't know at the time but found out later he was Turkish – came across and he leaned down to me and said this into my face. "You will do what you're told. Your little girl is waiting for you with our friends, and when you finish here you will get her back."' She shook her head. 'I was totally dizzy with shock. What was he talking about? My baby was with my childminder where I'd left her that morning. But just looking and listening to the set-up there made me think that they were telling me the truth. I don't know who these people were but they were frightening, and I was terrified in case they were telling the truth. I immediately took my phone out and called my childminder and tried to act all calm and asked whether everything was all right, and she said yes, and that my friend came for my baby and she gave Elena to him.' She shook her head. 'I mean, fuck! I can't believe she was that stupid. She gave my baby to someone she didn't even know.'

I shook my head in disbelief. I know what that moment feels like. The cold, stomach-dropping fear that your child is gone.

Jackie went on to talk about the film and her small part in it, which involved her being in bed when a knock came to the door. At first she'd thought it was a set-up, all staged.

'Then I realised it was really happening. They brought this Vietnamese guy in and they started to slap him around a bit. Then they bludgeoned him with a baseball bat, filming all the time. I felt sick rise in me, and I had to get out of there. I covered my eyes with my hands. But then I heard his screams and I took my hands away and I saw what they did. They hit him on the head and slit his throat and the blood squirted out across the room and ran down the camera lens, and that was it finished. The guy was dead.'

I'd seen a few grim things go down in my cop days, and heard a few blood-curdling confessions from sick bastards, but this was off the scale. Snuff movies, beating a man to death, right here in the city, hidden in plain sight. How can that happen in a city like Glasgow and the cops never get an inkling of it? Jackie was crying now, remembering, ashamed, terrified, a whole surge of emotions flooding through her, and still the agony of her missing child, and running away from these people. My heart ached for her and I didn't know what to say.

'What about the rest of the people?' I asked. 'The women in the minibus? Do you know what happened to them?'

She shook her head.

'No. I had to calm myself down so I could get through the afternoon and then leave calmly and get my child. But the cameraman liked me, and he'd been hitting on me before, and it was him who drove me back to Glasgow when it was finished. He said it would be fine if I kept my mouth shut, but that these guys were dangerous. He asked me to go out with him for dinner but I said no. I just wanted to get home to my baby.' She paused. 'It was the next day that he phoned me and asked me to go out again. He said that he was finishing with the filming and he was quitting the job with these people. So I agreed to go out with him that night. And while we were out he started saying to me that he had the films and the tapes and stuff and he had this idea that he would use the films for blackmail. He said he had other films, from a while ago, and that there was some cop or something who was part of the operation – the people smuggling. It was weird. I don't know why he told me all of that.'

'A cop?' I could feel my eyes widen. 'He said a cop was involved in people trafficking? Are you sure about this?'

She nodded vigorously.

'Yes. I am. That's what I was told. Definitely. I know who

he is. I've seen him. He was in the basement that day, and I hadn't seen him before. I'm not sure of his name though – but I think the photographer said something like Hewitt. But I can't prove he's a policeman. The photographer told me he was a policeman in Glasgow.' She stopped, her eyes darting around the room then at the door as though she expected someone to burst in and grab her. Then she leaned across so that our faces were close. 'But that's not all. There's cocaine too. A load of it.'

'What?' This was getting more complex by the second. 'Where? I mean what has the cocaine got to do with all of this?'

'It's all part of this gang's operation. They move cocaine. Sometimes using the trafficked people as mules.'

'Jesus.'

'So what about the cocaine? How does it fit into your situation?'

She didn't answer for a long moment, but she had a guilty look.

'It was in my flat. The cameraman told me if I could keep it in my flat for a couple of days he would give me two grand. He said he had a buyer for the cocaine, and he was going to blackmail people with the films. He was figuring it out. I don't know why I agreed, but I did. It was stupid – the stupidest thing I've ever done in my life. He brought the coke and hid it there in a cupboard. Along with the tapes. It was only for two days, he said.'

I almost knew what was coming, but I waited for her to say it.

'It was there for two days, in a cupboard. But now it's gone. All of it. The cocaine and the tapes. He must have come back when I was out and taken it, because the next day I looked and it was gone. These guys think I have it stashed somewhere. They were phoning and texting, but I said I didn't know what they were talking about. And that's why they took my baby. When I wasn't answering my phone I thought they would come for me, even though I hadn't given them my address. So I just packed up my baby and did a runner.' She pushed her hand through her hair. 'But somehow they must have been following me, tracking me. Because that day – the day of the crash – I was driving on that country road and when I looked in the mirror I could see someone was following me at speed. I tried to speed up, but my car is old. They were right at my back and I was terrified. I knew it must be them. Then everything happened so quickly – I felt the car getting shunted and I lost control of it and went into the ditch. I must have been knocked out for a few minutes with the impact. All I remember was the pain in my head and my leg felt like it was ripped open and I knew I was trapped. Then as I came to I managed to turn my head a little and look in the back to see if Elena was all right. But she was gone. That's all I remember.'

I watched for a few moments, expecting her to start

crying but she didn't. She just looked straight back at me, the dark terror in her eyes. 'He must have taken the stuff from my house. The cameraman. He left it there, and said he'd be back that night. But I never saw him again. He must have come in somehow when I was out and taken the stuff.'

'Christ almighty,' I heard myself murmur. 'Who is the cameraman? What's his name?'

'Lenny. His name is Lenny Dale. I don't know where he lives though. He says he's from Glasgow. I'm not even sure if that's his real name.'

'Did he give you any phone number or anything like that?'

'He gave me a mobile. But when I phoned it, the number seemed to be dead.'

'So who is he going to blackmail with the tapes? I mean, these guys aren't public figures – they're hoodlums, so blackmailing them won't do much good. Unless he was threatening them with going to the cops. But that wouldn't work, because he's the cameraman, and that makes him just as guilty as them. He's the one filming while they killed a guy.'

'Yes. He filmed it. I don't know who or what he was planning with the blackmail. I was stupid even to agree to it in the first place. Look what it's cost me. They took my baby. He was never going to give me any money for stashing it – he just wanted the stuff hidden at my house, to take the suspicion off him, then he did a runner with the lot.'

This was a lot to process, but one question had been niggling me from the moment I met Jackie, and it was now niggling me more than anything. I wanted to see the whites of her eyes when I asked it.

'Jackie,' I said, making sure she was looking straight at me and not fidgety and glancing away the way she'd mostly been since I'd sat down. 'I want to ask you something, and I need you to be completely honest with me. Understood?' I knew I sounded a little cold, but I wanted her to know that I wasn't interested in any half-baked truths.

'Of course,' she said, her face open and eager. 'Anything.'

'Your little girl, Elena,' I said, and waited a beat while I locked eyes with her. 'I checked the births registry, here in Glasgow, and across Scotland actually, and there is no baby girl born that fits Elena's age, or with you named as a mother. Can you tell me why that is? Do you have a birth certificate? Is she registered somewhere else?'

I watched as her face blanched and the willing look she had a moment ago faded. I waited. Her eyes dropped to the table, and she picked at the raggy skin around her chewed fingernails. The bar was quiet before, but now the silence was deafening and I half expected an explosion of emotion at any moment. Eventually she looked at me, and it was as though the wind had been punched out of her as her shoulders sagged and her eyes took on a look of sheer defeat. When she spoke her voice was barely audible, croaking.

'I . . . I . . . I didn't register her. There was no time. When she was born, I had to run. They were going to take her from me, so I ran. A couple of days after she was born, I ran. I had it planned. And I've been running ever since.'

Then the tears came. I had a million questions that needed answering, and it seemed the more I looked at Jackie Foster, the deeper the mystery ran.

CHAPTER EIGHT

I went back to my office even though it was after six in the evening, because that's where I do my best thinking. Something about sitting at a desk, often just staring at a blank screen on the computer, or zoning out watching the people in the street below, helps me figure things out. It kind of gives me an anchor, a normality, even when all around my head there might be chaos and regret and pain. If it hadn't been for work when my life hit the skids, I might not be here today. When my baby was stolen from me, because that's the only way to put it, there were days, weeks when I couldn't even get out of bed. After the initial frenzy of the police pulling out all the stops to find out where he was, the inevitable meltdown happened. And in time, it was work that got me through, gets me through. It gave me somewhere to go, and it still does.

I don't have a lot of friends – well, not close ones anyway. There were a couple of girls and guys from university and we had all been pretty tight for a while, but real life took over when we graduated, and apart from the odd dinner to catch up, we slowly drifted apart and moved on. Once I became a cop, that sustained me. It had everything I wanted – excitement, camaraderie among the officers, and every day another human story, another investigation to pick apart. That was enough of a life for me to be going on with, and I was happy, driven. Over the years I'd had the occasional lover, more often than not a guy would come into my life and last for a few months until I got bored with him, but I wasn't looking to build a nest by any means. That's why it was so out of character when I threw in my lot with Bob Bradley.

After my meeting with Jackie Foster, and the bucketload of terror that spilled out of her, I was trying to process it all, trying not to let the horror cloud my judgement and work out a way forward. Putting aside the porn movies, I now had to check out her story about going on the run with a newborn baby – far-fetched though it seemed. Back in the bar, when she'd eventually composed herself enough to tell me what happened, I'd asked her to give me real details, dates, addresses, so I could check out her story. She did. There was nothing exotic or fascinating about her tale, and it was the kind I'd heard in domestic bust-ups over the years as a cop. She told me she was living in London and in an abusive relationship with a wealthy coke-head boyfriend who would fly into rages and beat her black and blue. When she got pregnant, he told her his parents would take the baby, look after it, and they could continue living the party lifestyle, holidays abroad, endless socialising. She'd been shocked that he would even think that she would give up her baby, but within weeks, the parents were all over her, showering her with gifts, suffocating her, promising her the baby would be better off with them where it would have a real chance at life. Jackie had no money and no means to run, so she played along with it, until the final weeks when she contacted a friend in the Borders who came to her rescue. She had left in the dead of night, her friend waiting outside the house, and she never looked back. Jackie said she wasn't as afraid now of the ex-boyfriend or his wealthy parents because of the time and distance she'd put between them, though she still worried. But she hated herself because this time it was her own fault her baby was taken, and she would never forgive herself for that.

I had the details of the hospital where the baby was born, so there was something to look into. But first, I needed to look at her claims about the cop in the porn den.

If there *was* a cop at the centre of this, then it might explain a little of why the witness statement about seeing the aftermath of the accident was not passed on to HQ. Was the cop she was talking about the one in charge of taking the statement? It was hard to believe that a serving police officer would be involved in the murky world of people trafficking and cocaine smuggling, even if I did come across some shady cops in my day. But being part of kidnapping a baby? And snuff movies? That was just beyond the pale if it was true. But, even if it was, it didn't explain why, when HQ *did* eventually get the statement from William McPhee, it didn't set off major alarm bells. Why were HQ not all over this? Even if Jackie Foster had disappeared without trace after she left hospital, they still had a witness who had driven past immediately after the crash and had seen a child being taken. Why hadn't they acted? I checked my email again from Scanlon where it mentioned the statement from William McPhee. And the answer was right there. The police officer involved in the initial report was PC Hewitt. A little explosion went off in my head. That was the name Jackie had said. I sat back in my chair looking at the email, checking the time frame. When I saw McPhee's body this morning, it looked to me that he'd been dead for at least a couple of days. So that was it. Perhaps the reason Hewitt – if it *was* Hewitt – didn't pass the statement to HQ was because he had his own plans for this witness. If McPhee was the only witness to see the child being snatched, and he was now dead, then nobody could confirm that there was ever a child in the car in the first place. Case closed. But it was at least a couple of months since Jackie's kid was snatched, so why wait this long to get rid of the only witness? There was nowhere for me to look for an answer to that. But no doubt now, once detectives joined the dots after finding McPhee's body, they might find his witness statement, and start to ask questions – too late for Jackie's kid, though, who could be anywhere. I sat back, put my feet on the desk and worked out my next move. I had to find out who this cop was, where he lived and everything I could about him. And I sure as hell couldn't ask another cop. But that wasn't a problem. I opened my laptop – the one I use for the kind of work where I don't want to leave my fingerprints anywhere. Of course, it was illegal, and so was tapping someone's phone, running a check on their bank accounts and credit cards to find out what they've been up to. But it wouldn't be the first time I had crossed that line. I have a very basic threshold of justification for every dodgy thing I do. If the person I'm spying on is a nasty piece of work – cheating on a long-suffering spouse, or covering up a terrible crime, scamming an insurance company from sheer greed – then I'm in. I once tracked a guy and got him busted for causing his old mother's death when her house 'accidentally' burned down. I make no apology for any of it. Especially this one. And if this cop was everything Jackie Foster said he was, then he was getting the full twenty-four-seven treatment. By the time I finished with him, I'd know more about him than his own mother. In fact, if he was who she said he was, then I'd see that he was nailed to the wall, and I'd do it for free – any day of the week.

It took all of five minutes to get his name, address, date

of birth, and where he worked. Sure enough, there was a
serving cop called Thomas Hewitt working out of Milngavie
police station – the closest station to where the accident
happened. That fact sent a little jolt through me. What in
the name of Christ would possess someone in his position
to swim in the sewers like this? His bank account details
were next. He was well overdrawn, so he was a spender.
Then, trawling back two years ago, there was a substantial
overdraft. I was getting warm. Credit checks showed that
he'd been refused credit after non-payment of car loans. A
cop of five years' service, he would be on the kind of salary
that allows you to pay your mortgage, have a decent car
and have plenty left over to enjoy yourself. Especially if you
were single, which this guy was. So something was going
on here that had changed his life in the last eighteen
months.

I looked at my watch, then out of the window where the
snow had turned to sleet. I was feeling tired. Not ready-to-
flop-into-bed-and-sleep tired, but that jet-lag feeling that I
have almost constantly these days from restless sleep and a
troubled mind. It had been a long day, and I knew the darkness of the conversation I'd had with Jackie would keep me
awake tonight. So I'd have to wait until I was collapsing
with exhaustion before I went to bed. A wave of loneliness
washed over me as I watched the streets below, people heading home or out for the night. I had nowhere to go except
back to the desolation of my flat where everywhere I looked

I could hear the sounds of my little boy's laughter, the images of him in the bath giggling at the soapy bubbles on his little chin like a beard. All that I had left was the smell of him, and that was beginning to fade from the T-shirts and sweaters I kept in his room that still sat there like a shrine to him, because I will never give up the belief that he will come back to me, that I will find him. The day I give up that belief, I won't want to exist. I swallowed what could easily become tears if I wasn't careful.

I jotted down on my notebook the address of PC Thomas Hewitt. I knew the block of flats in the Merchant City. I made a call to Milngavie police office asking for him by name and was told he was off duty but would be back on at two in the afternoon tomorrow. So he would have to be home some time this evening, if he wasn't already. I switched off my laptop, put it in the drawer and locked it. Then I put on my coat and scarf and locked up. I slapped on the light in the corridor and pressed for the lift, watching it make its creaky clanky way to the fourth floor. One of these days, that lift will stop halfway down and I'll freeze to death before the morning comes. I changed my mind and took the stairs.

CHAPTER NINE

The Merchant City. It's where the wealthy tobacco lords, who got rich on the back of slavery, lived in their fine mansions and plied their trade in sprawling warehouses a couple of hundred years ago. When I grew up it was just changing from The Trongate – big sandstone tenements that were home to some of the poorest families in the city. From London Road to Argyle Street it was big discount warehouses and fashion shops where you could get rigged out for Christmas for under fifty quid, and credit offered all the way to hook you in. If the clothes fell apart by February that was tough shit, because this was where you were. The Trongate and the stretch that led into the city centre around Candleriggs was where you went for your clothes if you were poor, and the truth is it was the honest-to-God beating heart of the city back in the day. But now it had been rebranded the Merchant City, smart and gentrified, cobbled courtyards and atrium ceilings to the grey

Glasgow sky. And from champagne bars and gin shops to sushi restaurants nestling next to Cuban and Lebanese eateries, this was the place where you got dressed up to go out on the town. Changed days. As a cop on the beat from London Road police station I found myself in a few of these renovated flats over the years, the smart ones in the four-up tenements, where at one time there used to be set-in beds and grimy windows looking out at the smog. But this was the new, trendy, chic Glasgow, and people will tell you it smiles better. I'm not so sure it does.

I managed to get a parking space just across from the flats in Glassford Street where Hewitt lived three up. I kept the engine on to heat my numbing toes, and phoned his house phone from one of my burner phones. He answered. I hung up like I was a cold caller. He was home. Now what? I couldn't just go up and knock his door like a Jehovah's Witness, and there would be no mileage in that anyway. I had already seen several pictures of him online, from his cop ID card to his Facebook page, where he had a profile under a different name. He was also on Tinder where he was looking for 'fun and a bit of adventure'. That covered a wide remit, depending on your definition of fun and adventure. If what Jackie Foster said he was involved in was his idea of 'fun and adventure' then Hewitt was one screwed up guy and he deserved everything that was coming to him. It was just after seven, and as he was not on shift until tomorrow afternoon, my instincts told me that a guy like him would not be sitting in watching Netflix on the sofa. He'd be out on the town doing what young, single men do on a Thursday night. My stomach rumbled from hunger pangs and I remembered I hadn't eaten since midday. I'd give him an hour here, and if he didn't show, then I'd grab a takeaway and go home.

I scrolled down my phone for the mobile number Jackie Foster had given me, and pushed the ring key. Despite Millie's protests, I'd told Jackie she could stay in a flat I owned just off Maryhill Road and that I rented out long term. It had been empty for the past two months since the last tenants left, and I was hoping it would be occupied soon as the money always came in handy. It wasn't the best set-up to let Jackie stay there, and I suppose it was crossing the investigator–client line, but I didn't want her disappearing on me again, and she couldn't afford to stay in a hotel for much longer, so I told Millie I was letting her stay there. The usual warnings came with her reply that I didn't know Jackie Foster from Adam, and that her track record so far had unreliable stamped all over it. I hadn't even told Millie about Jackie's brief stint as a porn star, or any of the other horrifying things she'd told me, because that would truly freak her out. But I'd picked up the keys and handed them to Jackie when I dropped her off up at the flat, and she promised she'd stay indoors and wait for my call.

Her mobile was ringing out, and my vivid imagination

was seeing her bludgeoned body bleeding all over my steel-grey carpet. Eventually she answered.

'It's me, Jackie. How you doing? You took a while to answer. I was getting worried,' I said.

'Sorry, Billie. I was in the bath. I'm okay. I had a Chinese meal, and I'm just going to watch some television and go to bed.'

'Has anyone rung you?' I asked. 'I mean, any of the contacts from the agency or the other mob? Anything at all?'

'No. Why? Do you think anyone is following me?'

Her voice sounded suddenly agitated.

'No,' I said quickly to reassure her. 'I've no reason to think that. I was just wondering.'

'I don't think they'll call me,' she said. 'They're looking for me, that's for sure. They'll keep looking till they find me. But I don't care about that right now. I just want to know if my wee girl's all right. If someone could just tell me that.'

She sounded like she was ready to break down, and because of what she'd told me earlier about running all her life, I could see why. I could imagine her holed up in that flat, terrified to make a move, all the time worrying and agonising about her baby, because if she'd told me the truth earlier, then she'd been hiding long before she'd become involved with the sick porn-flick mob. My gut was telling me to go to the cops with this and let them run with it. Get her story out there. Somebody, somewhere, must know something. But it niggled me that perhaps they'd had the witness statement from McPhee and hadn't acted on it. What if HQ hadn't acted because Hewitt was part of the gruesome, murderous gang? Surely not, I told myself.

'Where are you?' Jackie asked, sparking me out of my thoughts.

'I'm trying to track down the cop. Hewitt. I want to have a look at him. He must know something. Or at the very least, he knows who's involved. I'm going to watch him for the evening; that's if he comes out of his house.'

'You know where he lives?'

'Yeah. That was the easy part.'

From the corner of my eye I saw the main door open in the block of flats and there was Hewitt coming out of the door. He stood for a moment, took a packet of cigarettes out of the pocket of his leather jacket and lit up. Then he looked up the street, first in my direction and then up towards Ingram Street, and started walking. I watched from my rear-view mirror until he was almost at the corner.

'I have to go, Jackie,' I said. 'Get some sleep.' I hung up before she had time to ask any more questions.

Then I got out of my car and walked briskly behind him, keeping a discreet distance as I watched him turn into the Corinthian Club bar. I crossed the street and waited a full five minutes, keeping my eye on the door in case he came back out. When he didn't, I crossed the road again, and went inside.

The Corinthian Club, by its very grand name, sounded like some exclusive den from the British Raj, where old colonials frittered away the hours, marinated in gin. In reality it was a former High Court building that had seen some of the city's worst thugs and villains sent down for their crimes. As a green detective constable a lifetime ago, I have vivid memories of trying to stand my ground in the witness box, giving evidence while a defence lawyer attempted to tear me to shreds. He didn't win. These days, The Corinthian is a four-storey playground for those who party hard, any night of the week, in its labyrinth of bars, brasseries, rooftop terraces and dance bars. A famous haunt of highly paid footballers, where they can take their pick from the array of eager young women dressed to impress in the hope of bagging a rich footballer who'll give them the kind of life they've only seen on reality TV shows. Fair enough. I just don't get it. The girls all look the same, with eyebrows like caterpillars and pillow lips that defy the principles of all those angry women who burned their bras in the sixties. I felt decidedly out of place in my black heavy wool coat and polo neck, with my jeans tucked into my leather riding boots, as I made my way to the bar. But it was a week night, and though there were plenty of women dressed like it was mid July, the place wasn't that busy yet.

I slid onto a high stool at the bar where I could have a clear view of the room, and cast my gaze around looking for Hewitt. I spotted him at the far end, at a table opposite three other men sitting in pine-coloured wicker chairs. Whatever else this was, it wasn't a Tinder date. I kept my eyes on them long enough to get the sense that two of the men might be Turkish. It was hard to tell, but it was beginning to look like Jackie's information about the foreign men was spot on. What was Hewitt doing with these guys? I needed to get closer, because I had a top-notch recording device in my pocket that picks up clear conversation from a few feet away. And I also had a hidden camera in the clasp on my bag that would give decent enough video footage to get a photo grab so that I could find out who these guys were. Times like this, I missed being a cop, because nine times out of ten in surveillance, I'd be working with another officer and we could pass ourselves off as a couple on a night out. I looked around the area where they were sitting to see if there was anywhere suitable for me to sit without sticking out like a sore thumb. Just then, a group of half a dozen thirty-something guys on a night out came in the main entrance and made their way up to the bar, standing smack in front of me, obscuring my view. I used them to disappear from the bar with my glass of soda, then walked across the room, passed a few other groups standing around podiums, and managed to find a seat three tables away from where Hewitt was sitting. A good-looking man on his own was on the table next to me, and he glanced up from his phone as I sat down. I hoped he didn't think I was trying to get close enough to pick him up. I did what everyone does when they're on their own with nobody to talk to. I took out my phone and began to look at it, while switching on my recording equipment. I placed my handbag on the table facing Hewitt and the others, and hoped for the best. They were absorbed in their own conversation, and didn't even notice I was there. The phone man at the next table looked at me again and half smiled. I didn't return it. The last thing I needed was someone coming over to chat me up. The music in the bar was low and jazzy rather than the thumping it would be later in the night, so I tried to tune my ears in to their conversation. The one closest to me – he looked Turkish – was talking the most, his brows knitted and lips tense as he seemed to be emphasising his point, gesturing with his hands. He spoke in broken English. He looked agitated and impatient. The big man next to him was trying to placate him, and I listened intently, hoping my device was picking up more. His voice was pure Glasgow hard man.

'Listen, Mehmet, for fuck's sake,' he was saying. 'You just need to calm the fuck down. We'll find her.' He glanced at Hewitt then at the others. 'It was your fucking man who lost her anyway. You were supposed to be following her everywhere, but you managed to lose her.'

This seemed to take the wind out of Mehmet's sails and

he said nothing. They sat in edgy silence for a few moments, then Hewitt spoke.

'The problem is, guys,' he said, 'we need to get this fixed. I'm under pressure now because of the witness. HQ are all over this. I've already been questioned by my own boss for not passing the information on.'

The big Glasgow man turned to him.

'What did they say? They're not making any connection between you and everything else, surely to Christ. I know cops. Believe me, they're not that fucking bright.'

Hewitt took the jibe and didn't answer back. No balls, I thought. Or he was just shit scared.

Eventually the other man, dark-skinned, thin-faced, tousled black hair, spoke. 'One thing the police will know, though, is that a baby was taken from that car. Even though the witness is now dead, that's still a problem.'

Nobody answered. My heart actually missed a beat. It was *them*. *They* took Jackie's baby. *They* got rid of McPhee. *They* were part of the brutal murder of an innocent Vietnamese man, who they'd trafficked for a sick movie for even sicker people. And here they sat, the scum of the earth, plotting their next move. If I'd had a gun, I could without compunction have removed each and every one of them from the human race.

CHAPTER TEN

I watched from my car across the street a little later, as all four of them left The Corinthian and went their separate ways. From the direction Hewitt was going in, I assumed he was heading to his flat. But I was more interested at that moment in the other three, who got into a blacked-out Merc, which was driven away by the big Glasgow crook who seemed to be running the show. I followed them three or four cars behind until they went through the city centre and up Charing Cross, and turned into the long wide stretch of Argyle Street that leads down towards Finnieston and the West End. They pulled up at a Turkish kebab takeaway. Then, to my surprise, all three went inside. I was pretty sure they weren't on the hunt for a good kebab, so I sat for a few moments before driving past slowly to see if they were at the counter. They weren't. Wherever they had gone when they went through the front door, they were no longer there.

I could see what looked like a plastic curtain across a doorway separating the front shop.

I'd seen enough for now. I took a picture of the shopfront and phone number. I was about to drive off when suddenly there was a loud bang on my window and the face of a man with a maniacal expression and bulging eyes pushed against the glass. I froze. Before my brain even registered to push hard on the accelerator, my driver's door was yanked open and I was being dragged out of the car by big hands digging into my shoulder with a vice-like grip. I struggled, still strapped into the seat belt, but the huge beast didn't seem to clock it. When he realised, he took one hand off my shoulder and clicked the belt free, and with the other hand grabbed me by the hair and pulled me out of the car. I could feel my legs go limp with shock as he pushed me up against the car and shoved his forearm under my neck, choking the breath from me. In that moment I glimpsed his face – big, fleshy pockmarked cheeks, brownish complexion and thick black hair.

'What . . . What do you want?' I managed to say, even though I already knew.

'Wait!' he said. 'You come with me!' He spoke in broken English.

He was thickset and powerful, but slow in the way he was trying to make sure I was held down, while attempting to turn me around. I knew what he was doing. He was trying to straighten me up and frogmarch me across the road to the kebab shop. If I went in there, chances were I would not come out. I resisted and tried to push him. I kicked his shin, but he didn't flinch. I grabbed the handle of my door and held on tight. He tried to prise my fingers off but I struggled against him. Then somehow I managed to wriggle my head in such a way that his forearm and the back of his hand were within biting distance of my mouth. I bit down hard. So hard that I could feel my teeth sink into his flesh, and he let out a yelp, stunned, as I clung on like a wild animal. I could see the shock in his eyes as I wriggled free. Then, before he could overpower me again, I was quickly behind him. I grabbed a handful of his thick hair and bumped his head twice, as hard as I could, onto the door sill of my car. I heard his skull crack. He groaned and tried to grab me again, but he was no match for how quickly I jumped into my car, pushed on the accelerator and sped off. I tasted blood in my mouth and retched and spat onto a handkerchief I grabbed from my passenger seat. When I was far enough away, I pulled into a side street and picked up a bottle of water from the seat. I opened the door, rinsed out my mouth, then spat again onto the road, my gut retching again. I sat back in the car, locking the doors, my heart pounding in my chest. I was more concerned that I might have caught something from biting into the beast's flesh than that they might still be after me. I quickly opened my glove compartment and pulled out the travel medical kit I kept there. I snatched a small bottle of disinfectant out of it and took a gulp, again rinsing my mouth, opening the door and spitting. I took a deep breath, put my foot down and drove off. I wasn't sure where I was going, but I needed to keep driving until I'd calmed down. Eventually I got up as far as Park Circus and parked the car, trying to work out what the hell had just happened. Who had this guy been? He was obviously one of the henchmen with the hoods who just went into the kebab shop, but I hadn't seen him earlier. I cursed myself for the schoolboy error I'd made, not checking all the cars around me as I'd pulled up at the kebab shop. Perhaps he'd been there the whole time for his bosses' security. Whatever. I should have checked. I could have been bloody murdered. I waited there in the darkness for a good fifteen minutes. I'd survived this time, but I vowed to be more vigilant.

I was still firing on adrenalin but resolved to go home and have a long hot bath after whatever microwave meal there was in my fridge. I turned my car around and headed for home. Just as I did, my mobile rang on the passenger seat and I glanced down at the screen. A mobile number I didn't recognise, and no name. I pushed the answer key, but nobody spoke for a long moment.

'Who's this?' My voice was sharp.

No answer.

'Okay. Whoever it is, I'm hanging up.' I was about to push the end key when I heard a voice.

'Billie. It's . . . It's me. Johnny . . . The guy from your office that day. In Mitchell Lane.'

From the slurring, I guessed it had to be the junked-up wreck who'd been sent to warn me.

'How you doing, Johnny?'

'Awright.'

Silence for several beats. Whatever he was phoning me for, it wasn't to tell me he was doing okay. But after what I'd just been through, I didn't have the patience for a jacked up heroin addict trying to work out what day it was.

'You phoned me, Johnny. What's going on? You got something to tell me?'

'Aye. You said I had to phone you if I heard anything.'

'I did,' I said, a bit brighter than I'd been. 'And have you heard anything that might interest me?'

'Aye.'

'Good. Well. Go on then?' Christ almighty! I wondered if anything he told me would even be half believable.

'Right. Can I meet you somewhere and tell you?'

I glanced at my dashboard clock. It was only nine. I knew exhaustion from the shock of what had just happened would hit me at some stage like a brick wall. But sleep could wait a little longer. I needed to hear what he had to say.

'Where are you?' I asked.

'Anderston. You know the flats?'

I did indeed know the flats, and on a freezing sleety

night in the dark, it's the last place I wanted to be going without a posse.

'Can you meet me in the street? Not in the flats. Meet me in Argyle Street, just before the flats?'

'Aye. Awright then,' he said. 'When?'

Christ. Wake up, son. I was shaking my head as I answered.

'Well, now, Johnny. You phoned me! But listen. Are you all right to talk? You sound a bit out of it.'

'I'm awright. I can talk. I just sometimes forget things.'

'Fine,' I said, turning my car in the direction I needed to go. 'I'll be there in ten minutes. I'm driving a black Saab. You know the kind? A convertible. But obviously the roof isn't down tonight.'

My attempt at humour was completely lost on him.

'I'll see you then.'

'Ten minutes,' I said and hung up.

I drove down to Charing Cross and headed to Anderston. The flats are a long five-storey job and the road into it leads to a square with another block of flats, kind of like a fortress keeping all the wrong people in the right place. But compared to some of the places on the edge of the city centre, Anderston was better, shabby-looking, but at least the GPs weren't afraid to visit on a call-out. I spotted the tall, skinny figure of Johnny close to a bus stop, smoking a cigarette. He was wearing the same thin bomber jacket that would have been fine for the summer. In his skinny jeans, his legs looked like sticks and as the light from my car shone on his gaunt face he looked even more emaciated than I remembered from our recent encounter. I pulled the car up beside him, and he stood shivering. I rolled down the window.

'Come on. In you come, Johnny.'

He looked at me a little suspiciously, then opened the door and got inside. He smelled of fags and unwashed clothes and days-old sweat, but his face was clean, though deathly pale, and now seeing him properly for the first time, I could see how young he was. He was a sorry mess of a boy, and not for the first time when I met junkies like him, I tried to imagine what his life had been like before this shit happened to him. Across the street there was a neon light in the chip-shop-come-café where I knew from my time on the beat I could get late-night food and a cup of tea.

'Do you want to go to the café? Are you hungry?' I turned to him.

He looked surprised by the offer.

'Aye. I'm hungry. I've had nothing since this morning.'

'Let's go then,' I said. 'I'm hungry too. We can talk in the café.'

He didn't say anything as I drove the car into the Anderston flats entrance, turned and came back up the road and parked in front of the café. In this neck of the woods, it was a good idea to keep your car where you could see it. We got out of the car and went into the café. The old guy looked up from the fryers but his face never changed; in fact, it was the same face and expression that I remembered when I walked this beat. The place was half empty – a few teenagers at one booth, wiring into burgers and chips, and an old couple at the back. I found us a seat by the window.

'What do you want to eat?' I asked Johnny.

He was sitting on his hands like a little boy taken out for a meal with his auntie, and I could see that somewhere in his sunken cheeks there was that kid who'd got lost, and it tugged inside my chest.

'Just chips.'

'Chips?' I snorted. 'You not want some fish? Or a burger or something?'

'Aye,' he said, shyly. 'All right then. A burger and chips.' He looked at me, then down at the table. Suddenly he looked sad and speechless. 'Sorry. I . . . I'm just . . . I'm no' used to somebody being kind to me.'

For a moment I didn't know what to say to him, and just sat there as the tears spilled out of his eyes. A broken soul who had been cast adrift from the rest of us who just about manage to keep ourselves on the right side of sanity, even when our worlds come tumbling down. I wondered what had sent this boy to this life, and if he would ever find his way back. A junkie's lifespan was short. So he didn't have a lot of time. I found myself reaching across and touching his icy cold hand.

'Come on, man! Get a grip. You're probably just hungry.' I hit him with a wry smile, hoping to break the moment.

'I'm the same when I need food. I'm ready to weep all the time.'

He wiped his tears away with the back of his hand and ran his other hand under his nose. Then his face brightened a little and he smiled, a chipped tooth smile with a mouth full of teeth that had long since lost their colour.

'You're awright, Billie. You are.'

The waitress appeared and I ordered a burger and chips and fish and chips for me. Tea for me, and Johnny asked for a chocolate milkshake. It's a junkie trait, the craving for sweet things.

I took my coat off and kept it firmly next to me and over my handbag. He was a harmless-looking boy, but he was a drug addict, and you didn't leave your bag anywhere within dipping distance.

'So,' I said. 'What made you phone me, Johnny? You heard something?'

He looked at me and I saw him scanning my face, his eyes resting on my neck, which I knew would be starting to bruise.

'What's wrong with your neck?' he asked. 'Looks all red. Like welts. Like somebody tried to choke you, Billie.'

Despite it all, in spite of the shattered, frightened way I felt, I smiled at him. If only he knew.

'Yeah,' I said. 'That's about right.'

'Seriously?' He looked concerned.

'Yeah,' I joked. 'You should see the other guy.'

He grinned, assuming I was making it up, and I was glad. He put the chocolate milkshake to his lips and began gulping till he was almost halfway through it, not stopping for breath as his Adam's apple bobbed on his skinny throat. I waited for him to put the glass back on the table. Then he stared into it, played with the straw in the froth before answering me.

'That lassie,' he said. 'That Jackie Foster lassie who I was sent to tell you to stay away from.' He paused, looking at me. 'She must have done something bad, or done the dirty on some dangerous people, because everyone's after her.' He looked out of the window and went silent.

'How do you know this? I mean, who is looking for her?'

'I heard people talking. A guy who knows one of the dealers, and he must know the people who are after her. Because it was him who sent me to you. They'd been following her and she came to your office. But after that they lost her.'

'Who's they?' I asked.

The waitress arrived with the steaming plates of food and set them on the table. Johnny surveyed his meal as though he didn't know where to start. Then he picked up the burger and took a huge bite. I had to wait until he got through that first mouthful before he was able to answer.

'I don't know,' he said, picking up the ketchup and squeezing it over his chips. 'I heard they were Turkish or something. Well at least one of them is, so I heard. But the thing is . . .' He lifted a chip and stuffed it into his mouth.

'They said something about a wean. Something about a wean being kidnapped.'

I was making my way through a chunk of delicious fish, not realising just how hungry I was. I almost choked.

'A baby? You heard someone actually saying that?'

'Aye. I heard them saying that she'll come to them – that lassie – because they've got her wean.' He looked at me, screwing up his eyes. 'Is that right? Did somebody steal that lassie's wean? Why would they do that, man? That's just fucking wrong.'

Johnny was definitely hearing snippets of all the right things, but I didn't think it was a good idea to confide in him about anything. Despite the feelings of compassion I had towards him, at the end of the day he was here to impart information to me for money, but he could just as easily pump me for info and sell it on to feed his habit.

I shrugged, stabbed at a few chips, and said nothing.

'She must have done something,' he mumbled.

'What does that matter to you?' I asked, a little too quickly.

He looked at me, struck by my tone. I didn't like his line of questioning. He was here to give me information, not gather it from me, and if I had to I would tell him that smartish. He fell silent, eyes to the table.

'I just wondered. Well, because I heard from another guy that these guys who are looking for the lassie were dealing in trafficked people. One of my pals met a guy – he's

working in the sauna, washing the towels and stuff – he's
a foreigner and he said he was trafficked.'

I was confused now.

'So what has that got to do with the girl Jackie Foster?
Did this guy mention her name?'

He shook his head. 'No, no. He's just a trafficked guy. A
slave, I suppose. He'll not get away from these people, so
he'll do what he's told.'

'But what's it got to do with the girl? And did he mention
the missing kid?'

Johnny sat as though he was trying to piece it together
and remember. My heart was sinking by the minute. Who
knew where he heard clips of information from in his
drug-fuelled stupor, and how he stored them in his fraz-
zled mind? Then his eyes kind of lit up.

'Oh. I remember now. It was Lainey, my dealer's bird. I
heard her saying something about looking after a wean
that wasn't hers for big Malky.'

'Who's big Malky?' Christ, this was complicated.

'He's a hard man. He's the man. Runs the saunas, brings
in the birds and the guys and stuff. He runs the coke
market too. But not for people like me, well, obviously. But
that's his thing.'

Somewhere in this tangled web of information there
were things that rang true. Big Malky. Was that the name
of the hard man I'd seen in the bar earlier? I had the footage on my camera, but hadn't downloaded it yet, and

I wasn't sure I wanted to show him the picture in case I couldn't trust him.

'So if you've heard a lot of stuff like this,' I said, 'did you hear anything about why someone kidnapped this girl's baby?'

He sat for a moment, his brain cells ticking over. Then he shrugged.

'Don't know. I heard she had something belonging to them. Maybe she stole their stash or something. Maybe a big load of coke. But she's got something they want and she did a runner.'

I didn't answer and we both ate our food. Johnny ate more than I expected – three quarters of the burger and a few chips. The way his eyes were drooping, he needed a hit, and if he didn't get one soon, he'd probably be chucking his dinner back up. Eventually, he spoke.

'So is this any use to you? My information?'

I nodded slowly. 'Yeah. I think it might be. But it's a bit convoluted, Johnny, like some of it you can't quite remember and in what order.'

'I know. I forget things a lot.'

I knew he was waiting to see if I would offer him some money, and at least he had the grace to wait and didn't ask for it upfront.

'I'll give you a few quid for your information. But I need you to find out more. Will you do that?'

'Aye. If I can.'

'This Lainey. Where does she live? Do you know if she has the kid, or did she have it at any time?'

'She lives in the Calton,' he said. 'But I don't know about the wean. I don't know if she's got it. That would be well dodgy, would it not? Suddenly having a wean that came from nowhere.' He grinned a broken tooth. 'I mean, even in the Calton!'

I half smiled. 'Yep. It would be hard to pass that one off. But could you keep your ears open for me? I'd like to know more about Lainey and who she's involved with. And this Turk bloke. Will you meet me again?'

His eyes lit up as I went into my handbag and took out three twenty pound notes. I folded them into my hand then reached across and squeezed them into his palm.

'Of course, Billie. I'll do anything I can.'

'Yeah, but be careful. Don't act too curious around these people. You know what I mean?'

'Aye. I know what you mean. They'd just dump me in the Clyde. Another dead junkie.' He looked at me, then out of the window into the drizzle.

We didn't speak for a long moment, and I waved the waitress over and paid the bill.

'I'm getting out of this, though.' Johnny finally broke the silence. 'I mean, I'm getting clean. I'm on a methadone programme, but I really want to get into a rehab unit, but there's too many people, too many junkies. But I want to get clean so I can go back and see my mammy.' He paused, swallowing. 'I miss my mammy. But I can't see her like this.' He spread his hands, gesturing to himself. 'She's got a bad heart. She says I broke it, and she's right. I did. But I'm going to make it up to her. I promised her.'

He spoke as though he meant it, and my heart bled a little for him. Because in the same time it would take you to shake his hand, he'd be stealing out of your pocket. And yet, somewhere inside him, he wanted to stop, to get off this death row roller-coaster where he was now. There was nothing really to say to a guy like this, and I'd heard so many stories like his before from drug addicts. Some made it through, but most didn't. I put my coat on and stood up.

'Okay. I best be going,' I said. 'Can I drop you somewhere?'

'Nah. I'll be all right tonight. Thanks for the money. Usually at night I have to go up the station and see if I can get picked up.' He dug his hands into his pockets and the muscle in his jaw tightened. 'Rent boy stuff. But I'm okay tonight. I'm sorted.'

'Good,' I said, because there was no other reply.

'But I'll keep listening out for you. And I'll phone if I hear.'

'Okay,' I said as I walked to my car. 'But be careful. I mean that.' And I did.

He gave a little mock salute, then turned on his heels and walked in the opposite direction, towards Cranstonhill.

CHAPTER ELEVEN

I lay in a bath so hot it stung my skin, but it was my way of winding down, getting to a place where I hoped sleep would come. The flat was so silent, yet in the shadows of my mind I could still hear him; his first-thing-in-the-morning voice calling out to make sure he wasn't alone; his cry in the night as the dinosaurs chased him, until I ran to his room and shushed him back to slumber. I lay watching the steam make little rivulets down the cobalt tiles, trying to push away the thought that he might be somewhere now, calling out to me, bewildered that I'm not there. And the worst pain of all, that he might be starting to forget me . . .

Every time I push the key in my front door, I have the same sinking feeling. Every time. My whole world was once behind this door, and when I twist the key in the lock it hits me square in the chest that none of it is there any more. My baby is gone. We think these things happen to other people, and when we read about it or watch the horror stories unfold on TV, we think we feel their pain. But we don't. Not until it happens. I look for answers every day. I've been searching for them for over a year now, because when it first happened I was so paralysed with grief and shock, I was told to leave it to the professionals. The police said they would find my son. People don't just disappear with a kid, as my husband had done. There were ways to track him down, I was assured. How could I have allowed that time to lapse without tearing the world apart myself to find him? The truth is I was incapable of doing anything. I've been through this guilt thing with my shrink over and over again, and she tells me it's natural to blame myself, but it's not my fault. But it *is* my fault. I took my eye off the most important thing in my life – my little boy. In the bigger picture, I was so wrapped up in my work, fighting my corner during the lengthy investigation into my shooting dead of the murderer, that I didn't see what was happening in my own home.

My marriage to Bob had been a mistake, and it had been staring me in the face for a long time. He'd been the charming, clever American I met at a party in London. I fell stupid in love with him and his dreams of being a writer, and we married over a summer lost in a whirlwind that made me believe anything was possible. But I knew nothing about him. I was a serving police officer, a smart one on a fast track to the top, and yet I married a man who I barely even checked out. I didn't even know his parents – all he told me was that they were back in the USA and that he didn't speak to them. He'd come to London to study, then dropped out of university to follow his true path as a writer. When I look back on it, I hate myself for my naivety. Less than a year into our marriage, I watched him become a lazy, feckless individual I barely recognised. He said he was writing, working on the great novel, but he spent his afternoons and evenings in bars in the West End, hanging out with the arty set, but not actually writing anything. He said his novel was a work in progress. And then came the drunken, violent mood swings, the temper, the resentment – always followed by intense love making full of regret and sorrow. All this time I was working hard, becoming recognised as a detective who could go all the way. My work sustained me. Bob was someone I came home to, but we were drifting apart, and he grew more and more volatile. I was going to tell him it was over the day I took the pregnancy test, but when it came out positive he had fallen to his knees in tears clutching my stomach – he was so happy that we were going to be a family. I told him how I'd felt, that I was leaving him, and he pleaded with me to give him another chance. For a while it worked. He was great with our little Lucas, our blond, blue-eyed boy who I felt such adoration for it ached my heart. Bob was an obsessive father, caring, fun and loving too, but almost to the point that I sometimes felt a little excluded. Because I had to go back to work, and Bob stayed home to look after Lucas, the pair were inseparable. The pressure of working as a cop in a big city – the nights, the long hours, the disappearing for days undercover – that became my life too, and when I came home and had some time off, Lucas had sometimes been a little sullen, maybe because of my absence. Guilt washed over me every single day I went to work.

Then, in one pivotal moment, my life turned upside down. After I shot the child-killer there were months of a massive investigation into every area of my life, the possibility of me being faced with court, the pressure, the meetings, and sometimes drinking to get through my evenings. I should have seen that my life was beginning to unravel, but I didn't. Then one night when I came home, Bob was gone. And he'd taken Lucas with him.

There had been no note, no phone call, nothing. His mobile was no longer active. They had just disappeared. The passports were gone, and so were most of Lucas's clothes, as well as Bob's. The panic of that moment when I went into my bank account to find it emptied, was confirmation that Bob must have been planning for a while. How could he do this? Scanlon was on the scene minutes after I called him, and he found me hysterical on the floor, weeping, losing control. Then the police investigation came sweeping in, the sympathy from my superior officers, the female liaison officer holding my hand, telling me they would find them.

One day turned to two, and there was still no sign of them. I knew the police could only do so much, because my son was with his father, so it was not as though he'd been abducted. But in reality he had. Unknown to me, Bob had put Lucas on his American passport, and then the bomb-shell dropped four days after they disappeared. Bob had used his passport to fly to France, and from there they'd taken a flight to the USA. I still remember the look on Scanlon's face when we were told that. Lucas was in America. The stark realisation dawned that I might never see my son again.

For days afterwards, I kept going, but it was like wading through cement, trying to keep myself upright, falling down with exhaustion. There was nowhere to go with this. My husband had taken his son to his homeland in the USA, and no matter what doors Scanlon and I rattled and which authorities we phoned, this was a distant far-off land, and there seemed to be no sense of urgency. People go missing in this country every day, every hour, we were told. We were logged in their system. That's what you have to do, ma'am. We contacted a US website, a forum with people to talk to, who linked us with organisations who helped track missing people. It was big business. They felt sure they would find him. But nothing. Bob could have taken him anywhere. You can disappear anywhere in the world, in Europe or in the UK. But America is so vast that anyone can vanish for ever, reinvent themselves, with no footprint of who they were. And that is what we were faced with. I even hired a private eye in Baltimore. I didn't know if I was looking in the right place, but Bob had said he once lived there. I even went there, met with the private eye, paid the upfront money – he only took half of it because he felt sorry for me, but I sensed I could trust him. And he did try. He was still trying nearly two years later, keeping me informed on every line of enquiry. He tracked Bob's life back to his high school, his family, his friends. He found he was trouble all the way. His parents could not be traced in the town where Bob had gone to school. And each day, no matter where I'd been or what job I'd been involved in, the first thing I did when I came home to this empty house was go to my laptop, onto the website looking for hope from others who were searching for missing loved ones, and then check for my private eye's emails. I became obsessed with it, and it finally broke me. I didn't want to live without my son. I was suicidal, but I didn't have the guts to do it, and I phoned Scanlon who came over and took me to the private doctor the next day. I lost my job, my livelihood. Scanlon told me if I didn't start shaping up, I would never come back from this, and I might lose my son for ever. He told me I had to keep believing. He sat up with me late into the night holding my hand as I wept and told him my life was over. And eventually he made me realise that I had to find a way back if I was ever going to find my son. But in the meantime, I had to keep living, earn some money. Scanlon's ex-detective mate had become a private eye and suggested it might be the kind of work that would suit me. I picked myself up, and I was doing even better than I imagined. Some days, there were nearly two hours when I hadn't thought about Lucas, and that hurt too. But I kept going, because if he was somewhere waiting for me, I would find him. But I tortured myself with negative thoughts. What if years went by and I couldn't find him, and he grew up somewhere far away? And tonight, as I lay in the bath, I asked myself: what if he ends up like Johnny, broken and clinging to life in the dark side? How would I ever know where to find him?

I woke up to the sound of my mobile ringing, and reached across to grab it from the bedside table. It was Scanlon's name that came up, and I suddenly remembered I had phoned him last night to see if we could meet.

'You having a lie-in, Billie? I've already done fifty lengths of the pool.'

'That's just showing off,' I yawned, my fingers touching the bruising on my neck.

Something about Scanlon's positive attitude to everything made me raise my game no matter how low I might be feeling. I was groggy. I'd finally dropped off to sleep around two, but it was fitful and restless, and full of faces pushed against the window of my car, and men trying to choke me to death.

'I got your call, but I was working,' he said. 'I'm not starting till six tonight, but I'm up for a meet.'

'Great. Where and when?' I said. 'I've got some things I want to show you.'

'You been traipsing around more murder crime scenes?' he joked. 'I heard about your run-in with big DCI Wilson. The McPhee death.'

'I've been doing my own digging,' I said. 'And despite what you hear, I wasn't traipsing around the crime scene. Christ. Wilson. He's such a wanker.'

'I know. That's some shit with McPhee, by the way. It's been kept very low key. I've got a couple of things to tell you on it. You want some lunch?'

'Definitely,' I said, checking the time. 'I've got to run into the office briefly, then I'll meet you in the town. I'll call you later.'

'Great. See you then.'

He hung up before saying goodbye, and I lay staring at the ceiling, knowing that if I didn't get out of bed straight away, chances were I never would.

CHAPTER TWELVE

The Willow Grove café down past Charing Cross is wedged in between two shopfronts, and looks like it has been put together with a collection of furniture and artefacts from all over the world. Inside, it's a long narrow room that gets darker and more secretive the further in you go – the kind of mysterious little place you'd find behind the souks in Marrakesh or somewhere in the Middle East. I love it so much that if I'm there when it's busy, I feel resentful that people have discovered my secret café. But today it was quiet, apart from a thin, bearded hipster sitting at a table near the counter, engrossed in whatever he was writing in his notebook. For a moment it made me think of Bob, the way he would swan around cafés and bars, looking the part, when he was actually just bone idle. I pushed the thought away as I spotted Scanlon on a sofa down a couple of stairs at the back. He looked up and his face broke into one of those smiles that always made me feel that I'd never be truly alone. I went across the gloomily lit room to greet him.

'Dark in here, isn't it?' Scanlon grinned. 'I know you love this place, Billie, but I think it's a bit creepy. Kind of feels like if I didn't finish my avocado salad I'd get dragged downstairs and suffocated with a load of wet lettuce leaves.'

I plonked myself down on the opposite sofa and chuckled. I was wearing a cream wool polo-neck sweater to hide the bruises on my neck, because right now I didn't want to discuss it with Scanlon. I knew he'd push me into reporting what happened last night.

'It's a Glasgow café,' I said, 'but not as we know it. Well, certainly not when we were walking around here as beat cops.' I took off my coat. 'Oh, by the way, I had dinner in that chip shop we used to go to down the road in Argyle Street last night. Remember the torn-faced guy at the fryers? His face is still tripping him.'

Scanlon laughed. 'I remember him. Jeez. You private eyes get to all the fancy places.'

'I was also in The Corinthian earlier,' I joked. 'Trying my best not to look like a private detective.'

'You're up to something, Billie, so spill it.'

'I will,' I said. 'A lot to tell. But you first.'

He tossed a menu across the table to me. 'Let's order some grub first, I'm starved.'

I knew the menu well, and after a cursory glance ordered

some crab salad with some of their home-made toasted sourdough bread on the side. Scanlon had chorizo in a chilli tomato sauce on flatbread. Green tea for me and white coffee for him.

'So what's the score with big Wilson?' I asked.

Scanlon steepled his hands and sat back on the sofa. His face was saying wait-till-you-hear-this, even before he spoke.

'Well,' he said, 'there's something dodgy going on with the way this whole McPhee situation has been handled. I mean, the very fact that a witness statement was not passed on at the time – that stinks.' He spread his hands. 'Of course, it could just be a case of some cop back in Milngavie not passing it on straight away because he got distracted by a phone call or something – that's how they're playing it. But I'm not buying that.'

'Why?'

'Just the fact that they're playing it down. You would have expected the officer who failed to pass it on to get his arse kicked all over HQ, but I don't think that's happened.'

'You mean Hewitt?' I said. 'He must have been questioned though. Maybe there's a lot happening behind the scenes.'

'Could be. But the whole thing – the McPhee death. They just want to close the case and get the hell out of it.'

'You mean in case anyone gets a hold of the information

that McPhee was actually a witness to the child being taken?'

'Yeah. If a newspaper got wind of that, the shit would hit the fan,' he said. 'But McPhee had no family, no friends really, so they're very quickly putting it down to suicide and hoping it all goes away.'

I looked at Scanlon as he went quiet for a moment, and I got the distinct feeling he was holding something back. I let the silence hang for a bit to see if he would burst. I've known him a long time and he's seen the best and the worst of me. He'd feel guilty there was something crucial he wasn't telling me. I waited. Then he spoke.

'Look, Billie,' he said, letting out a puff of frustration. 'There's something else.'

'No shit, Sherlock.'

He spread his hands. 'Listen, if this gets out, there will be all sorts of crap.'

I half smiled, again with the sarcasm.

'You mean there's a scandal in the police force, and they actually don't think anyone will be talking about it? Come on, Scanlon. You know what it's like. There are more fishwives in the police when it comes to gossip than anywhere else. So whatever it is, if it's not already out there, it will be before the week's out.'

He nodded. 'I know. I'm bursting to tell you, so I can't hold it in any longer.' He leaned across the table, glanced furtively around at the empty café and I almost laughed at his paranoia.

'Hewitt. The cop. You know who he is?' His voice was a whisper.

I sat for a moment searching Scanlon's face for clues. Then the penny dropped. I could feel my eyes widen.

'No way,' I said. 'Are you kidding? He's Chief Superintendent Hewitt's boy? Kenny Hewitt's son? Christ almighty!'

'Sssh,' he said, his hands in a pipe-down gesture. 'You can imagine the arses clanging shut all over the place.'

'But this must already be going around like wildfire. It's only a matter of time before it comes out.'

'That's why they're trying to close it down. That's what really stinks. Anyone can make a mistake or overlook something. But covering up what looks like a mistake is worse than shameful when there's a missing baby at stake. It's like they've just closed the investigation into the kid.'

I knew any signs of a cover-up would really rankle with Scanlon. All the time we'd worked together, he was much more of a purist than I was. I hadn't even told him that I'd seen the DCI planting evidence that time, but I know if it had been him that day, he would have raised it with the boss. Whereas I kept it in reserve, in case I ever needed it for ammunition. And if I needed it, I would not hesitate to use it.

'So what stage is it at just now – with McPhee? Is there a post-mortem?'

'Yeah. It's been done. It looks like it could well be suicide, and it might have been. But there's something not right about it.'

'What are the other cops saying?'

'It's being talked about. In whispers. They know there's a cover-up. But the thing is, because the girl retracted her claim that her kid had been stolen, there isn't a lot they can do about it. Some of them are saying that maybe McPhee was mistaken, maybe he'd had a drink – apparently he had a bit of a drink problem. But the main thing, is they're burying it.'

'What about Hewitt? Do you know anyone who has spoken to him? His mates?'

He shrugged. 'He seems to be toughing it out. Saying these things happen. Pressure of work. He meant to send it straight away, but got distracted and didn't. But as long as the investigation into the missing kid has stopped, he knows he'll get away with it.'

We sat for a long moment, thinking of the scenario, the investigation that would be going on at HQ, and how they were trying to cover their backs. But when you stripped it down, right now they seemed to be in the clear, because Jackie Foster took back her statement. No missing kid, no investigation. End of story.

The food and drinks arrived and the waitress set them down on the table. Once she'd moved away, I leaned a little closer.

'Scanlon,' I said, almost in a whisper, 'I've got information here that is so explosive, I'm not even sure how to start telling you, or even if I should.'

Scanlon picked up his sandwich and tore off a chunk. He gave me a look that was somewhere between incredulous and hurt. He put his mug of coffee to his lips and took a drink.

'Don't give me that crap, Billie,' he said, mouth full. 'What are we doing here if we can't talk?'

I put up my hand in a gesture of peace.

'Of course,' I said. 'And I want to tell you, because this stuff is just off the scale – especially given what you've just said. But I need you to agree that you won't do anything about it once you know.'

He chewed slowly and narrowed his eyes.

'That bad, eh?'

I nodded. 'Yeah. That bad. And if it's true, it's worse than bad.'

'Then maybe you should be seriously thinking about bringing in the cops, Billie. I know how you are. I know how you operate, with your own rules. You can be reckless. But if this involves finding a kid that really did get stolen, then you know as well as I do that it's the cops who should be taking it on . . .'

His voice trailed off at the end because he could see by the expression on my face what was coming.

'You mean like they pulled out all the stops to find my

Lucas?' I knew it was a stupid, barbed comment that served no purpose, but it just came out, because deep down it was what I really thought.

Scanlon put his head back and stared up to the ceiling.

'Aw, come on, Billie,' he said. 'Listen. I'm with you on that – a hundred per cent. You know I don't think enough was done in the early, crucial stages for your Lucas. And I think the cops failed because of that. I'm not going to defend them. But if there is something big going on here with this Jackie Foster kid that you know about, then you can't do this on your own.'

I said nothing for a moment and let it hang there.

'I'll get help,' I said. 'Just maybe not from the cops.'

He nodded. 'Okay. Whatever you think is best. But if you tell me things, for God's sake don't think I'm going to go behind your back and get the force involved. If you don't want that, then I'm okay with that.' He looked me in the eye. 'I promise.'

I nodded, ate a mouthful of my crab salad, and drank some tea.

'Okay. Then strap yourself in for this.'

'I'm strapped in.'

'Jackie told me she had worked for an escort agency, and also got a job making films. Porn films.'

'Porn films?'

'Yep. Shot in a basement somewhere on the edge of the city. But she said she could show me the location.'

'And she was in these films? Having sex?'

'Yeah. Well, sexual acts. Four films. But it turned out to be more than a porn movie – the last film she made. It was a snuff movie.'

'What! Are you serious? She said that?'

'She did.'

'And you believe her?'

'I do. Not because I want to believe her. But because she told me something that's a bombshell. And she would have no reason to mention this guy's name if it wasn't true.'

'What guy?'

'Hewitt. That was the name she said. A young cop. She told me that he was on the film set, that he was there when they shot the movies. And that he is part of whatever this gang does. Which she says involves people trafficking and drug smuggling.'

Scanlon sat back and puffed as though he'd been punched in the gut. He shook his head, looking at me, his eyes narrowed, trying to process the information. Eventually he sat forward so he could be closer to me, and opened his hands.

'Okay. How about you tell me everything she said? The lot. Her story.'

I looked at him and I knew he was hooked, desperate to hear it, but I also knew he would be torn about what to do when he did hear it.

'Okay,' I said finally, 'I'll tell you. But it goes nowhere. You have to promise me, Scanlon.'

He tightened his lips. 'Come on, Billie. You know me better than that. I'll say nothing. I promise.'

'Okay,' I said.

I told him everything – well, except about last night. His eyes popped when I mentioned the possibility of people being trafficked.

'She saw the minibus? The people?' Scanlon interrupted.

'She saw them. And she saw a Vietnamese boy who was later in the film that she'd been a part of. The snuff movie. She saw them beat him to death. But she was so shocked that she was beginning to wonder if it was real or staged. But it was real.'

'What?' He sat back. 'Billie. This is far-fetched.'

'Exactly. So far-fetched it could be true.'

'So what did she tell you about the cop?'

'Not much. Only that the cameraman told her his name was Hewitt.'

'Fucking hell!'

'I know. I couldn't believe it myself. I mean, I saw Hewitt's name on the witness statement email. But I assumed, like everyone else, it was a lapse. Now, if what she's saying is true, then the reason he didn't pass it on is because he was part of the whole thing. Jackie had no way of knowing that Hewitt's name would come up in an email about a witness who had seen someone taking her baby. She doesn't even know there *was* a witness, because she was lying trapped in the car. So she has to be telling the truth.'

'Christ almighty. It's hard to believe anyone would do that, never mind a cop.'

'He was in debt, Scanlon. I looked into him. He's owing money everywhere. So maybe he was desperate.'

'But snuff movies? People trafficking? Covering up a baby being stolen? You're right. This is off the scale.'

'But you can't do anything about it. You promised.'

He nodded. 'I know. I won't. If I told my bosses this, they'd think I was on drugs or something.' He paused, and I could see his brain working. 'So what about the cameraman? Who is he? You have a name?'

'Yeah. She gave me a name. I'm checking him out.'

'Find him, then you're going somewhere. But do you really believe all this stuff?'

I shrugged. 'I don't have any reason not to believe her. I know it sounds crazy, but I have checked a couple of things out and they ring true.'

'Like what?'

'Like the foreign guys she mentioned – maybe Turkish or Moroccan. As I said, I dug out some info on Hewitt and tracked him down to his home.'

'So you also followed him?' He rolled his eyes to the ceiling.

'Yeah. That's what I was doing in The Corinthian. I followed him there and he met with these two guys – they were Turkish. I sat near them. I photographed and videoed them in the bar.'

'You filmed them in the bar? That was risky, never mind illegal. You need to watch yourself, rattling cages with these guys.'

I spread my hands. 'What's another risk?' I said. 'My life is all about risk these days.' If only he knew.

'So did they say much?'

'Some stuff. But I've got good footage of them, and I followed them to a Turkish kebab joint up the road and they disappeared. Not Hewitt, he went his own way, probably back to his flat in Merchant City.'

'You have the footage?'

'Yep. I thought maybe you could get some checks on facial recognition in case they are players or hoodlums or whatever. There was a big Glasgow guy with them. Obviously some kind of hood, but I didn't recognise him. Can you have a look for me? See if he comes up anywhere?'

He raised his eyebrows and made a face.

'I'm going to have to, am I not?' He shook his head. 'But I need to be mega careful. Because if there's a bigger picture here that is being closed down, then I might find doors closed everywhere, and I don't want my prints anywhere near a private investigation by you.' He sighed. 'It's going to be awkward. But I'll try.'

'And there's more,' I said.

'Christ. More?'

'Yeah. I met with this smackhead – the one who tried to

warn me the other day at my office? So he calls me last night to say he had information and could I meet him.'

'Hence the dinner in the chip shop in Argyle Street.'

'Yeah. He told me something about his dealer's girlfriend looking after some kid – not hers – and some other things he'd heard.'

'Really? You got a name? Address?'

'Not quite. The Calton. But I hope to get more specifics soon. Maybe even today if he gets lucky.'

We had finished our food and coffee and sat for a few moments in the stillness of the café, not saying anything. We were like that as friends, comfortable in each other's company in silent moments. But I caught Scanlon giving me a long look and was conscious that he had flicked a glance at my sweater which I was sure hid the bruises on my neck. Eventually, I looked at him, feigning surprise.

'What?' I said, trying to keep my face straight.

He pursed his lips the way he did when he knew someone wasn't being straight with him.

'So what's with the strangle marks on your neck, Carlson?' He shrugged. 'Are you planning on telling me or what?'

'Oh,' I said, giving him a sheepish look. 'I hoped you wouldn't notice. It's not important.' I looked away from him and sighed as my fingers went automatically to my polo neck.

Before I could object, Scanlon had leaned forward and gently touched just under my chin. I didn't stop him as he eased the sweater down a little. I saw his eyes widen with surprise and then burn with anger.

'What the fuck, Carlson! Who did this?'

I pulled back a bit and put my hand on his, and we stayed like that for a few seconds, our hands touching. The tenderness of the moment stirred something in me, perhaps even more so after the brutality of last night.

'It was last night,' I said, blinking the scene away. 'I had a run-in with some gorilla outside the kebab shop. One of their mob. Bastard nearly choked the life out of me.'

'Christ!' He let my hand go. 'What the hell were you thinking, tracking these guys on your own? You wouldn't have done that as a cop. You'd have had a partner.'

'It was just automatic. You know how these things are. One step follows another and stuff. I had no idea he was there, in the street – I should have checked.'

He shook his head, still looking straight at me.

'How the hell did you get away?'

I smiled and shrugged. 'I bit the bastard.'

'You bit him!' His voice went up an octave.

I chuckled. Something about offloading to Scanlon made it not as terrifying as it had been.

'Yes. I bit him so hard on the wrist that I could taste his blood. It worked. He screamed. But I retched my guts up afterwards.' I gave him a mischievous look. 'I didn't know

I was that much of an animal. But he was trying to drag me into that kebab shop and I knew if he did I would never come out of it alive.'

He put his hands up to his face and rubbed his cheeks. Then he gave me that look again, that affectionate, caring look he always had that picked me up so many times when I was rock bottom. Nobody ever looked at me the way Scanlon did, and sometimes I wondered if I was missing something in our relationship. But I batted the thought away.

Eventually, I checked my watch, picked up my jacket and pulled it on.

'Come on. We should go. You've got villains to catch all over the mean streets.'

He puffed out a sigh and we both stood up and headed for the door.

CHAPTER THIRTEEN

The cameraman's name was Lenny Dale. But he was nowhere on the radar. I'd spent much of yesterday trawling through the internet, but found no trace of a Lenny Dale that would fit the profile. A professional cameraman would be out there, he'd be showcasing his work, looking for commissions. That's how these things worked in the industry, an old boyfriend with dreams of being a Hollywood cameraman used to tell me many moons ago. If you wanted to get on, be picked up to work on TV or independent production companies, you had to be networking. Unless, of course, like Lenny Dale, you were shooting seedy porn flicks in a dingy basement warehouse that ended in a bloodbath. I was getting nowhere fast on this, and time was not on my side. Every day that passed, with Jackie's baby still missing, reduced the chances of finding her. I know. I've been there. And given what happened to me the other night, if that mob I saw with Hewitt were holding the kid, there's no telling what they could do, or where she might be by now. If she was lucky, she was actually in the Calton, as Johnny had said, in some drug dealer's house, however shitty that might seem. The alternative – that she could be far away, sold abroad by ruthless people traffickers – didn't bear thinking about. I'd tossed and turned in my bed last night going over all the scenarios, and none of them were good. My nightmares were full of car crashes and babies being dragged away; and always just before I woke up, always a little boy waiting at the end of a long dark tunnel with his arms outstretched. Shattered from fitful sleep, I'd got up early and out of the flat as quick as I could, as though I was running from ghosts. On days like this, I needed to be in the city centre, streets teeming with ordinary lives. I needed the drone of the traffic, the vendors selling papers, where every day the beat goes on, no matter the desolation, no matter the darkness you feel. In my office, there was normality, a routine, an escape from the nightmares. And there was Millie this morning, badgering me to get on top of things. Clients looking for a private eye were stacking up, she told me, and Jackie Foster wasn't the only show in town. She was like that, Millie, a tough, thrawn woman who had no time for navel-gazing introspection. And she should know. She buried two of her children before they were teenagers after a drunken motorist mowed them down on their way to school. You never really get over that, she told me once on a rare occasion she opened up. But you had to keep living for the ones who didn't get this far. She was right, too. But she knew me well enough by now to know that I wouldn't let this Jackie Foster case go, that I would chase every thread and lead until the end.

I'd been ferreting away on the internet all morning, and as the clock on my office wall was hitting midday, Millie put her head around the door.

'I'm going down to pick up a sandwich. Will I get you something? My shout to buy.'

'Sure.' I was suddenly feeling hungry as I'd had nothing but coffee all morning. 'I'll have that chicken thing you get.'

'The toasted panini with the cheese?'

'Yeah, that. And tea would be good, thanks.'

I heard the door close and Millie's footsteps along the hallway. I was about to call Jackie for a check-in when my mobile shuddered on the desk and her name came up on the screen.

'Jackie. I was actually about to call you. Are you okay?'

'Yeah. I'm all right. Didn't sleep much. I can't sleep really, since this all happened.' She paused. 'But I've found something for you. About the cameraman.'

I held my breath in anticipation.

'You did?' I said. 'I've been digging around for nearly twenty-four hours trying to get a handle on him, but there's nothing. Like he's invisible on every check. Are you sure that's his real name?'

'Not any more, I'm not,' she said, sounding a little elated. 'I found something. It must have dropped out of his pocket. It's a card. Like a bank card. It's got a name on it that's not Lenny Dale. But it's his picture.'

Something inside me was bursting with excitement. Even though I knew it was far too early for that, but it was a breakthrough.

'That's a result, Jackie. Where did you find it?'

'It was at the bottom of my bag. He must have dropped it in there at some stage. It must have been a mistake, because he told me his name was Lenny.'

'Great. I'll head up to the flat right now, and pick up the card. I'll bring you some lunch.'

'Thanks. That would be great.'

'Will be there in less than twenty.'

I pulled on my coat and picked up my car keys from the desk, then headed out of the door and dashed downstairs. I could see the bakery below the building was packed with lunchtime customers at the takeaway counter, and Millie was being served. I pushed my way past indignant, hungry customers, as the woman handed her the bags of sandwiches.

'Millie. Sorry. Can I take these? I mean yours too? I'm going up to see Jackie. There's been a little development and I need to go there.'

Millie pursed her lips and handed me the brown paper bags. Then she turned to the assistant.

'Can I have another chicken panini, please?'

'You're a star, Millie,' I said. 'Thanks. I'll be back in a while.'

Millie sighed and shook her head, turning to the shop assistant and shrugging as I pushed my way back and out of the door.

I pressed the buzzer at the apartment where Jackie was staying, even though I could have let myself in with my own key. I had to respect her privacy, as I had allowed her to stay in the apartment and told her to make herself at home.

'You don't have to buzz to get into your own house, Bil-lie,' she said as she opened the door and I stepped in.

'What the heck. It's only fair.' I held up the brown bag. 'Lunch. Go and put the kettle on. I hope you like chicken and cheese panini.'

'That would be great,' she said as she walked into the kitchen. 'I didn't eat much yesterday. I feel nauseous when I eat. I think it's nerves.'

I didn't answer, but I knew how that felt. Dark smudges under her piercing blue eyes gave her a tired look, even though her demeanour seemed brighter than before. When the kettle pinged, she poured boiling water into two mugs with tea bags, and we carried our lunch into the living room. There was a fleeting moment when on the face of it we could have been two old friends having a catch-up lunch, instead of the broken souls we were. Jackie knew nothing of my own private hell, and I wanted it to stay that way, no matter how relevant it might seem. My grief was mine alone and sharing it wouldn't make it any less painful.

She had no television on and the place was eerily quiet. On the coffee table sat what looked like a bank or credit card, and she picked it up and handed it to me. I didn't recognise the colour or logo, and as I examined it closely I saw Arabic writing. There was what looked like an account number, but there was also a photograph, thumbnail size, on the top right-hand corner, which you don't see on bank cards. I strained my eyes. Below the photo was the name Thomas Barton. And the name was repeated again at the bottom.

'Strange-looking thing,' I said. 'Like a bank card or something.' I held the card out to her. 'Is that definitely the photo of the man you knew as Lenny Dale?'

'Yeah,' she said softly. 'That's definitely him. He looks exactly like that, so it must be recent.'

I flicked the card around, but everything on the back of it was written in Arabic. The card opened up a whole new thread in the investigation. I now had a photo of the cameraman and a name. I needed to find out what the card was, and who this guy was. If I had still been in the police, there were people up in Fraud that would be able to run this through quickly and get some info on it. But that wasn't an option. I could ask Scanlon to find a way to have it looked at, but he was already pushing into areas for me he shouldn't be into and I didn't want to get him in trouble. There was only one other guy I could approach, and I wasn't even sure if he was still in the country. Javed Singh, of Pakistani parents, was born and brought up in Glasgow and a total wide boy. He was a businessman to the clients he dealt with in a Glasgow and Bradford exporting business, but he was also a fraudster. Javed could knock up a credit card within a couple of hours of scamming a number from a true one, and a criminal could go out and use it without any problem. He'd been a valuable contact and informer, and he got away with most things he did because he was useful to the cops, slipping them info on bigger gangsters. You could call it grassing, but Javed would see it as business. The last I heard was that he was lying low after a deal went belly up and some heavies were chasing him for money. That was three years ago though. Knowing Javed, he'd be over that by now. I checked my phone for his number and was glad to see I still had it. But I didn't want to make the call here.

'I'm going to hit the road after we have lunch, Jackie, and have this checked out,' I said, taking a bite from the panini.

'Will you be able to track it down?'

'I know somebody who does that kind of thing, so maybe.' I watched her as she ate the sandwich and sipped from the mug of tea. 'Can you think back to your visits to the film set – were there any conversations or anything you might have seen between the cameraman and any of the others? Can you just put your mind to that? I mean, did they seem to be good friends? Was there any banter or stuff like that? Did they eat together?'

She nodded. 'Yeah. They all seemed to be friends, or at least acquaintances, and talked a lot to each other. I was kept away in another area of the studio where we ate and made coffee while waiting for our stint on the film. But I could see them through a kind of bamboo wall, you know, like one of those trellis things you sometimes see in your garden. Lenny – or Thomas – was always the centre of the conversation. He was keeping them amused with his chat. But the director was in charge. He was the Turkish guy. He was the big boss. It was him who gave all the instructions when to start, stop and stuff.'

'Did you ever hear his name?'

She looked like she was thinking back and said nothing for a moment. Then she spoke.

'I heard the name Mehmet. But I don't even know if it's a first or second name. I mean, I was only in there about three times in total. I just wanted in and out. The escort agency was my job, not the filming.'

'Did you go back to the escort agency after you made the last film? The one with the Vietnamese guy being murdered?'

She looked at me, shook her head.

'No. No way. I just wanted to run a mile from all of it. Because the escort agency must know them. It was one of the girls there working on the reception who told me about the porn films.'

We sat in silence for a moment, the rain rattling on the window as we ate the paninis. It crossed my mind that she might not be telling the whole truth about the cameraman.

'Jackie,' I said, and waited until I could look her in the eye. 'Did you and the cameraman . . . I mean, did you sleep with him? Is there more to this?' I put my hands up. 'I'm just asking because if you did, or if there's anything else you know about him, then you really have to tell me.'

She looked at me, then at the table. She put her sandwich down.

'I didn't sleep with him. No. He wanted to. We kissed a bit, on the couch, after we came back to my apartment – the night he stashed the stuff there. But that was all. He said he liked me, and that he could take me somewhere away from all this. My baby too. That we could have a holiday or something. But I couldn't get involved with him. It was stupid enough to let him stash the stuff in my flat.'

I sighed. 'You should tell me stuff like this, Jackie.'

'I forgot, actually. And then I just didn't think. I'm sorry.'

'So how did you really get the card? Did he really drop it in your bag? Or did you steal it?'

She looked shocked. 'I didn't steal it, Billie. I'd be too scared to do that. My bag was on the couch, and maybe it was open and the card fell out of his trouser pocket when he was all over me. That's all I can think. I don't know how it got there. I promise you.'

I believed her. We finished our lunch in silence. I felt I had to say something to lift the mood because I needed her trusting me and sticking with me, not running out. If she ran out again, chances were they would find her and that would be the end of the road.

'Okay, I'm going back to dig up anything I can get on this Thomas Barton. Having a picture of him is a real bonus. You did good. I wasn't getting on at you or anything, but I really want to run this to ground and get to the bottom of this mob so we can get your baby. You understand?'

'Yes.' Her eyes filled up. 'I just want my baby back, Billie. Every day I feel she's getting further and further away.'

Her voice trailed off as she sniffed and looked away. There was nothing I could say to her, because nothing anyone says is a comfort to you when you're helpless and lost like this.

'I know,' I said.

I could have told her the information I already had about Hewitt and his connection to the top of the police, and also what Johnny had said about a woman in the Calton with a kid who'd just turned up from nowhere. But that would be a mistake. I didn't want to give her that much hope because the road to finding this kid was still a dark alley, and I was nowhere near out of it.

But I wanted to know if any of the guys – including Hewitt – in the pictures I took at the Corinthian were the same guys she knew from the film shoots. I knew it was risky to take her this much into my investigation, but I needed to know.

'Jackie,' I said, 'I'm going to show you some pictures I took of some guys while I've been doing my work. See if they're the same guys. If they are, then you do nothing about it, okay? You sit tight where you are. Are you okay with that?'

She nodded but said nothing. I took my camera from my bag and scrolled back and brought up some of the pictures on the screen. I stood next to her as she examined them. It didn't take long.

'That's them!' she said, excited. 'That's them! The cop guy, the Turk and the others. I don't know their names, apart from the Mehmet one. But those are definitely the guys I saw at the shoot. Jesus! The one on the far left, the young one – that's the cop who I was told was called Hewitt. You found them? You actually sat close enough to them to take pictures?'

I could see that somewhere in her mind she was wondering why I didn't confront them, but she was smart enough to know that's not how it works.

'Great,' I said. 'You're sure?'

'I'm sure. Positive. I only saw them a few times, but I know that is them in the picture.' She paused as I put my camera back in my bag. 'Can I ask where you saw them?'

'Doesn't matter where, Jackie. They were in a pub, talking, that's all I can tell you. But it's a big help that you have identified them. So I want you to hang fire and just wait.'

'Do you think it will help find my baby?'

The look in her eyes made me feel perplexed. It would be stupid to give her a lot of false hope.

'It's a step, Jackie. That's all. Just do what you're doing, and know that I'm throwing everything I've got at this.'

It seemed to be enough.

'Thanks,' she said.

'Okay. I'll be in touch. Stay in the house and try to get some rest,' I said as I left.

CHAPTER FOURTEEN

I called Millie on the way back to the office and asked her to dig out anything she could on a story about a guy that got jailed for possessing a haul of child porn movies in Glasgow six or seven years ago. The name Yates was all I could remember, as I wasn't involved in the case, but I did recall how outraged the officers were at the time when his sentence was something like a paltry three years. He'd have been released in half that, so he was out there somewhere. I also put a call in to Javed Singh, but his mobile was answered by a woman who said he was out of the country on business and would be for some time. With Javed, that could mean anything, so it was looking like that avenue to find out more about Barton's bank card wasn't going to work.

'Colin Yates files in your email.' Millie looked up from her computer as I walked into the office.

'That was quick, Millie. You're worth your weight in gold.' I took my coat off as I went towards my office.

She gave me a look that said she'd heard it all before.

'How was lunch?' she asked.

I shrugged. 'Good enough. She had some helpful information for me, so it's something to run with for the moment.'

Her eyebrows went up a little, but her face said I was wasting my time.

'Oh. That insurance company called. They want to know whether you're taking on the case?'

I stood for a moment, thinking back to my phone call with the company and the details of the case. It required me to go to Perthshire to talk to the widow and ask a few questions that had arisen from their suspicions. I needed to talk to them further for details, but it would have to wait.

'Sure,' I said. 'I'll take it. I'll give them a call myself in a bit, Millie. I'll just need to juggle a few things around.'

'Yeah,' she said. 'The juggling again. Maybe they'll give you your own TV show.'

'Couldn't do it without my lovely assistant, though.'

'Aye right.' Her face cracked a smile. 'You want coffee?'

'Would love it.'

I went into my office and hung my coat on the stand in the corner, and went to my desk, clicking on the email about Yates. On the screen there was an image of Colin Yates and a headline screaming *Snuff Video Perv Jailed*. And below, a strapline reading, *Cop's fury at soft sentence*. The story told of how police found dozens of DVDs of snuff films with hideous, brutal killings on them when they raided his flat in Shawlands, Glasgow. Yates had claimed they didn't belong to him but had been left there by a previous tenant and he'd thought they were just ordinary videos. He hadn't reported them or handed them over to police as he was afraid. The article said he'd eventually cracked under questioning and admitted he had been told they were child porn films, not snuff movies – he'd done it for money and he regretted it. There were details of his connections and travels to Thailand and East Asia and how he'd become embroiled in the porn movie industry. He was jailed but there was no more information aside from that. Newspapers moved on so quickly, and unless you were a violent killer or a major drug dealer, you could slip out of jail without being noticed and be back out in the community. I turned to my other laptop to see what I could find on Yates, his bank account, recent transactions – all the illegal stuff I have to do sometimes. He'd been spending some cash in Glasgow, so it looked like he might be living at a new address, which thankfully was listed. I didn't think he'd be happy to have a private eye popping up on his doorstep, so it might be a good idea to do a bit of a recce. But first, I wanted to run the name Thomas Barton, the cameraman, through the computer. I ran it along with Yates's to see what I came up with. There seemed to be no connection. There were plenty of Facebook Thomas Bartons but none of them looked like the picture on the card

Jackie gave me. That would have been too easy. I went back to my other laptop and ran some illegal checks, and to my surprise a Thomas Barton came up with bank accounts with an address in Glasgow up in Maryhill Road. When I keyed into them I could see he was massively overdrawn and there had been no activity for over a year. So something had gone wrong and he was in hock, if this was the right Barton. One of the debtors was a camera shop for some online video cameras. This had to be him. Then I saw something in Arabic. I had no idea what it was and looked further but found nothing. I keyed in Thomas Barton, Turkey. Nothing. Then a piece on people trafficking on the Turkish border came up about a Brit who was in Turkey smoothing the way for people to make the journey to the UK. There were no pictures, though, only an anonymous side shot that looked similar to him. I was intrigued. This was going somewhere. I was beginning to see that Barton might be at the heart of the trafficking. If he was involved in trafficking human beings, then it wasn't a huge leap of the imagination to think that he might be involved in filming snuff movies where some poor innocent got bludgeoned to death. Whatever was going on here, I was in, hook, line and sinker. But first up was a visit to Shawlands to see if I could dig out Yates.

Yates's address was close to Shawlands in a big old triangular tenement building at Eglinton Toll which reminded me of the famous Flatiron Building on New York's Fifth Avenue. But that's where the similarities to Manhattan ended. Shawlands is in the Southside of Glasgow, but it has never really felt like Glasgow to me. Kind of like Glasgow's relative who lived down the road but didn't really get invited to family parties. When I went there as a cop, by the time I had crossed the Jamaica Bridge and down Kilmarnock Road, I always felt like I was leaving the city. Apparently, many years ago all this area was more of a village than a real part of the city, but these days it's home to a mixed bag of families, many of them Asian, and hipster youngsters on the early property ladder as you can get more house for your money in Shawlands.

I waited in my car just a few yards along from the entrance to Yates's building to see if there was any traffic in and out. I was more vigilant now, checking over my shoulder frequently, even in the city centre. My eyes flicked up and down the street in case there was anything to arouse my suspicion. I could see there was enough going on to let me slip in the main security door when someone was on the way out. I switched off my engine and got out of the car, hung around outside the building and in less than a minute I saw someone coming down the dark hallway. The woman didn't give me a second glance as she stepped past, and I slipped in. Yates's flat was two floors up. I was actually itching to knock on the door and just take the bull by the horns and start asking questions. But the cautious part of me, and there isn't a lot of that, told me to hang back. I looked all the way up to the fifth floor but there was no movement in the stairwell, so I took the stairs two at a time until I got to the second floor. The door had no name plate, probably intentional, as Yates would be trying to keep a low profile, given his background. I stood, catching my breath and listening, but could only hear the muffled sound of a television. Then suddenly I was startled by the clinking of locks and the door across the landing opened. I froze for a second as a thirty-something guy in a quilted jacket came onto the landing. I braced myself for trouble, almost waiting for him to attack me. Christ, I was edgy – perhaps a bit of delayed shock from last night's attack.

'You looking for somebody?'

I was relieved that he sounded more helpful than suspicious, so I gave him my best bewildered look.

'Er . . . Yes. I was looking for Colin Yates. But I think it's the next floor up.' I put my hand on the wooden banister and half turned as though I was going upstairs.

'Yates?' the guy said. 'That's his flat there.' He pointed to Yates's door. 'But he's not in. I saw him going out about fifteen minutes ago.'

I nodded. 'Okay. Thanks, I'll come back.'

I turned and found I was facing the guy, who was now giving me a longer look.

'Do you know Colin? Is he a friend?' he asked.

'I don't know him very well,' I answered, wanting the conversation to end.

'He's not a friend then?'

Jesus! I didn't expect the Spanish Inquisition. Talk about nosy neighbours. Sometimes they're useful, sometimes not. I didn't answer, but gave him a look that said enough with the questions. But as he was waiting for an answer I just shook my head.

'Right,' he said. 'He's a bit of a weirdo.'

My inner smile came right to the surface and I couldn't stop it. I looked at him and he smiled back.

'He hardly ever goes out, you know. Never talks to anyone. Only time he's out is to go to the shops or going down the Aldo's café. Every day. Always at this time, that's where he goes. I followed him one day, just because I was curious to see where he went.'

I was bursting to say, Who's the weirdo, mate? You're the one who's been following your neighbour. But it wouldn't have been a good idea. If he was telling me about his neighbour, then he couldn't be trusted not to run off at the mouth, so he wasn't getting to know any of my business.

'Thanks,' I said, and turned towards the stair and left ahead of him, aware he was following on the stone stairs behind me.

As I opened the main door and stepped out, he gave me a quick glance then walked briskly up the road. I knew Aldo's was close enough around the corner, so I waited until the nosy neighbour was well into the distance, then headed for the café.

I had studied Yates's picture on my laptop screen often enough to know that I'd be able to spot him in a crowd. Through the window I could see Aldo's was busy with teenagers and a couple of families. But within a few seconds of scanning the place, I spotted him in the far corner in a booth by himself. I stepped inside, and the warm air, thick with the smell of frying, wafted across to me, and I'd be lying if I denied that it made me hungry for café stodge on a cold winter's day. I stood for a moment and glanced around to look for an empty table, but the only one I was interested in was the table next to the booth where Yates sat. I walked towards it, careful not to look closely at him, but could see he was engrossed in some Danish pastry that he was slicing meticulously into strips. He hadn't looked in my direction. I made a snap decision and slipped into the booth opposite him and he looked up, alarmed at my invasion as he glanced at the empty table across the aisle. I put my hand up by way of apology. I spoke softly.

'Colin Yates?' I locked his startled eyes.

'What ... what the f—' He glanced around as though looking for someone to intervene and remove the intruder.

'It's okay, Colin. Don't worry. I'm sorry. I just need to talk to you.'

His eyes narrowed and his face flushed.

'What the fuck! Who are you? You can't just barge in here. Into . . . into, my space.' He spread his hands to demonstrate that this booth was his.

'I'm sorry, Colin. But I just need to talk. Just give me a moment to explain. I'm a private investigator—'

'Fuck! Fuck right off.'

'Please. Just bear with me. That's all. Then you can tell me where to go. Just give me a minute to explain.'

He sat fuming and I could hear his breathing hard and angry and a little desperate. His eyes dropped to the pastry he had so surgically prepared and he looked crestfallen. I had ruined his day. No doubt about it.

'Explain about what? What do you want with me?'

'It's not about you, Colin. Please. Just trust me. I'm not here about you, I promise you. I just wanted to run a name past you and see if you can help. A client of mine is in big trouble and a name has come up.'

'My name? Not my name,' he said defensively. 'I've served my time. I've done nothing wrong. My life has changed. I managed to waste it myself. Please. I don't want to get involved in anything.'

For a moment I thought he was going to cry. His lip trembled and his face crumpled a little. But then he tightened his lips and regained his composure.

'It's not about you. I'm trying to get information on a guy, and when I was digging up some old files and looking through some newspaper articles, your name came up.

About the videos you were charged with those years ago and why you got jailed.'

'I've done my time.'

'I know, I know. But this is much more serious than anything you were charged with. I just want to run a name past you. In case you can shed any light on him.'

He looked at me and I could see that, despite his anger and shock, he was curious enough not to do a runner.

'Thomas Barton,' I said, keeping my eyes on his.

I let the name hang there and watched his expression closely. He held my gaze for a few seconds then his eyes flicked down at the table. He recognised the name, that much I was sure of. I waited, but he didn't answer.

'You know him? Barton?'

He nodded, the muscle in his jaw tightening. Again the silence. I spread my hands a little and raised my eyebrows.

'Is he a mate? Did you work together at any time?'

He puffed. 'He's a prick. I don't want to be involved in anything to do with him.'

'You're not involved, Colin. I'm just trying to gather a bit of info on Barton. He's a cameraman, a photographer. Is that how come you knew him?'

His brain was ticking over, and I felt he was trying to work out a lie or a line to throw at me that would let him off the hook. There was nothing in Yates's demeanour that warmed me to him, and the fact that he sold child porn movies made him all the more sickening to me. Only in very dark moments did I ever consider that my Lucas, if he'd been abandoned or lost somewhere, could ever end up in one of those films. But I had to put that to the side. I needed to make him talk to me.

'I don't know what you're doing,' he said, 'or why you're looking at Barton. But all I'll say to you is, just watch your back. He's a polecat and he's mixed up with some very dangerous people, doing some very dangerous shit.'

I waited to see if there was any more. But there wasn't. Whatever he'd been doing in recent years, he obviously knew Barton well enough to know he was not just a cameraman.

'People trafficking? Drugs smuggling? Shooting snuff films?' I was leaning across the table so close to him that I could almost smell his fear. 'Am I close?'

He swallowed and his breathing became shallow. Then he nodded his head slowly.

'I don't want anything to do with that bastard. He's a parasite.'

'Can I ask you a question, Colin?' I didn't wait for an answer as I quickly added, 'Do you know if he ever worked in Turkey smoothing the way for refugees to come to UK – actually helping the traffickers?'

He nodded again. 'Parasite. Fucking parasite. He came to me last year and wanted to get me involved. No way. No fucking way would I do that.' He wrung his hands. 'Look. I sold movies. That was my crime. My shame, no doubt. But I made money, and I was stupid and ruthless and I'll have to live with what I did. But that shit Barton's doing? That's just evil.'

He picked up his coffee cup and sipped from it, then took a piece of pastry and stuffed it into his mouth. Maybe he needed the sugar. I took a moment to let him eat and get his breath back. I didn't want him to know it, but what he'd told me was a big breakthrough. Barton was everything Jackie had said he was.

'When did you last see Barton? Hear from him?'

He sighed. 'Maybe about six or seven months ago. I didn't know what he was up to, and assumed he was just doing the videos. I'm not going to judge him for that, after what I did. I mean, I was selling the shit, the child porn. I'm ashamed even to say it. So he called me and asked me to meet him for a coffee. I did. It was in here, actually. Then he told me what he was doing. Said there was big bucks in it if I came in with him.'

'Doing what?' I asked. 'What would you be doing if you came in with him?'

He shrugged. 'Distribution. Storing. That kind of stuff. But once he told me about the people trafficking I thought, no way. I would never get involved in that. And definitely not for snuff movies. But Barton said it was easy money. I was shocked, to be honest. I knew he was a money-grabbing arsehole but I was shocked he'd be involved in people trafficking and using refugees for those movies. It's . . . It's just beyond evil.'

'So you told him no. That you weren't interested.'

'Yep.'

'You heard from him since?'

He shook his head. 'No. Not a cheep. And I don't want to either.'

We sat in silence for a long moment. Then I took the card Jackie had given me out of my pocket. I held it up.

'This the Thomas Barton you know?'

He nodded and peered at the card. 'Can I see it, please?'

I handed it over to him, and he studied it, then flicked it over and looked at the back. He shook his head, incredulous.

'The Turks. He's involved with them. You know what this card is?'

'Do you?' I asked.

'He told me he was involved with a group of Turkish businessmen and that there were millions of pounds floating around and he was buying into it. He said he had a bank card that could get him access to loads of cash, as long as he kept delivering.'

'Sounds bizarre.'

He shrugged. Held up the card. 'Maybe. But what else can this mean?' He paused. 'Where did you get it, by the way? I know it's not my business.'

'He mislaid it,' I said.

That would have to be enough, and it was. We sat for a moment and I watched as he picked up the remaining pieces of his pastry and ate them. Then he took a long drink of tea from the mug and looked at me.

'So what do you want from me?' he said. 'Sounds like you already know plenty.'

I waited a few moments as I considered my next move. Yates hadn't been difficult to crack, as he had confirmed everything within ten minutes of meeting him. But I couldn't be sure if he was onside with me enough for me to trust him with more information.

'Do you know these Turks? Or any of the people Barton was involved with when he asked you to come in with him?'

I could tell from the look on his face that he knew who they were, so if he denied it then the conversation would be over.

Finally he nodded slowly, examining the backs of his hands. 'I know who they are.' Then he looked at me. 'But if you're smart you don't want to be rattling their cages. Trust me on that.'

'You mean the Turk?'

'Not just the Turk.'

'There's a Glasgow hood involved too,' I chanced. 'You know him?'

He nodded but didn't speak.

'You have a name?' I asked.

He looked at me. 'You don't have a name? You're the private eye here. If you don't have the name of the main man you're investigating, you're in trouble. You need to know that these are dangerous people. You can't just go wading in there noising these people up.'

'I don't have a name,' I said, feeling I had to justify myself. 'But I will by the end of the day, hopefully. But I have a picture of him. In fact, I have a picture of all the people involved.'

He looked surprised. 'Can I see?'

'Colin,' I said, as I brought my phone out of my bag, 'I'm doing a lot of trusting here. I mean, how do I know what you'll do with this information?'

He shrugged and puffed a little.

'Well, you don't.' He half smiled. 'But it's a chance you'll have to take. But I'm not going to go calling anyone telling them that you're looking for them, that's for sure. I don't want to be anywhere near it.' He raised a finger of warning. 'And if you're smart, neither should you.'

I looked at him, then out of the window where the afternoon light was fading.

'I have to, Colin.'

'Why?'

'I just have to. I can't tell you. But I'm not going to let this go.'

He studied my face for a long moment, trying to work out why this meant so much to me.

'Show me the pictures.'

It was risky and I knew it. But there was something about Yates sitting here, living his life the way he did, like a recluse, full of regret, that made me think maybe there was a scrap of decency about him after all, or there had been before he'd sold his soul. Maybe he was looking for a way to make amends. Or perhaps I was being naive. But I opened the screen, pulled up the pictures I had taken, then held it towards him. He examined them, then I expanded them, homing in on their faces.

'I don't know who the young guy is, but I know who the Turk is, and the man with him, and also the big man. He's Malky Jackson. He's a vicious bastard. He runs the women and the trafficking operation. He started out just running the traffic, the slave trade. But now he's branched into the movie game. Big business.'

'Where's he from?'

'As far as I know he lives in a penthouse down in the quayside. Well, he used to. He owns a couple of bars and lap-dancing places. And he keeps some of the girls in the flats where he runs a prostitution racket.'

'What about the Turk?'

'The one on the left of your picture, I don't know when he got involved. But the Turk on the right, he's the main man. He runs the network from the refugee areas picking people, making the promises and shit. Jackson has a haulage business going to and from Europe. Big containers, that's what he uses to bring the people in. It's mostly about the slave trade for him, but if they're making snuff movies with them then he won't give a shit about that. They're just money to him. I'm surprised none of the immigrants have died in those big containers, but I suppose it's just a matter of time, because according to Barton he's bringing in more and more every week.'

We sat for a moment, saying nothing, and I saw that Yates was angry and disgusted. For a man who used to distribute child porn he had no place taking the moral high ground. But I wasn't here to judge, just to milk him for information.

How did I know that he wouldn't pick up the phone and alert Barton that I was on his tail? That's the problem in this kind of job – sometimes you just don't know. Sometimes you just go with your gut and hope you get lucky. This was one of those moments.

'Okay,' I said. 'You've been helpful, Colin, and I'm grateful for that. Look, I can't go into details about my investigation because that would be all sorts of wrong. But you seem like a decent enough guy, and I get the impression that if you knew what Barton had done and the reason I'm looking at him, then you would be totally on my side. But, as I say, it's not fair to divulge what I'm doing. Wouldn't be fair to my client, and it could jeopardise everything.'

His eyes darted from the table to me.

'What – you think I'll leave here and go warning Barton that some private eye is looking at him?' He shook his head. 'Well. You don't know me. And I don't know you either, or even if I can trust you. But I can tell you something. When

Barton told me what he was doing I was sick to my stomach, and that's the truth. I wouldn't go anywhere near the bastard. He's filth. That's all he is. Pond water.' He paused for a second and glanced at me again. 'I told you, you want to be careful, noising these guys up. They're dangerous.'

I let it hang, then I went with my gut feeling.

'Colin. If I was to ask you to help me track him down, would you do that?'

He took his time, looking beyond me as though he was imagining what the consequences of his next answer would be. Then eventually he spoke.

'I don't want involved with anything that brings in cops. I don't want anywhere near that.'

'No cops,' I said. 'I'm not dealing with the cops. I'm working for a client.'

He looked at me quizzically, but he was smart enough to know I wouldn't say any more about who I was working for. I felt I had to sell this better.

'All I'm going to tell you is that Barton is part of something that is, well, how can I put it, the worst thing you can imagine, and it involves my client.' I knew it sounded a bit convoluted. The worst thing you can imagine is all relative to who you are, and for me, stealing someone's baby is the worst horror you can ever imagine, but Yates might have a different threshold of terror. I hoped I'd said enough. Eventually he spoke.

'Okay. I'll help you,' he said, to my surprise. 'I have a

phone number for him and I know where he can be found. Or where he used to be found. If he's up to his arse in something then he might not be there any more. But I can give you the information I have. That's all.'

That was good enough. I took the phone number and address down on a piece of paper and shoved it into my pocket. I stood up.

'Thanks,' I said and hoped he knew I meant it. 'You've been a big help.' I hesitated a moment, then chanced my arm. 'If there's anything else you can think of, then give me a shout if you can.'

I gave him my card and he turned it over in his hand, looking at it then up at me. He raised his chin a little in acknowledgement but didn't say anything. I turned and left.

CHAPTER FIFTEEN

My flat overlooks the lush gardens on Blythswood Square, surrounded by classy sandstone apartment blocks, once the swanky homes of the city's cotton and shipping merchants. The square at the top of one of Glasgow's seven hills oozes money and respectability. But just around the corner is the notorious red light area – known as The Drag – where prostitutes hang out, hawking their drug-addled, skinny bodies to pay for their next heroin fix. Sleazy punters looking for cheap sex have cruised this area for decades, but a couple of generations ago, the prostitutes who hung around here didn't look like the emaciated waifs of these days, barely able to stand up in shop doorways. Back in the day, the ladies of the night might have been passable enough to be procured by bellboys from the clubs and hotels on the square to pleasure rich clients in town for the night. But the end game was still the same. At the end of each encounter, the women were diminished a little more as they went back to their pitch to wait for the next customer. These days, it felt more desperate, more lowlife, and always, always, there was a parasite pimp or dealer waiting in the shadows for his hooker to come back with her dough. Every time I stand at my window it makes me feel still, and a little desolate inside. And tonight was no different. It was already dark by the time I got home, and the rain turned to sleet was making the streets brown with slush. But in the padlocked gardens it was still a blanket of white with only the snow on branches of the sycamores beginning to melt and drip. I suppose my father bought this flat because it had a calmness about it, close enough to the buzz of the city and far enough away to think you were somewhere else. I used to wonder if maybe he bought it because it reminded him of back home in Sweden, where he grew up in a fine apartment in the centre of Stockholm. There was probably a lot of his life when he longed to be back there instead of bang in the middle of Glasgow, which must have seemed a million miles away from where he was raised. He died before I ever got the chance to have conversations like that with him, and there is a bleakness in me because I never had those teenage years you are supposed to have with parents when you are becoming an adult and getting to know them on a different level. I try not to go to these places in my head, and I'm usually successful about moving on, and pushing hopeless thoughts away. But tonight, looking at the snow in the square and the silence in this big shadowy house, it takes me back . . .

I was only twelve when I was put on a plane and sent to Sweden. It was a place that had wonderful childhood memories of warm summers, swimming in lakes, walking in never-ending forests of pine and spruce trees that seemed to go all the way up to the sky. But most of all, my memories were of the quiet patience of the people. They were different from the people I was used to back in Glasgow, who could be brash and funny, and always talking. They were different from my mother, who was half Irish and funny and clever. They were like my father, who always seemed calm and understated, who never shouted or lost his temper. And yet inside there must have been all this turmoil that made him leave me and my mother the way he did. When you're twelve you cannot even begin to understand that. And I still don't. But when you're twelve and you've lost both your parents in the space of a year, you don't have any thoughts other than fear and grief and wondering what has happened to your world.

I went to live with my Aunt Lilly in Sweden, the only alternative being put into a Glasgow children's home. Even though my aunt clearly didn't want me, she would never have forgiven herself if she'd abandoned her only brother's child into care. She actually told me this, though it was much later on, when I had become a troubled teenager living in her home. The first night I arrived, she didn't even come to the airport to meet me, but sent some man from the village to pick me up. I remember the trip to her house, which was three hours from Stockholm, where I had only visited with my parents when I was very young. Sometimes, when I can't sleep and my demons haunt me, I can still see myself that night, gazing out of the window of the car as the roads and landscape and lights from the city passed in a blur until we reached the edge of the coastal town of Vastervik where she lived in a smallholding. Aunt Lilly didn't greet or embrace me as I got out of the car. She stood in the doorway, her expression cold and distant, her blonde hair cut in a Cleopatra-style bob, with sharp cheekbones and striking good looks. I wasn't sure if I should move towards her, and it was only when her friend took my bags out of the boot of the car that she eventually cracked a smile and beckoned me over. She didn't ask me how I was or how was my trip, or any of the stuff that when I look back maybe she should have asked. But I could see that there was a sadness about her too, a distance, and I didn't know why. As time went on, she seemed slightly bitter about most things, whether she was reading the newspaper or watching television. I don't think I ever remember her laughing out loud. But that first night, sitting in that little, neat living room with the log fire and the coloured throws on the sofas, it was the quietness, the heavy silence that got me. I was fed and sent for a bath and shown my room. There was no anger or gruffness, just a coldness, and perhaps that's because I didn't ask any questions or have any conversation. I tried to speak a couple of times, but there was a lump and a tightness in my throat because I was holding back the floodgates of grief. Eventually, when I was told it was bedtime, she simply said we had to make the best of what we had, because that was what her brother, my father, would have wanted. And that was it. I can still feel my face on the pillow that night, wet with tears, bewildered that my life had come to this and hoping that when I awoke in the morning none of it would be true. But it was.

The upside of the grim existence I had been thrust into was that when I went to school, I fitted in in terms of appearance with the rest of the blonde, white-faced, blue-eyed children. But I was by no means one of them, and was ostracised as an outsider for not really being Swedish. I learned to tough it out. And in time I made some good friends, but I was never really one of them. I even grew to love much about the country and the people, and, in time, like most children, I adapted and began to accept that this was my home. By the time I was fourteen I was well accepted and running with a crowd of teenagers who were pushing the boundaries on every level. We were smart, educated kids, some from families with money, but all hanging out in that teenage way, drinking, smoking, sexually fumbling their way through adolescence. In all of that, studying came easy to me, and I excelled at school. But when it came to university, I chose to go back to Glasgow. I had made some really good friends in Sweden, but just being there was a reminder of everything I had lost. I yearned to go back to the warmth of this big city where the people were different, and loud and overstated. So I came back to Glasgow for the first time since I was twelve, back to the flat that had been my childhood home. It was once filled with my father's jazz music and my mother's paintings in every room. And although it was beautiful and luxurious, it was empty and sad, until the arrival of my heart and my life, my Lucas. The last I heard from Sweden, my aunt was in a nursing home, and the house and farm she lived on for years would be mine in due course. I should visit her some time, and show her the kindness that she had never shown me.

My mobile rang on the coffee table and startled me out of my reverie.

'Billie? Is that you?'

It sounded like Johnny.

'Who's this?'

'It's Johnny. Have you forgot me already?'

I smiled at his dig, glad that despite the shitty life he was living he could still find a bit of that Glasgow swagger.

'Of course not, Johnny. I was just making sure. You never know in this game. How you doing?'

'Awright. Listen – mind I told you about that wean? In the Calton?'

My heart skipped a beat.

'Yes. I do. You got news?'

'Aye. Well, I think so. It's a wee lassie. I saw her this afternoon. There's something funny going on. Because that woman I was talking to you about, my dealer's bird – Lainey. I don't know her, like. I mean, I've only seen her three or four times. But I never knew anything about her having a wean. I've never seen a wean with her in the house before, or even anywhere else. I might be wrong. But I think I would have known if she had a wean. You just know stuff like that.'

I hoped Johnny wasn't too spaced out. He sounded quite coherent, but you had to be careful around addicts, even ones who seemed smacked out of their heads. There was always a cunning about them that they had learned as part of their addiction. If they could sense you wanted to hear something, they would tell you what you wanted to hear if it meant a few quid.

'What kind of age are we talking about, for the little girl?'

'Dunno. But not a new baby or anything. I think maybe about a year or something, maybe a bit more – maybe two.'

'And you saw her? Where was this? In your dealer's house?'

'Aye. He lives in a flat in the Calton. I didn't think his bird lived with him, but seems she does, well, just now anyway. You never know. But there is a wean in there.'

'Maybe she's looking after the kid for someone, like a sister or a friend?'

'Aye. I didn't want to ask. I only saw the wean for a minute or two when the bird had to take a phone call and she left her sitting on the floor in the kitchen when Jimba was sorting me out with some stuff.'

The very image of this, of a kid sat on the floor of a smack den with a parade of junkies in and out all day long, made my chest tighten.

'What was the kid like, Johnny? I mean, was she crying? Or did she seem okay?'

'I didn't notice too much. I didn't want to draw attention that I was interested in her. She was crying in the beginning, but the bird gave her a biscuit and she stopped.'

My mind was already going into overdrive trying to work out how I could get into that house, even just to have a look. But in a place like the Calton, you didn't just walk into a street and knock on doors. Behind every window you were being watched by neighbours protecting each other, watching for cops or social security snoops or any chancer who might come in and move into your turf. You didn't walk in there if you didn't belong.

'Are you there, Billie?'

'I am. Sorry, Johnny. I was thinking of a way I could get in to see the kid. But it's pretty impossible in the Calton.'

'Billie, do you think this wean I saw is that lassie's? That Jackie lassie that they wanted you to stay away from?'

I had to be careful about saying too much to him. Any time he'd brought the kid up before I hadn't made a big deal of it, but it looked like he was beginning to piece things together. Even in his drug-muddled mind, there was someone smart underneath it all.

'I don't know. I've no way of knowing really. And look, Johnny. You can't go asking any questions either. You'll get yourself in a lot of trouble if you start doing that.'

'I know. I'm no' daft. But that's fucking wrong if they've got that lassie's wean, and the wee thing is sitting about in that shithole. Christ! If I ever have a wean I would never have her near a place like that.'

Part of me wanted to ask for more details about inside the house, but the thought of it would only torture me. And anyway, when I was a cop I'd been in those stinking houses full of people all smacked out of their heads. So I very much got the picture.

'Do you have an address, Johnny? I'm not going to go there, but just an address would be good.'

'Aye. It's a top flat. Number twenty-three Balbeg Street. Most of the houses are boarded up in the block but you'd be able to see it. It's got a steel door. In case the cops come barging in – gives Jimba time to get rid of his stuff.'

'Good. Thanks, Johnny,' I said. I knew he would want paying for this information, but I couldn't do it tonight. 'Look. Can we meet tomorrow? I want to drop you a few quid for your tip.'

'Aye. That'll be fine. But, Billie? If these cunts have stole that lassie's wean, I'll help you. I don't want money.'

'Thanks, Johnny. How about I call you in the morning and we can meet for a chat and a coffee.'

'Aye. Great.'

I hung up, touched by Johnny's enthusiasm to do the right thing, but hoping he didn't start asking questions when he was full of smack. He could end up dead if he opened his mouth in the wrong company.

CHAPTER SIXTEEN

Wherever I go in my dreams, my first thought when I wake up is always the same. Lucas's absence fills every room. In the life I used to live, in the me I used to be, he is everywhere. If he hadn't climbed in beside me in the night, spreading himself across my bed, I would wake to the sound of his giggling in another room, or the roar of him chasing imaginary monsters along the hall. In the beginning, when he was taken, the silence killed me, and as soon as I was awake I would have to switch on the television or radio for a noise to fill the emptiness. But these days I can trust myself to lie in bed for a few minutes, listening and remembering, because that is all I have now. Until I find him. But I cannot allow myself to dwell for too long in that desolate place in my head, or I will never get out of bed. So, quickly, my thoughts turned to Jackie Foster, and to her pain, and to where the hell I was going with this investigation. I cannot let her down. Before I drifted off to sleep last night, I was

figuring out my options. Digging out Barton from whatever stone he was hiding under was my initial plan. But
even if I did find him, he was never going to come clean.
That would involve him putting his hands up and going to
the thugs with their drugs and films and forgetting whatever plan he'd cooked up when he'd stolen from them. And
it would make him a dead man. No doubt the coke would
already have been moved on by now anyway, because
nobody steals another person's cocaine haul unless they
plan to sell it for themselves. I asked myself if I was making
the right decision by not going to the cops. But that was a
minefield. Bringing all of them in would result in a major
shakedown of everyone involved and would put Jackie's
baby at risk. And the police had a dog in this fight anyway,
because they had covered up the McPhee witness statement, so it wasn't in their interest to bring all of that out
into the open. Scanlon would disagree with me, no doubt,
but I didn't want to risk it. There might come a time when
I had no other option but to go to the police, but that wasn't
right now. The more I thought about it, the more I came
back to what my gut was telling me. I had to play these
guys at their own game. They were hoodlums, so it would
take a better one to beat them. Paddy Harper came to mind.
The big gangster who controlled the north side of the city
had been in jail for the past eight years for attempted murder, and had only been released a few months ago. I didn't
know him, but our paths had crossed when, as a young

detective, I investigated the brutal beating of a thug who Harper had hit so hard he'd blinded him in one eye. The thug had bullied his teenage son and humiliated him to the point that the boy was suicidal. I told the truth in the witness box and my testimony helped Harper get off with probation instead of jail time. There was widespread fury among the cops that I hadn't embellished my evidence to get Harper put away. Plenty of cops lied in the witness box, but I wasn't one of them. I got pelters from my boss. Harper approached me after the case and said if I ever needed anything then I should get in touch. I told myself I never would. I never needed to. But maybe it was time. I didn't have a contact for him, but I knew where to find someone who did.

It was getting light as I got out of bed, and from the window I could see the snow in the square gardens was melting and patchy from the rain. I wished I could close my eyes and take myself back to before all this happened, to the time when I had Lucas and a whole day to look forward to. 'Until I find you,' I whispered to myself as I have done many times when I wake in the morning. 'This will be me until I find you.' I blinked back the darkness and pulled open the curtains. That was for another day. I would go and see Harper. This would either work or it wouldn't, and there was only one way to find out.

The Balmore Bar wasn't the kind of place that welcomed new visitors. Not that there were many tourists. It was the kind of place that if you happened into it by mistake, you backed out very quickly after all heads had turned towards you with suspicious glares. In the middle of the notorious tough housing scheme of Possilpark in the north of the city, the customers were locals and they were protective of their own people and their turf, whether they were the hard men or just punters. There were only a few people inside when I arrived, two playing pool and a couple of older worthies sat at the bar. All eyes turned towards me when I came in the swing doors. That's not the kind of thing that would ever faze me, and I went up to the bar and ordered a soda and lime. The barman served me, but stood for a moment, waiting for the question, because there had to be a reason for a woman not from around here to waltz into the Balmore at this time of day.

'I'm looking for Jimmy Murdoch. Has he been in?' I asked, sipping my drink.

There was no answer for a moment. Then he shrugged.

'Not today. Was here last night. Who's asking?'

'Me,' I said, giving him a long look.

He snorted and flashed a half smile.

'You got a name, Me?'

I let it hang for a couple of beats.

'I have, if you know where to find Jimmy. You got a phone number for him?'

'Aye.'

'Good. Well how about you call him and ask him if he's free.'

'You polis?'

'No.' I shook my head.

'You know Jimmy? Is he a friend?'

'You polis?' I said, mocking his earlier question.

He gave me a sarcastic smile, then went across to the phone mounted on the wall behind the bar.

'I'll phone him. Who will I say is asking?'

'Just say Billie.'

'Billy? As in King Billy?' he said, eyebrows raised. I could see the two men at the counter were engrossed.

'Yeah.'

'Billy,' he repeated.

'That's right. If you just tell him I'm here and would like to talk to him if he's got a minute.'

He shrugged and I watched as he keyed in the digits on the phone.

Then he spoke.

'Jimmy. Davey at the Balmore. There's a bird—A woman here asking for you. Name is Billy? Wants to talk to you.'

I didn't hear what Jimmy said, but the barman looked across to me and held out the receiver on the grimy cream cord. I walked to the other side of the bar and he stretched it across to me. I turned away towards the toilets as the whole bar was listening to me.

'Hi, Jimmy. How you doing? Sorry to bother you. But I'm looking for a contact number.' I lowered my voice. 'For Paddy. You got a number?'

There was a pause for a moment. Then he spoke.

'Aye. But better if I get in touch with him and give him your number. Been a long time, Billie.'

'It has, Jimmy.'

'You all right?'

'I'm all right.'

'Good. I'll ask Paddy to phone you.' He paused. 'I wouldn't be hanging around in there though. Not the place for a good-looking woman like yourself.'

'Sure. I'm just leaving. If you ask your man to phone me, Jimmy, I'd really appreciate it.'

'I will. You watch yourself.'

'Always.' The line went dead.

I called Johnny on the drive back to my office and was about to hang up after a dozen rings, when I heard his voice.

'You all right, Johnny? Took a while to answer.'

'Aye. I was sleeping.'

It was midday on my dashboard clock and even by junkie standards that was a lie-in.

'Sleeping? The day's nearly gone,' I breezed. 'Did you have a late night?'

'A bit. To tell you the truth, Billie, I got wasted last night.

I've been trying to cut the smack right down, but it just happened last night. I had a bit of money.'

I was immediately suspicious that he suddenly had money, as it flitted across my mind that he might have sold my information. No. If he'd done that, he'd have had to admit that he'd met me, and no matter what he told them, he'd still be dead meat.

'You up for a cup of tea somewhere?' I asked. 'East End? I'm out and about. I'll buy you breakfast.'

'Aye. That'd be great,' he yawned.

'I'll meet you in Di's café down the Gallowgate. You know it?'

'Aye.'

'See you there in fifteen minutes.'

I hung up, wondering what kind of nick he'd be in when he arrived.

I parked my car where I could see it and sat by the window at Di's café. The squally shower had washed away the remnants of the snow, and the grey, heavy sky seemed appropriate for the depressing backdrop of boarded up shops and businesses in the fringes of the Merchant City, the part that hadn't yet been given a makeover. Despite its dreariness, I'd come to these places any day for a coffee rather than be perched on a high stool leaning on a shelf of a trendy barista bar looking out at Buchanan Street. I think better in places like this, where appearances don't matter. And just as well. I saw Johnny crossing the road, bouncing on rubbery legs as he approached the café. I looked up when he came in the door, and he gave me a nod as he walked to my table and sat down. He stank. Big time. He was wearing the same sweatshirt that was grubby at the cuffs two days ago and was now stained with what looked like curry sauce down the front. His hollow cheeks were the colour of whey, and as he sniffed and drew the back of his hand across his nose I could see he was trembling.

'You feeling all right, Johnny? You're looking a bit rough.'

He sniffed again, glancing over his shoulder as though watching for someone to pounce.

'Aye. I've got the fear,' he said. 'You know what I mean? Paranoid as fuck, man. Shouldn't have had that smack last night.'

I looked at him, knowing that the only thing that would sort him out fast was another hit of something. And a little alarm was going off in my head that this guy was my only inside track in the hunt for a missing baby. Christ!

'Let's get some breakfast into you. Maybe you'll feel better when you eat,' I said, waving the waitress across.

He looked up at her, shifting nervously in his seat.

'Can I get a burger and chips? And a Coke? And tea?'

He glanced from the waitress to me, wondering if he'd over-ordered. I smiled and ordered a bacon roll and coffee for myself. When the waitress turned away, Johnny fidgeted with the salt in his trembling hands. I hoped he wasn't about to have a complete meltdown.

'You sure you're all right?'

'Yeah. I'll be fine when I eat,' he said. 'But I'm definitely not doing that shit again. I made my mind up, Billie. I'm going to see the doctor today. I know I'll not get a rehab place or anything right away, but I need to get some help. Maybe even go to NA – you know Narcotics Anonymous? Or somewhere with people to talk to.'

I wasn't expecting the full Samaritans-style disclosure but I felt for this edgy shadow of a boy and wondered at what stage of his life he'd thrown himself to the wolves like this, or whether someone had done it for him. I made my mind up to call my GP friend this afternoon to see if there was anything he could do to push his case on. Probably not. But it was worth a try.

'So,' I said, feeling I had to try and divert his attention from the paranoia. 'Have you seen anything else? You know, down in the Calton? Any news.'

He brightened, nodding. 'Aye. There is, actually. That's part of the reason I'm in the nick I'm in just now.' He paused. 'I don't see the dealer all the time, especially as I've been trying to just rely on the methadone, and I've not got much money. But yesterday, he phoned me and said to come down and do some drops for him. You know what I mean?'

I nodded, but didn't reply.

'Well, there were five drops, so I got a few quid out of it.

And that's how I ended up getting into the smack last night with my wee buddy. But anyway, while I was in the dealer's house in the afternoon, I heard him talking on his mobile. He went down into the hall but left the door open and I could hear him. He said something about them needing to move the wean, because his bird was fed up with her. She wanted to go out and do stuff but she was stuck with this wean who needed feeding and stuff, and looking after.' He paused, looked at me. 'So that made me think for sure that this wasn't his bird's wean. Definitely not. She wouldn't say that if it was her own.'

This was dynamite stuff, and if it was true, we didn't have a lot of time.

'Did you see the kid yesterday?'

'Aye.' His eyes widened. He went into his jacket pocket and took out his mobile. 'I even took a picture.'

I hoped my mouth hadn't dropped open with shock.

'You took a picture? Jesus! Inside your dealer's house?'

'Aye,' he said, grinning through his gap tooth. 'It was done dead quick. His bird came into the kitchen and sat the kid on the floor then went away, and my dealer was in the other room, so I just snapped away.'

'Christ, Johnny! That was seriously risky,' I said. 'I didn't want you to do anything like that – anything that could put you in danger.'

He looked a little deflated. 'I thought you'd be pleased. Look!'

He brought up a picture up of a little dark-eyed girl with matted hair and a snotty nose, sitting on the grimy vinyl floor. It felt like my heart actually stopped in my chest.

'I *am* pleased, Johnny. Totally amazed. It's a huge help.' I looked at him. 'But it was really dangerous for you.'

He shrugged. 'The shit I was shooting into my veins last night was dangerous too, Billie. Who gives a fuck!'

We sat for a moment and I looked again at the picture.

'Can you WhatsApp it to me?'

I heard it ping on my phone a second later, and I desperately wanted to rush out and see Jackie to ask her if this was her baby. But I knew I couldn't do that. She would totally freak out if it was, and we still wouldn't be able to go and get her.

The waitress came with the food and we ate in silence for a while as I watched Johnny wolf down the carbs. He drank almost the full glass of Coke in a oner and asked for another straight away, needing the sugar rush. It was weird, but I could see him perk up like a string puppet before my eyes, and by the end of the meal he had stopped trembling and was more relaxed. I looked at him as he sipped his tea and bit into a piece of cake.

'You should see that doctor today, Johnny,' I said. 'I mean it. Look, I don't know you from Adam, but from what I see you're a decent enough guy and you need to find that guy again.'

He nodded. 'I know.'

I wanted to pay him for being brave enough to take the picture, and if this was really a picture of Jackie's baby there was no amount of money that would be enough. But, of course, I couldn't tell him that. And I couldn't pay him a lot of money, because, despite what he promised himself, he would end up blowing it on heroin. When we finished he sat back, hands in his pockets.

'Listen, Johnny, I want to give you a few quid for your help on this. It could mean a lot to my investigation,' I said. 'But I'm worried if I give you money you'll do what you did yesterday and just get out of it.'

He nodded. 'I know. But I won't. I'm going to get out of the squat I'm staying in, and rent a place in the unit. If I pay a week's rent upfront, it'll be good for me, so I'm not dossing just anywhere. It's when you're just dossing you get involved. I've got a social worker and stuff, and I can talk to him and see if he can help me out. You know, maybe in time get me a council flat or something. But I have to start somewhere.'

I wanted to believe him but I'd heard it before from people like him who'd never made it.

CHAPTER SEVENTEEN

The last time I saw Paddy Harper was in a newspaper photograph after he was released from prison. The story was that he'd been freed early, and that he was still a wealthy man with properties and business across the city and in the south of Spain. The article hinted at retribution for the men who had turned Queen's evidence against him and put him inside. He'd made no comment, and afterwards it seemed he melted into the background as a businessman. The allegations he was a gangland kingpin were now part of Glasgow folklore. I had only met him a couple of times before he got jailed – the first time was as a detective after I gave the evidence. Then weeks later, out of the blue, Paddy approached me in a restaurant while I was having dinner with my husband. He looked me in the eye as he leaned towards me, and whispered that I had done the right thing, which was rare, he said, for a cop. And he added again that if there was ever anything I needed, then to contact him.

Anything, he'd emphasised. I did bump into him and Jimmy Murdoch a couple of times over the following months in a Glasgow bar, where the clientele was a broad mix of lawyers, cops, villains and journalists, all drinking together. From what I could make of him, he was almost charming, if you didn't know his reputation.

I spotted him in the Ashton Lane bistro, a Belgian place, which I knew was discreet and kind of out of the way. He was drinking coffee and sitting on a bench seat in the corner of the still mostly empty room after the lunchtime traffic. He stood up as I approached and stretched out a hand.

'Billie,' he said. 'How you doing? Good to see you.'

I wasn't quite sure how I should play this, so I thought it best to keep to small talk for the moment. I shook his hand, and he motioned for me to sit down.

'I'm fine, thanks, Paddy. I hope you don't mind me getting in touch.'

He looked back, disarming me a little, as though he could see something in me, and he waited a beat before he shook his head.

'I told you, Billie. Remember? Anything I can ever do for you.'

I nodded, and was glad when the waitress came up, as I wasn't quite sure where to begin. I'd never had an actual conversation with this man sitting opposite me, his grey eyes and silver hair giving him an older, benign look, but the scar running down the outside of his jaw telling another story. I ordered a flat white coffee from the waitress and watched as she left, then turned to Paddy.

'Thanks, Paddy. I appreciate that.' I took a breath, feeling a little uneasy and unsure of whether I was doing the right thing. I clasped my hands on the table, conscious he was studying me.

'To tell you the truth,' I said, 'I'm looking to see if you might be able to help. Or maybe even to pick your brains? I don't know if you know, but I'm not in the police any more.'

He nodded slowly. 'I saw. I read about it – the inquiry.' He shrugged. 'Whatever happened that day, as far as I'm concerned you did the right thing. Shooting that fucker meant one piece of scum was off the face of the earth.'

I looked at him, then at the table.

'I'm a private investigator now. I left the police a couple of years after all that shit. Even though I was cleared, it didn't feel right, you know, some of the people around me, stuff like that.'

He nodded. 'I heard you left. I talk to some of the good cops from time to time, and they told me.' He looked at me. 'For what it's worth, Billie, it's their loss. You were a good cop, and they're a bit thin on the ground as far as I'm concerned.' He paused, almost smiling. 'So you're a private eye now? I heard that too. What's that like? Not too many women in that kind of job, is there? I don't suppose it's anything like the movies, is it?'

I smiled, feeling a little more relaxed.

'No. Nothing like the movies. Not that exciting most of the time. Much of it is mundane, stake-outs, that kind of thing. But I do like the investigating side of it, finding things out, getting things sorted for people. I get all sorts walking through my door.'

'I bet you do.' He paused. 'Is that why you're here?'

My cue. 'Yes. I'll be honest with you, Paddy. I've got a case I'm investigating. And I know that some very heavy people are doing a lot of bad things. If I was a cop, the full force would be wading right in there and sorting it out. But there's reasons I can't go there.' I paused. 'I'm probably not making much sense.'

He put a hand up. 'Billie, just tell me what's going on. What do you need? If I can help, I'll make it happen.'

'It's . . . well . . . It's . . .' I cursed myself for stuttering and not knowing where to begin. 'There's a girl came into my office. Young woman. In a real state. She says her baby was stolen. Someone, some hoodlums, she claimed, involved in some terrible shit, took her baby – to try and get her to give them stuff that she can't give them.'

His eyebrows knitted in confusion.

'Is it drugs? She owe them money? I can't imagine any-one who would take anyone's kid to get money from them.'

'It's worse than that. It's complicated. And it involves cops.'

There was a definite glint in his eyes now.

'Cops? A baby stolen? I'm intrigued.'

I took a breath. 'Okay. Let me start again. You might have seen a story a while ago about a car crash and a girl saying she'd lost a baby? Then the story died.'

He sat back, his mind picking up the thread.

'I do remember. Crash out near the switchback. Girl was cut out of the wreckage, and some stuff about a missing baby. But then it seemed to go away, didn't see any more about it.'

'Because she changed her story. That's why. She told police there was no baby.'

'And now she's told you there is.'

'Yes.'

He folded his arms. Then nodded the waitress across.

'I might need another coffee for this. So just tell me everything you know, Billie. And if there is something I can do, then I will.'

'Okay.'

Over the next few minutes I told him everything, and he sat nodding, surprised when I mentioned Malky Jackson. I saw red mist in his eyes at the mention of people trafficking, snuff movies, and then the baby. And then McPhee's apparent suicide. I even told him about being attacked by the thug outside the kebab shop, and he winced and looked genuinely angry when I pulled back my sweater to show him the marks. Maybe I was wrong to spill it all out to a guy like him, a man I didn't know other than by reputation, but I had to trust my gut. Time would tell. When I finished, he sat for a few moments, his fingers drumming on the table as though he was picking out notes on a piano. Then he inhaled through his nose and sat back, pushing out a sigh, shaking his head.

'Malky Jackson. Fucking pond life. Always was. I'm not surprised he and his lowlifes got one of their thugs to rough you up. You must be getting too close.' He glanced at me. 'You know him? Anything about him?'

I shook my head. 'I don't remember him coming up on my radar when I was a cop. But I could be wrong.'

'He's been around a while, but only in the last three years, moving up the food chain, if you know what I mean.' He paused. 'Can't believe the bastard is into the smuggling racket, stacking them poor people into containers. But he'll have seen how money can be made in that game, and Jackson doesn't give a shit how he makes his dough.'

I knew from my cop days that Paddy had made a lot of money smuggling in cannabis, and rumour had it also heroin, but he was never convicted of anything. I wasn't going to point that out to him right now. In the past years, even before he was sent down for attempt murder, he was already out of the sewers and into property, giving him a tag of respectability.

'So what do you think?' I asked breaking the long silence.

He narrowed his eyes.

'So you think the baby is in the Calton? You have the address, right?'

'I do.'

'Okay. I have to think about the best way to tackle this, Billie. You've got an address for Barton?'

'I have. It's over the water in Kinning Park, flats by the river. I haven't been to his house yet.'

He nodded. 'I might pay him a visit. You want to come along?'

All the alarms going off in my head were saying No, I don't want to be anywhere near Barton's home when he gets a visit from your boys. But the reckless part of me wasn't listening.

'Let me know when you're going,' I heard myself saying.

A trace of a smile moved on Paddy's lips and he looked at me with something that might have been admiration that I had truly crossed to the other side.

On the way back to my office my mobile rang on the passenger seat, and I automatically glanced across but there was no name. I pushed the hands-free button on my steering wheel but didn't speak.

'Billie Carlson?'

'Who's this?'

'It's Yates. I need to talk to you. Not on the phone. Can you come to my place?'

'Sure. Now? What's up?'

'I've got some information. About Barton.'

'I'm on my way.'

I swung my car around on the Broomielaw to head back down to the Jamaica Bridge. But as I did, there was an almighty bang and for a moment it was as though I had lost consciousness. The side of my head hit the driver's window and jerked my neck so hard that the searing pain almost made me pass out. But it was over so fast I couldn't work out what had happened. Then I saw a big angry guy coming towards me, and I suddenly realised his car must have hit me square on the driver's door as I'd made the U-turn. I was dizzy and barely taking in the scene, but I could hear him shout and curse as he marched towards my car.

'You stupid fucking bitch! You didn't even look where you were going. Fucking swung right round! Fuck! Look at my car!'

I sat for a moment, hearing it, but the ringing in my ears from the impact was making it all seem hazy and distant. I could barely remember swinging my car around, but I must have done, or I wouldn't be sitting here with this guy bawling at me, his eyes jumping with rage and indignation. I stared at him for a moment, then I listened to the sound of traffic honking horns, backing up already along the Broomielaw. Get out of the car, I told myself, but I could feel my hands shaking. The side of my head was pulsing with pain and I reached up and touched it, wincing. My fingers were wet. I was bleeding. Christ. The only relief was that I'd been bumped in an accident, and it wasn't an attack. I glanced up and out of the window and his shouting seemed to calm down when he saw the blood that was now trickling down my cheek. I must have looked helpless and about to burst into tears because suddenly he stopped yelling.

'Are you all right, hen? Sorry for shouting. I'm . . . I just got such a fright. Are you all right?'

I looked up at him, still in a daze, and nodded. Then I heard the sound of a police car coming from behind me and saw one speeding towards me from my driver's mirror. Jesus Christ! The car pulled up at the side of the road, half mounting the kerb. I could hear the police radio crackling and felt momentarily somehow dazzled by the flashing lights. I took a breath. Pull yourself together. The next few minutes were a blur as the policeman leaned in the window, asking me if I was okay, and giving me a cloth to wipe the blood. He told me to come out of the car, and I got out a little unsteadily, and glimpsed the female cop who was with him raise her eyebrows. They ushered me into the back of the police car, and I knew I was going to be breathalysed. While I was there, trying to get myself back to some kind of normality, I could hear them asking what had happened, and suggesting I go to the hospital. Then I remembered. Yates. Shit. I was supposed to be on my way to see him. I looked at my watch, but couldn't even remember what time we'd had our conversation. Everything was coming at me in images – my conversation with Paddy Harper, my driving down from the West End, and then bang. I was piecing it together. I had to get out of here quickly.

'Do you want us to take you up to the hospital?' the cop asked. 'You've taken a dunt on the head there. You're bleeding.'

'I'm okay,' I said quickly. 'Look. It's my fault. I took my eye off the ball for a moment.'

They said nothing and handed me the breathalyser. I blew into it, knowing it would come up clear. It did, and after a couple of minutes with the sound of the radio crackling and instructions all around me like some kind of surreal dream, the cop turned to me.

'Okay. You'll be charged here with careless driving. What the hell were you thinking about?'

If only you knew, I thought. I shook my head, looking and feeling contrite.

'I don't know, officer. It happened so quickly.'

More paper being rustled, then he turned to me and read me my rights. I made no reply. I've seen this too many times. After a decent amount of silence I asked, 'Can I go now?'

The cops looked at each other.

'I'm not sure you're safe to drive. Are you dizzy?'

'No. Honestly. I'm fine. I was a bit dizzy when it happened. The knock to my head. But I'm okay now. I'm not going far.'

'Where are you going?'

'I'm going to see a friend. Southside.'

They looked at each other again. Then shrugged.

'Okay. If your car is driveable, you can go. Once you give your man out there the insurance details. But I have to issue you with this fixed penalty for careless driving.'

I opened the rear door.

'Thanks, officer. I'm sorry.'

I felt stiff and sore. My neck was in agony, but I couldn't show it here. The big guy looked at me.

'Are you all right?'

'Yeah. Bit painful, but I'm fine. I'm really sorry about this,' I said, managing to seem as though I was composed. 'Look. Here's my phone number. If you get in touch with me there I'll give you all my insurance details.' I paused, jerking my thumb back at the police car. 'But I've been charged with careless driving.'

'Sorry to hear that,' he said. 'But it *was* careless.'

'I know,' I said.

I yanked open the car door, which had got twisted and now squeaked, and got in.

'I'll be in touch,' he said.

'Okay.' I steadied myself and started the engine. I had to get out of here. I drove off.

I was still feeling a little shaky, swigging from a sweetened sports drink I had in my glove compartment for emergencies. It was working. I knew I had to get to Yates to find out whatever it was he wanted to tell me. As soon as

I was through with him, I'd go straight home, check out my wound, and see where we were.

As I approached the street where Yates lived, I could see an ambulance, police cars and flashing lights up ahead. I pulled to the side of the road and as I did, saw DCI Harry Wilson and a young detective talking to the nosy neighbour I'd encountered at Yates's landing. The neighbour suddenly spotted me, and his eyes widened as he frantically started pointing towards me.

'There she is. That's her. She's the one I saw. She was at Yates's door.'

The big DCI turned around and his face fell when he saw it was me. I could see him mouthing, 'Fuck Me!' Then he turned and strode towards my car.

'Carlson. What the actual fuck are you doing here?'

'What's going on?' I ignored his question.

'Colin Yates. Perv. Murdered. This guy behind me says you were at his door yesterday.'

I looked up at him, then out of the windscreen, not quite believing how the past hour of my life had unfolded.

'Well? Were you?'

I nodded.

'What the fuck! That's two stiffs in three days, Carlson! One common denominator! Out the car!'

I looked at him, and really wanted to tell him he couldn't make me. But I stepped out of the car, the bashed door squeaking as I closed it. He glanced at it, then at me, eyes squinting at the blood on my face.

'What the fuck happened to you?'

'Crashed my car.'

'Fuck me!'

He shook his head, then peered at the blood and the swelling I could feel on the side of my head. To my shock he reached across and gently lifted my hair up to have a closer look. I jerked my head back a little, and I saw him glancing down at my bruised neck. Then I felt my legs go weak and as I steadied myself on the car, he grabbed hold of me.

'Hold on a fucking minute, Carlson! You're bleeding like a fucking sheep! You need to get that checked out.' He paused, then reached across to carefully pull the top of my polo neck down. 'What's with the fucking bruises in your neck?'

'It's nothing,' I said, pulling away.

He yanked open my car door and eased me to sit down on the driver's seat, then pointed his finger at me.

'Don't fucking go anywhere.'

He turned and strode towards a couple of uniformed cops.

CHAPTER EIGHTEEN

I stood at my window gazing out at the deserted
Blythswood Square, hypnotised by the squally rain sweeping across the rooftops, flowing over guttering into puddles.
There's something calming about watching the incessant
rain, even though it hangs over the landscape with a kind
of brooding. The last couple of hours had been completely
surreal, like watching someone else stumbling through it.
It was only now that I was back in my flat in the stillness
that I was able to think straight. I could still see big Wilson's face that moment outside Yates's building when I
turned up. The thought of it brought a slight smile to my
lips now.

'So what the fuck's going on, Carlson?'

Wilson had climbed into the back of a marked police
Land Rover which I'd been ushered into after our encounter. I didn't answer. Truth was, I didn't quite know where to

start, and there was no way that I was going to spill my guts about my investigation. I also wasn't comfortable sitting that close to him in a confined space, not for any reason other than that I was edgy and didn't like it. I shifted myself a little closer to the door.

'Look, Harry,' I said, turning to him, 'you know the score. You know that I can't tell you anything about an investigation I'm working on, any more than you can tell me about yours.'

He glared at me. 'I'm on a murder investigation. And you walked right into it. That's what *I'm* doing.' He paused and raised his eyebrows. 'So I think you'd better start explaining yourself a bit.'

'I'm not a suspect,' I hit back, so he would know I wasn't about to buckle. 'I told you. I am working for a client, and Yates's name came into the frame. I spoke to him yesterday, and then he called me and asked to see me. As I said, I crashed my car, and got delayed. So by the time I got there, it was too late.'

'Carlson, I need you to tell me what you were talking to him about.' Wilson's tone had a pleading edge to it. 'We're trying to work out why Yates was shot. It wasn't random. It's no robbery. This was a hit.'

I shrugged. 'The kind of stuff he was involved in – you know from the court case – who knows how many enemies he had? Probably plenty of people wouldn't mind a pop at him.'

'You mean the snuff movies and all that shit he was done with? Is that something you're working on?'

There was a part of me that wanted to tell him, wanted the full force of the cops to be all over this hunt for Jackie's kid. But I knew that was not how it would pan out. I'd seen them operate on my own case, how slow they were off the mark, how frustrating it was to hear that they hadn't covered a lead or had failed to do something concrete. Those kinds of stories seldom had a happy ending, and I was living proof of it. There was no way I was going to throw Jackie or her kid to them. I just wished I could trust them but right at that moment I couldn't, so I kept silent.

He sighed heavily and took a long frustrated breath in, pushing it out through gritted teeth.

'Okay. Have it your way. But you can't just walk away from this the way you did with the McPhee suicide. This—'

I cut him off because I couldn't resist it.

'Was it suicide? McPhee? Is that what the post-mortem came up with?' I said it so I could study his reaction.

He gave me a long look that told me he was wondering how much I knew.

'Yep. That's what the PM said.' He glanced away from me out of the side window and then looked back at me. 'Tell me this. Is there a connection on the case you are working on with McPhee and Yates?'

I managed to keep my face straight. Wilson was just

fishing and he clearly didn't even have a clue if there was any connection. The only connection was the fact that somebody bumped McPhee off because of what he witnessed, and somebody bumped Yates off because of what he was about to tell me.

'No,' I said, looking him in the eye. 'Look. Can I go now? I've given my statement to uniform, and I'm knackered. I want to go home and have a lie down.'

He nodded. 'Okay. You can go, Carlson. But you should get that bump on your head looked at. You want someone to drive you up to the hospital? And listen, it's none of my business, but those marks on your neck. Are you in some sort of trouble?' He sounded as though he actually cared, and that felt a little weird.

'No,' I said. 'I'm fine. It's a graze, and I'll have a rest when I go home. But thanks anyway.'

I got out of the Land Rover and went to my car, aware that the nosy neighbour was still hanging around and staring at me until I reversed and drove out of the street.

I was still feeling a little wired with the shock and what had happened afterwards, but I decided that a long hot bath might not be the best idea given the head injury from the crash. So instead I took a shower hot enough to relax me in the hope I would find sleep at some stage. The last couple of days had been a bit overwhelming. I watched the early evening news on television with a microwave dinner of poached salmon and vegetables perched on my lap. They were leading with the Yates shooting, and dragging up all his back story of distributing child porn and snuff movies. But they had no leads, and the only talking head from Glasgow Police was a press officer. Wilson would be in his office glowering that he was getting nowhere. I knew how he felt. I agonised over Yates being bumped off before he got the chance to tell me whatever was so important that someone silenced him. It made me wonder if he'd been more involved in the whole affair than he was admitting. And that in turn made me even more edgy. Because if they had shut him up, then they might figure out that it was me he was going to tell whatever it was he had to tell. And that made me a target. Again. Especially after the attack outside the kebab shop. The people who had sent hapless heroin addict Johnny to warn me that day still had no idea where Jackie Foster was. But if they still believed she was holding their snuff movies and coke, they would keep looking for her. If they were smart, they'd be thinking they might not be done with me yet. I found myself glancing up at my front door, and got up from the sofa and went across, pushing the three bolts across, and triple-locking the heavy oak door, just to feel safe. Then I thought of Jackie. Call it instinct or sixth sense, but I suddenly felt the urge to call her. I hit her number on my mobile and waited. It rang one, two, five, six times, and no answer. I hung on. Nothing. Then it automatically cut me off when there was no answer.

I gave it a minute then hit the key again and waited. Eventually she answered and I heard her voice. Christ!

'Billie? Sorry. I was in the shower,' Jackie said.

I breathed a sigh of relief.

'Had me worried there, Jackie. Are you all right? Just checking on you. I mean, you haven't been out or anything, have you?'

'No,' she said, sounding a little puzzled. 'You told me to stay in.'

'That's good.' I didn't want to sound paranoid, so I added, 'I'll call up with some food and stuff for you tomorrow – tide you over for the next few days.'

There was a heavy silence, and I sensed she was maybe a bit down. I know how it breaks you every day that there's no news, until one day you learn that this is what you have to live with. But for Jackie this was fresh and raw, and she was nowhere near learning to live without her baby. Eventually she spoke, and I could feel the agony in her voice.

'Is there any news, Billie?' she asked. 'I mean, like, anything at all? Any information?' Her voice tailed off and my heart broke for her. 'I keep hoping, every time you call.'

'I know,' I said softly. 'I know how tough this is for you, Jackie.'

I wanted to tell her I had some leads, even that I had a photo, but I knew she would want to know everything. But I also knew that I had to give her some crumb of faith because when you hear nothing day in, day out, it can start to seriously mess with your head. I had to choose my words carefully.

'Jackie,' I said, 'I'm looking at a couple of people, and as you know I'm still trying to track Barton. But I can tell you that one guy I spoke to who knew Barton, has just ended up dead.'

'What? Dead? Seriously? Who was it?'

'A guy called Colin Yates. He was jailed for distributing snuff and porn a few years ago. I went to see him. And now he's dead. He called me earlier and said he had something to tell me. But when I went to see him, someone had got there first. Police were all over the place, and Yates was found murdered in his flat in Shawlands.' I paused. 'You ever hear of a guy called Yates while you were dealing with these people?'

'No,' she said. 'I don't know the name. It was always just the same people. The foreign guys, the hard man, Barton and the cop, Hewitt. I never saw anyone else.' She took a breath. 'What do you think this means?'

'I don't know,' I said, and that was the truth. There was no point in elaborating my fears to her.

'If Yates is dead because he talked to you, Billie, that means they are watching you. And maybe watching me too.'

'I wouldn't worry about that.' The last thing I wanted to tell her was about my bruising encounter with the maniac who tried to choke me. 'Meeting Yates was a recent development. If they were after me, they know where my office is. They've already been there, so if they wanted to get at me they would come back,' I said, more in hope than belief.

'Okay,' she said. 'Do you think it's still safe for me to be here?'

'Of course,' I assured her. 'Nobody knows you're there, and you can't be out in the open in the city. You never know who you might run into. Just sit tight. I'm working on things. I'll see where it takes me.'

I had the feeling she was silent because she couldn't speak. I was right. Finally, her voice choking with the lump in her throat that was trying to stem the heartache, she pleaded, 'Billie, please, please find my baby. I . . . I don't know how much longer I can take this.'

I had heard that voice inside my own head so many times in the beginning, when all my hopes had hung on the police search for Lucas. The pleading, the tears, the desperation that it was out of your hands and you were relying so much on other people, takes you to dark places and there are days when you can't see any future that is worth living.

'I know, Jackie. Try and get some rest. Just stay strong. For your baby. We'll get there.' I said it as much as to convince myself as her. 'I'll see you tomorrow.'

CHAPTER NINETEEN

I was at my desk in the office even before Millie arrived bang on nine, and when she popped her head around my door she gave me a look somewhere between concern and surprise.

'You been here all night?' she asked, half joking, eyebrows arched. 'Everything okay?'

'Yeah,' I said, taking my eyes off my computer screen to look at her. 'Just up early and thought I'd come in and catch up with some things.'

As she crossed to my desk and picked up my empty coffee mug, I quickly minimised the window I had been studying. It was an email from my private investigator, Dan Harris, in Baltimore. I didn't want Millie to see what I'd been obsessing about since six this morning when I switched on my laptop in my flat. It's not that Millie was unsympathetic or anything – far from it. She knew how broken I was, and how every day Lucas was gone was a day he would be growing further away from me, learning to live without me. And she knew that the longer he was gone, the more difficult it was going to be to find him. She had always been a hundred per cent supportive. But this was my own private hell, and I didn't want to share every scrap of information with her, because I didn't want to see the look of futility I sometimes saw on her when I got excited over news from the USA.

This morning's email from Harris had sent a surge of adrenalin through me. Every time I opened my laptop and there was an email from him – few and far between most days – my heart leapt. Most times it was to say he was chasing a lead, poring over the latest documents from various agencies, involving other search websites. It was a process, he had always said, a long slow process, but it had to be done. Today was different. Today, the subject line of his email was 'College friend, Cleveland, Ohio'. I had opened it up and quickly read it, barely taking anything in, then I'd gone back to the beginning to read it again and again. Harris said he'd found some college friend of Bob's from way back and he'd tracked him down to Cleveland. His email was brief but the gist of it was that this college friend told him he had actually bumped into Bob two months ago. He was living in a trailer park out of the city and he had a kid with him, a little blond boy. Harris said he was going there in the next twenty-four hours. I'd sat back, staring at the screen. Jesus! It could only be Lucas. It had to be. Someone actually said he saw Lucas, a little blond guy. I pictured him. I needed more. I needed to know what he looked like, whether he was crying, and how he was living. Was he skinny? In minutes I was driving myself crazy, and my first thought was to jump on a plane and go there with Harris to see for myself. But I had to force myself to take a breath. It was two months ago that this guy had bumped into him. A lot can happen in two months. I called Harris, apologising for getting him out of bed in the middle of the night, and he was very patient about it. Let me go first, he told me. He was taking a plane there, if not tomorrow, then the next day for sure. He said there was no point in coming all the way over to find they'd already moved on. When I hung up, I sat dumbfounded, my mind tormented by a blur of images and scenes of my little boy being dragged from pillar to post. Eventually, my mobile ringing brought me back.

'Jackie,' I said, my mind only half on the call. 'You okay?'

'Yes. But . . . But I've got something to tell you. Have you seen the news? I just saw something on the news. I had to phone you.'

There's a television mounted on the wall of my office. I keep it on but with the volume down low, just so I can see the headlines popping up, and if something interests me I turn up the sound. It's kind of a company thing, that you keep it on just to feel you are still in the world and not bogged down all alone three floors up in the heart of the city. Right now, some government minister was talking, so whatever Jackie had seen, the news had moved on.

'I haven't seen anything. What is it?'

'There was a girl that came up on the Scottish news. A picture of her. A young girl. Missing from a children's home. It's her.'

'Who?' I asked, a little confused.

'It's Hannah – the girl I told you I met at the film set. She told me her name was Hannah. But on the telly it says the missing girl is called Tracy. But I'm sure that's the same girl I met.'

My mind was flicking through the news from recent months, and some memory popped into my mind of the story. It happened. A lot. These kids were punted into homes and into the system, and many of them were already way beyond playing by the rules. Some disappeared at night to get involved in drugs or stealing, and some of them went to work as prostitutes. I could hear Jackie breathing. Whatever she knew she was bursting to tell me.

'I think I remember some teenager going missing a few months ago. So what are you saying?'

'The picture on the television, they must be doing something else about the search or something. I missed most of that because all I could think of is that it was her – the girl I met. She was really young. But she was there. At the film set.'

Alarm bells jangled all over my head.

'You saw this girl? At the porn film set?'

'Yes, I told you.'

'Jesus! When? Was she in a film?'

'Yes. But I didn't see it. It was before the snuff film with the Vietnamese boy, maybe a few days before, I'm not sure. They told me not to come in the next day as they were making a different movie. I remember now the girl was told she was getting five grand. She said she was going to London. To run away. That five grand was going to be a new life for her. She was excited.'

'Did you see her or hear anything about her after that time?'

'No. I wasn't expecting to see her as she said she was going to London. But that's the thing.'

'What's the thing?'

'Barton told me they'd made a film with her, but he went all dark and stuff when I asked him whether she got paid.'

'What do you mean "all dark"?'

'Like he was hiding something.'

'Like what?' I asked, but the flutter in my stomach told me I already knew.

'A snuff film maybe.'

'Christ! Why do you think that?'

'I don't know. I didn't think much of it at the time, but now that I see that she's disappeared it makes me wonder.'

'But she said she was going to get her money and go to London.'

'Yes, I know. But it was just Barton, the way he went that

day. He said they made the movie and that it was one of the tapes he gave me. He said it was really important and that's why he was locking it away in my flat so nobody could get it. I said that she'd told me she was going to London and he went all quiet. I never thought much about it at the time, and since then I've been so wrapped up in my baby being stolen. But now I'm worried.'

A fifteen-year-old girl part of their sick snuff films. This changed things for me. This girl's picture was out there and they were still looking for her. Somewhere she maybe had a family, a mother like me waiting and hoping, maybe in completely different circumstances, but still waiting with the same ache in her heart. I couldn't just hold onto this. But before I did anything or made any moves, I had to go and see Jackie.

On the way up to see her my mind lurched from what she had just told me, to the email and the phone conversation with my private eye minutes earlier. What if this was really happening? What if there was a chance I turned up there in Cleveland, spent a few weeks and followed a trail? But then I'd done this before, last year, along with Harris, trailed and followed leads only to come home seven grand down and empty, even more than before. I'd promised myself then I'd leave it to him.

Jackie opened the door on my gentle knock and I could see from her face she was agitated and troubled. I followed her into the living room then to the kitchen, where she filled the kettle and switched it on. She turned to me.

'Is there anything on my baby? I know you would have told me, Billie, but I just wondered. This morning when I saw that girl's picture is the first time I've been distracted for weeks. First time I've not thought about Elena every moment of the day. I can't get that girl, Tracy, out of my mind now. Her face. She was so pretty, so thin though, and troubled.'

We stood silently with only the hissing of the kettle. Then it pinged and she made us two coffees and we moved into the living room and sat down.

'So, Jackie,' I took a sip of the coffee and placed it on the table, 'I need you to go through every single detail you can remember of Tracy. What day you met, what time, how it came about. Every single detail of what she said. Everything.'

She nodded. 'I've been thinking,' she said, 'trying to piece together every moment.' She looked at me, then turned her head to the window. 'It was the third time I'd been there. Before the people arrived on the minibus – the trafficked people. That day was the last day I was there. But before that, it was kind of okay. I mean, I'm not proud of what I was doing, but I was getting good money. So this girl turned up, came to the door, and one of the guys introduced her. He said he'd met her in the town.'

'Can you remember which guy?'

She shook her head. 'Not by name. But it wasn't Hewitt.

It was one of the other guys, one of the Turks. He said he'd seen her in the town and asked her if she wanted to make some money.'

'Do you think she was working the streets? As a prostitute and that's how he met her?'

'He didn't say. But I suppose so, because when she was in the back room with me and we were having a cold drink, she told me she was working as a prostitute in the city centre. That she got picked up regularly because she was young.'

'Did she say her age?'

'She said she was seventeen. But I think she looked younger and I told her. She just shrugged. And it was then she told me that she'd grown up in a broken home and that she was going to be different. She said this job would give her enough money to go to London and find work, proper work. She seemed quite smart. I'm surprised she was only fifteen.'

'So what else happened that day?'

She shrugged. 'I did my bit and then once I was dressed I just left. Every time I went there the first thing I wanted to do was go home and have a shower. I felt grubby and disgusting every time.'

'Was the girl still there when you left?'

'Yes. She was going to get organised to be making a film, she said the next day. But I don't really know when the film was actually made.'

'So what happened then? The next time you went. Did you go back again after that?'

'Yes. I went about two days later and that was when the bus arrived with all those people. That was when I saw the guy . . . you know . . . being beaten to death.'

'Can you remember when you arrived, did you ask anything about Hannah? Like whether she was coming back?'

She nodded and sat quietly for two beats.

'Yes. I asked it in the room where they sat. I asked where the girl was and a couple of them just looked at each other but didn't answer. I asked Barton later, and he shrugged and said not to ask questions. It didn't cross my mind that something had happened, because at that point I hadn't seen what they did to the refugee, so I just assumed the girl had got her money and moved on. It was only later, after I knew about the snuff movie, that I thought maybe something bad had happened to her. But I told myself they wouldn't risk doing that to a girl from Glasgow who might have friends waiting for her who she'd told where she was. The people they killed were trafficked, and probably people back home never even knew where they were – so they could get away with it.'

I nodded. She sounded as though she was trying to convince herself, but I could see she felt guilty. There wasn't much she could have done, and she would know that, and as time went on she'd had more on her own plate with her kid being stolen. But I could see that now, in the cold light of day, after seeing the picture on the television, she was feeling she should have done something. We sat for a long moment not saying anything, but this was a game changer. I couldn't sit long on this information working out what to do. I needed to move fast.

CHAPTER TWENTY

Sometimes you don't know if you're doing the right thing, and all you can do is rely on your gut instinct. That's been how I've lived all my life, and one or two of my decisions based on my gut turned out to be wrong, but fortunately for me the consequences were not grave. Unless you count the child killer I shot square in the chest twice. Some people would tell you I was wrong about that, and it did have consequences that may actually have changed my life, consequences that in the long run I could never have imagined, because it was after that my life began to unravel. But in my book, my gut was right that time, in that snap moment when I fired my gun. And I had to get this one right, because if I didn't, the end game didn't bear thinking about.

I drove back from seeing Jackie, having left her knowing she would spend the afternoon beating herself up for not doing something when she had met the teenager the police were trying to find. She was already thinking the worst. I'd told her that whatever had happened – if anything *had* happened – to Tracy, it wasn't her fault. But it didn't help. She wanted to go to the police, but she was afraid because then she would have to go back over everything she'd told them after the crash, and her credibility with them was already shot. She said they would never believe her if she suddenly pitched up with another story of a missing girl. I had to agree with her, though I didn't say anything. So the way I saw it, I had two choices. I could call Scanlon and go to the cops, hand everything over to them and let them run with it mob handed. I could see the drawbacks a mile away, not least that my tip-off would first have to go through the various police red tape before they'd move. We didn't have enough time for that. But at least it would be legit. The other choice was to get Paddy Harper involved. I had a vague plan in mind, if he agreed. But if it all went pear-shaped, it could quickly end in a bloodbath. There had to be a way to get Jackie's baby back without causing an all-out war. Because if that happened it would be too late. I picked up my phone from the passenger seat and glanced at the screen as I stopped at traffic lights. I took a second to finally make up my mind. I pushed the recent calls key and took a deep breath as it rang.

'Billie. How's it going? I was going to call you today.'

'Paddy,' I said. 'Can we meet?'

'Sure. When?'

'Now would be good.'

'Something up?' He sounded concerned.

'Yes. I think it needs moving on quickly.'

The pause was just a second or two but it seemed longer, and it crossed my mind that he was reluctant. Then he spoke.

'Okay. I'm in the city centre now. How about we meet in Starbucks, Buchanan Street. On the precinct.'

'Great. I'll be there in ten.'

I hung up and slung the mobile on the passenger seat. I decided to ditch my car in the private parking space I had at my house in Blythswood and walk down to Buchanan Street. As I pulled over and switched the engine off, my mobile shuddered and rang on the seat. I could see Scanlon's name on the screen.

'Billie. You all right?'

'Yeah. What's happening?'

'I've got something to tell you, but I've only got a moment. Can we meet later?'

I hesitated. I wasn't sure what the outcome would be with Harper, and where I might be once I told him what I knew.

'Yeah,' I said finally. 'Sure. Can it be a bit later on, though, as I'm going to see someone now. What's happening?'

'Okay. Just briefly. There's a developing situation here. We made an appeal last night on that missing girl – you remember the runaway from the children's home? Her name is Tracy . . .'

My stomach knotted. 'Yeah.'

'Someone from an escort agency has been in touch and she's told us that the girl was making porn films in some basement somewhere outside of the city.'

'Shit!'

'Yeah. Exactly. Especially since she's completely vanished.'

'So, what you going to do?'

'We're working on it, but we don't know where the place is. Do you?'

'No. I don't. Jackie said she could take me to it. But it hasn't happened yet.'

I knew what was coming.

'Listen, Billie. You know I haven't said anything about what we talked about, about what you told me. But I think this changes things. Maybe you should come in and talk to the guys. We should work together.'

I froze for a moment. This was not how I wanted to do things. As soon as I walked through the doors of a police station I relinquished any control I had over my investigation, the outcome, finding and rescuing Jackie's baby. I did feel guilty about the missing girl. But I wasn't ready to just throw my lot in with the cops yet.

'I don't know, Scanlon,' I said. 'I hear what you're saying, but I . . . I would have to talk to Jackie. I don't think it would be fair just to throw her into this. She needs to find her baby.'

'I know she does. And we can help her, Billie. You need to

be realistic here.' He sounded pleading, and a little frustrated, and it occurred to me that he might have already spoken to someone about it, but I knew he would never betray a confidence.

'Let me talk to her later. But I have to go just now. I'm already late. We can speak in a couple of hours.' I hung up, knowing that Scanlon would be staring at his mobile, troubled that my tone was dismissive.

Harper sat on the faux leather chesterfield sofa at the far end of Starbucks, well away from the window that looked out to the pedestrian precinct. He listened intently, as I sat opposite telling him about Jackie's frantic call this morning on the missing girl, and then how my cop friend had just phoned to tell me about the escort agency development. When I finished telling him my options and fears that we were running out of time, he took a long moment before he answered.

'So what are your thoughts, Billie? How do you want to play this?' He looked at me, the softness of his expression belying the kind of ruthless scenarios he must have been running in his head.

I wasn't remotely sure what the right thing to do was, and everything had a major risk to it. But we had to do something.

'I think we should look at visiting the weakest link in the chain,' I said, sounding more decisive than I felt.

'Hewitt?' he asked.

'Yes. If you go for Malky Jackson or any of the gang at this stage, everything could explode very quickly,' I said. 'And we have to get Jackie's baby back before that happens.'

He nodded, looking beyond me, then back at me.

'There's something else, Billie,' he said. 'I was going to call you this afternoon when I had more information. But now we're here, I can tell you.'

I looked at him, curious.

'Barton,' he said. 'We took his flat apart last night, and there is absolutely zilch in it of interest to us. So whatever he did with the films and the coke, it's gone. I'd say long gone by now.'

I wasn't surprised, but the way Harper was looking at me, he had more to say. He leaned in closer.

'We know where he is,' he said quietly.

'Shit! Really?'

He nodded. 'The fucker's in Turkey, if you'll pardon my French, Billie.' He paused. 'We tracked him down.'

'You found him already?' My eyes widened. 'How the heck . . .?'

Harper half smiled and shrugged.

'I have connections there who moved stuff for me back in the day. Barton was easy to find, as it turned out. He probably thinks if he's far enough away from here then he's safe.'

I was impressed.

'Amazing, Paddy! What's he doing?'

'He's not doing much at the moment, but we just tracked him and found him this morning, so he's around the place, meeting people and stuff. He's obviously got something to sell, or a deal to be struck. The films maybe. Or the coke. Though I don't know how he would have got the coke into the country.'

I was trying to process this. I didn't care about the coke, but if he had the films, then that was important.

'So what happens now?'

'My friends are just waiting for me to tell them to move on him. But someone is watching him twenty-four seven. If he's got anything with him we will get it.'

I shook my head, astonished at how swiftly a crook can move and make things happen. It would have taken the cops a week to have anything like this result.

'This is brilliant, Paddy.' I smiled at him. 'You've missed your vocation. You should have been a cop.'

He chortled.

'Not corrupt enough,' he laughed.

We sat for a moment then he spoke again.

'So, your call, Billie. Which way do you want to move?'

I knew that somewhere in my psyche I wanted to move to Turkey and team up with Harper's shady contacts who could grab Barton. I wanted to be there when they held his feet to the fire and I wanted to tell him what a sleazebag he was, shooting porn flicks in the first place, but that filming innocent victims being murdered was beyond evil.

I wanted to be there in the hope that he would hand the films over, and to witness him being chucked into the Bosphorus strait, tied to a lump of concrete. That would be justice. But I knew it was fantasy, however morbid.

'Hewitt first, I think.'

He nodded, fished his phone out of his pocket and pushed a key.

'Jimmy. Meet me at the top of the precinct. Bring a couple of the lads.'

I had a fair idea how this was going to develop. Harper would be seeking answers from Hewitt, and he wouldn't be asking nicely. Much as I would love to see Hewitt being slapped into submission, I had to pull this back a little. I had already crossed a line getting a hood involved, knowing that his tactics would be bruising. But I really didn't want to be part of whatever bloodshed might follow. I'm a private investigator, I told myself, not a gangster. But I also asked myself what I would do if the only way I could get Lucas back was to bring in a bunch of criminals. Whatever it takes, was the answer. And that's what I told Harper as we left the café together. I made a phone call to Milngavie police station and asked for PC Hewitt. He was out on an enquiry, they told me, but he would be back and in the office until eight this evening when he finished his shift. I gave this information to Harper.

'Good. Do you think he'll come home to his flat after work?' he asked.

I shrugged. 'Anybody's guess. But I would imagine he would come home and change out of his uniform if he was planning to go out.'

Harper nodded, ran his hand across his chin.

'You got an address for him?'

'I do. It's a secured entrance.' I gave him the address in the Merchant City, and he noted it on his mobile.

'Good,' he said. 'We'll be waiting for him when he gets home.'

I looked at him, incredulous, but said nothing.

'You want to be there? In his house?'

I stood for a moment watching the hordes of people going about their daily business in the middle of Glasgow while we were planning, well, I wasn't quite sure what we were planning if I'm honest, but it was a world away from what their days would bring.

'Yes,' I said.

It wouldn't be the first time I'd broken into a house as a private investigator – sometimes it goes with the territory – but it wasn't something I would admit on my list of services. Lying in wait in someone's home with a couple of hard men at my side was a step too far, even in my book. But whatever it takes, I told myself.

CHAPTER TWENTY-ONE

In the end, a decision was made that it would be better if I wasn't actually in Hewitt's flat, lying in wait. It was Harper who had made the call, and I wondered if he did it to protect me from any potential fallout, rather than, as he suggested, because my presence in the flat was surplus to requirements. He actually said that. Like he was planning a board meeting rather than whatever reception party he was plotting in Hewitt's Merchant City flat. Whatever his reasons, I was glad, because when it came down to it I had to bear in mind that if this all went belly up, the last place I would want to be seen was in the middle of a flat with a bunch of gangsters attempting to extract some truths from a serving policeman.

I was parked across the street and watched as Harper, Jimmy Murdoch and two other men somehow managed to get in through the secured entrance as though it was their own place. It was dark and I shivered as the icy rain lashed across the deserted streets. The clock on my dashboard showed eight twenty-five, and I kept checking my mirrors for any sign of Hewitt. Nothing. Then I saw the glare of headlights and a car turned into Glassford Street and slowly headed down in my direction. I automatically slid myself down as low as I could as the silver Mercedes whispered past me and slipped into a parking space outside Hewitt's building. It was the same car I'd seen the men get into after they'd left the Corinthian that night. I watched as the headlights went off and the engine cut. Nobody was getting out for me to be able to confirm it was them, and I wasn't going to chance getting out of the car in case the gorilla who I'd bitten was in the car with them. I squinted around, wondering if there was another car anywhere as back-up. I hit Harper's key on my mobile and he answered straight away but didn't speak.

'Paddy,' I said. 'A Merc has just pulled up outside and I'm certain it's the same car those guys were in the other night when I saw them in The Corinthian. I don't know what's going on, but it must mean something.'

'Okay,' he said calmly. 'Maybe they're also waiting to greet Hewitt when he arrives.'

'You already in?' I asked.

'Yep. Nice place he's got here.'

I didn't answer because there was really no answer to that. I pictured Harper and his men sitting in his living room, or behind his front door, or holed up in the bedroom.

'I'll let you know if they move.'

'Fine. I've got a car out there too with a couple of lads in it in case anything happens.'

'Oh,' I said, glancing along the lines of parked cars, wondering where they were. I didn't have to know, and perhaps better if I didn't.

Then, from the corner of my eye, I saw a dark blue Peugeot come around the corner and down the street towards the flats. As soon as it was close enough for me to spot in my passenger mirror, I could see the face of Hewitt.

'Hewitt's just driven past me, Paddy.'

'Good.'

I watched as he parked a few cars beyond me but on the same side. He stepped out of the car, dressed in a black puffer jacket with a dark scarf around his neck. He glanced around briefly and crossed the road towards his flat. Just then, the doors of the Mercedes opened and two men stepped out, one from the passenger seat and one from the back. They were about thirty feet from him when he noticed them, and I caught the startled look on his face. Whatever they were doing here, Hewitt wasn't expecting a visit. I relayed what I saw to Paddy and kept watching. Hewitt slowed his stride as the men approached just outside the entrance to his flat, and in the street light I could see that he wasn't smiling. The big Turkish guy looked angry, and Jackson, deadpan, said something to him. Hewitt spread his hands and seemed to take a key from his pocket as he moved closer to the door. Whatever was being said, it looked like he was inviting them in, or they were inviting themselves in. Hewitt pushed his key in the door and stepped in, the others following behind.

'Shit, Paddy!' I whispered. 'They're all coming in.'

'Fine.' He hung up.

As the door closed I rubbed my face with my hands wondering what holy hell was about to erupt when Hewitt walked inside his flat. I didn't have to wait long.

The first thing I heard was a gunshot. Then more shots were fired, rapid, three, four, five. My eyes traced the sound to the third-floor window where I knew Hewitt's place overlooked the street. In the next few seconds the front door opened and several panicked residents rushed out. I watched as some of them were on their mobiles, probably calling 999, one or two filming the block of flats. I had to get out of here fast. Suddenly there was a sound like a shotgun blast and the window onto the street shattered, shards of glass and frame making the people below run for cover. Then, as I switched on my engine and eased my car out, I froze. People screamed as a body came flying through the raggy gap where the window had been torn out. It was a split second image, like a flicker from some TV disaster footage, the kind of thing that you know you will never be able to unsee. There was a sickening thud as the body smashed onto the pavement. The last thing I heard was the screams and howls of the people standing aghast in horror.

By the time I was out of Glassford Street and into Ingram Street I could hear the wail of police and ambulance sirens. I drove fast and headed down towards the Broomielaw and just kept driving, not knowing where I was going. As I got off the Clydeside Expressway and onto Byers Road, my mobile shivered and buzzed in the passenger seat and I could see it was Scanlon. I pushed the answer key on my steering wheel. But before I could say anything, it was him who spoke.

'Billie. Where are you?'

'Heading to the West End.' I hoped I sounded calm.

'Listen. I can't meet you. There's some shit happening in the city centre – shooting and a body out of the window. I'm on my way there. Might be terrorist related.'

I didn't reply.

'Billie,' he said, after two beats. 'It's in Glassford Street. Did you not say that's where Hewitt lives?'

'Yeah, his flat is down there. Near the bottom.' I felt as shady as they come, and I hated myself for it.

'I'll call you later,' Scanlon said, and hung up.

Two hours had passed and I still hadn't heard from Paddy Harper. All that was running on the TV news was an incident in a flat in Glassford Street, and there was at least one fatality. The police had a major operation on the go and from the pictures the area had been taped off, and the place was awash with officers. There were a couple of people speaking to camera telling of their shock at what they'd witnessed. But none of that was what was making me pace up and down the living room of my flat. No. I had made the most stupid of all mistakes, a rookie error that even the most witless criminal wouldn't have made. I had been in the area in my car. That meant I would be on CCTV street cameras somewhere. And once police went through the procedure of door-to-door and the usual stuff that went along with the beginning of an investigation, they would be looking at street camera footage. Every car's number plate in the vicinity would be checked and contacted – including mine. I couldn't believe I had been so stupid and failed to take the elementary precaution of making sure I was nowhere to be seen. How in hell had I forgotten to do that? I beat myself up. I had taken my eye off the ball, swept up in the excitement of the email from my private eye this morning, focused on the possibilities of that, and I wasn't thinking straight. Now it was only a matter of time until the police came knocking on my door.

I watched the news, switching channels to check for updates, wondering if they were going to say the incident happened in the flat of a serving police officer. But nothing. All they were saying was that the fatality was a man in his forties. The investigation was ongoing and forensics experts were all over the flat.

My mobile ringing on the coffee table jangled me out of my paranoia. It was Harper's name on the screen.

'Billie.'

I didn't reply.

'Listen. I have someone here who wants to talk to you. Where are you?'

'Who . . . What?' I found myself speechless.

'Come to the flats in Lancefield Quay. Last on the block. Go to the fifth floor. Someone will meet you outside.'

'But. What . . . What happened?'

'Tell you when I see you.' He hung up.

I stared at the phone as though there was an answer there. What the hell was going on? It was Paddy's voice, for sure, and on his mobile. But what if someone had a gun to his head and was forcing him to tell me to come and see him, and I was just walking into an ambush? But it didn't feel as though I had an option. I pulled on my jacket, picked up my car keys and left the flat.

I was glad to see Jimmy Murdoch standing smoking a cigarette outside the Lancefield Quay flats. He clocked my car as I pulled in a few feet away from the entrance, and walked towards me when I got out.

'I can't tell you how glad I am to see you, Jimmy,' I said. 'I didn't know what to expect.'

He glanced at me from the corner of his eye as we walked to the entrance.

'Did you think it was a trap?'

'It crossed my mind,' I said.

He turned and smiled. 'And you still came anyway. That's ballsy.'

I didn't answer and followed him as he pushed the button on the lift and we stepped in.

'What happened, Jimmy?' I asked. 'I'm almost scared to ask.'

He blew out from pursed lips. 'Shitstorm and a half, that was.'

'I saw,' I said. 'Christ, who was the guy out of the window?'

'Some Turkish fucker. He caused all the trouble. But Malky Jackson is running the show. There was a bit of infighting amongst themselves. Paddy will tell you more.'

'Who shot the Turk?'

'Malky's boy. Fucking sawn-off shotgun. I mean, who does that these days in the middle of the city centre?'

I nodded but didn't say anything because I didn't know how to answer that.

The lift pinged and the doors opened on the fifth floor and we got out. The hallway was carpeted and neat. These flats were new and well-heeled now, but I knew a good number of them were used as knocking shops. When we got to the flat he rapped on the door a couple of times and it was opened by one of the other guys I'd seen going into the flat in Glassford Street earlier. When we walked down the hall and into the living room I came face to face with Hewitt. I thought for a moment there was a flicker of recognition on his chalk-white face. He wasn't tied up. There was no gun to his head, and no injuries. He just stood there like someone who had seen a ghost, or as though it had suddenly dawned on him that he'd been in the wrong place too long.

'You know who this is, Hewitt?' Harper said.

'You were a cop,' he said.

I didn't answer, but glanced at Harper.

'So tell her, Hewitt. Tell her what you told me. The short version.' Harper nudged him and he flinched.

I looked at him for a long moment, waiting for him to answer, but he said nothing.

'Where's the kid?' I asked, deadpan.

He opened his mouth to speak and I could see his lips trembling.

'I don't know and that's the truth. They moved her this morning.'

'Who's "they"?' I asked. 'Are you not part of "they"?'

He shook his head vigorously.

'Not any more.' He turned to Harper. 'Definitely not now after the shit in my flat. They'll be after me now too.'

I didn't really want to hear his sob story. I was only interested in where the kid was, and how fast we could get to her.

'Where have they moved her to? You need to find out. What's going on?'

'There was a falling-out this morning. I don't know

what's going on, but they know you are looking for the kid and that Jackie came to you.'

I didn't want to say that I already knew. I wanted to leave Johnny out of it as much as possible because I was worried about what might happen to him.

'So they could have found me. They could have come for me any time.'

'It's Jackie they want.'

'They think she has the films, but she's already told you she hasn't.'

'They don't believe her.'

'So they steal her kid?' I spat the words out and glared at him. 'What kind of lowlife are you, Hewitt? And you, whose old man is a chief super. What do you think he's going to say when he gets to hear about his beloved son?'

'They'll be looking for me right now. The whole force.' He turned to Harper. 'You kidnapped a policeman. Do you know how serious that is?'

'Shut the fuck up,' Harper said, deadpan.

The arrogance of Hewitt made me burn with rage so much it was all I could do to stop myself walking across and punching him out. I stood watching for a long moment until he had no option but to look me in the eye.

'Snuff movies,' I said with disgust. 'You were making snuff movies, Hewitt. Never mind that you're a serving cop. What kind of lowlife do you have to be to get involved in something like that?' I paused, as his eyes dropped to the floor. 'You think the cops are looking for you now? Wait till they hear how you've been moonlighting, you piece of shit.'

I felt myself shaking with anger, and I could see Harper and Murdoch glance at each other then back at me. I'm sure if I'd asked them, they'd have handed me a gun so that I could deal with this scumbag in much the same way as they would have done. The silence hung heavy in the room, then Hewitt finally lifted his eyes from the floor and looked at me.

'It . . . It . . . Things just spiralled out of control. It was never meant to be like this.'

'Yeah. Tell it to the jury,' I spat. 'But you listen to me, arsehole. You need to get on the phone and call one of these pricks and find out where the kid is.'

'I don't know if I can.'

'You have to,' I said. 'Either that or I'm going to call HQ and tell them exactly where you are and what you've been up to your arse in. So just make the call.'

'And say what?'

'Christ! It's up to you. Tell them you've found the films or some other crap. Make it up. Just make it happen. You need to know where the kid is. Now. And what about the girl who is missing – Tracy. Is she already dead?'

His face went even whiter.

'Can I have a glass of water?' he said. 'I feel dizzy.'

I watched as Jimmy went to the kitchen and came back

with a glass of water. I looked at Hewitt, the cold fear all over his face, and I wondered what has to happen in your life that it goes so shit off the rails that you end up in the kind of company he was keeping. No matter what he said or how he helped us, he was well and truly finished. The truth would come out eventually and he would be seen for what he was. No matter what promises were being made in this living room. He took a few gulps of water, sat down at the table, and pulled out his mobile.

'Who you going to call?'

'One of Jackson's men. The guy I deal with. It was him I got involved with in the beginning. I'd ... I'd borrowed money. And I got sucked in. I was gambling.'

I looked at him and hoped I conveyed that I really wasn't interested in his feeble excuses.

'So what are you going to say?'

He took a breath and let it out slowly.

'I'll tell him I've got the films and that they have to bring the kid and we will exchange them.' He shook his head. 'But shit, man, if this doesn't work, I'm a dead man walking.'

'Just get the kid, Hewitt,' I said.

I glanced at Harper. Hewitt was a dead man whatever he did.

CHAPTER TWENTY-TWO

I had the TV on at a murmur to break the silence in my flat. It was almost eleven by the time I left Lancefield Quay, but I could have driven all night, because the last thing I wanted to do was go home. My head felt ready to burst with the events that had unfolded in the last few hours and I knew that sleep would never come. I poured myself a glass of red wine and stood in silence at my living room window, watching the sleet fall steadily in the gardens. It was eerily quiet, the only flicker of life outside the odd car slowing down, cruising around, probably looking to find whatever it was they were searching for among the women who walked up and down the square or sheltered in doorways. Now and again a car would stop and a woman would come out of the shadows and lean in the open window, then she would open the door and get inside. None of this was new to me, living here for so long, but every time I saw it, every time I watched a woman climb into a cruising car,

I wondered if a little bit of her died inside. Just watching it was bad enough.

I ran a bath and while it was running, I checked my emails on my laptop in case there was any update from Harris. There wasn't. I toyed with the idea of phoning as it was late afternoon there, and maybe he'd picked up some more information, but I decided against it. No news was good news, I tried to convince myself, not very successfully. I looked at my phone, and saw that I had several missed calls and texts from Scanlon. By this time, the police HQ would be all over the place trying to work out how to manage the news that the blast and body that took a swan dive in the city centre had actually come out of the window of Hewitt's flat – a serving policeman. And he was now missing. The jungle drums would be beating through every police station across the city and beyond, because once they worked out who the Turk was, they would find out he was a gangster and people trafficker. So as well as hunting for Hewitt, they would have to work out what the hell this guy was doing in his flat, and how he ended up dead. The press would get hold of this before the morning. It was only a matter of time, and the dots would be joined and cages rattled all the way up to Chief Superintendent Hewitt and the Chief Constable. If I wasn't going to sleep much tonight, I wasn't alone.

I had left Hewitt in the company of Harper and Murdoch in the Lancefield Quay flat, as Harper told me I should make some distance between them now. That made me think he was going to get the information he needed to find the kid, then get rid of Hewitt, and not in a good way. But I left it for him to handle. I was about to head into my bath, when my mobile rang. It was Harper.

'Billie.' His voice was low, almost a whisper.

'Are you still in the flat?' I asked.

'Aye. We'll keep him here tonight. He's not made the call yet. It's too late to start hunting people down, so we'll have to leave it till the morning.' He paused, as though he was waiting for me to say something, but I didn't. Then he went on. 'Listen. I've just had a call from Istanbul. They've got a hold of Barton.'

'Really?'

'Yep. And he's got stuff on him. Films. DVDs. We're not sure what's on them but my boys are checking it out. If it's what we think it was, then we will get them back here.'

'Barton's not talking at all?'

'No. But he will.'

'I take it Hewitt knows none of this.'

'Of course. But we have to act fast. We will know in a few hours what's on those tapes and we will have Barton talking. Then we'll call you.'

'Great. Thanks, Paddy.'

'How you feeling?'

'Kind of speechless, if I'm honest. Just trying to go over the events of the past few hours.'

'Yeah. Rough enough. I'll tell you all about it soon.'

'How did your guys get out of that flat alive – I mean if Jackson's men were shooting people?'

'It all got a bit crazy, but that's for another day. Right now we need to get Hewitt moving on how we can get this kid. If we've got the tapes, then we have something to bargain with – or so we can make them believe.' He paused. 'Get some sleep, Billie. You looked tired.' He hung up.

After another troubled night, tossing and turning, I was up early, showered, dressed and ate breakfast in my kitchen while scrolling through the newspapers to read their take on last night's shoot-out in the city centre. Much was being made all over the front pages of a body either being thrown or falling from a third-storey flat. They were saying that the deceased, who police were not naming, also suffered shotgun wounds to his stomach and was pronounced dead at the scene. None of the newspapers mentioned whose flat it was, which I thought was peculiar. Surely some of the neighbours would have told newspaper reporters that it was a policeman who lived in the flat. There was also no mention at all about Hewitt being missing, which I could understand. All of them declared the shoot-out to be part of drug turf wars. I could see the police were spinning this to keep reporters from getting to the heart of the matter – that the policeman who owned the flat had vanished. They wouldn't be saying it publicly, but I knew the shit would be hitting the fan all over HQ because of what happened and because of who Hewitt was. I wished I could be a fly on the wall in the briefing room this morning. It was while I was mulling this over that my doorbell rang. I put my mug of coffee on the table and waited a moment, then the bell rang again. I got up from the table and went along the hall into the living room where I can discreetly peek out of the window and see who is standing on my front step. I wasn't surprised to see DCI Harry Wilson and Steve. I knew this was coming, but I thought they might have called me rather than just pitch up at my door. The fact that Wilson was there meant they were suspicious. But I was disappointed that Steve hadn't called to give me a heads up. I thought I knew where his loyalties lay, and it wasn't in my bed even though he'd shared it a few times. I went to the door and called out 'Who is it?', because I know they'd have expected that.

'Billie. Harry Wilson. We need to talk to you.'

I opened the door and the pair of them stood there, classic frontline detective look – dark suits, rain jackets, faces grey from lack of sleep. I almost knew what the script would be. They wouldn't be able to tell me anything, but, the fact was, I knew more than them. I just had to be careful.

'Can we come in?'

'Sure. What's up?'

The DCI looked at me and raised his eyebrows, bored.

'Are you serious, Billie?' His lip curled a little as they

walked in the doorway. 'Last night. What were you doing in Glassford Street?'

I looked at both of them but didn't answer. I hoped my glare at Steve was enough to convey my wrath at his treachery, but I walked towards the kitchen.

'You guys want some coffee?'

They followed me but didn't answer.

In the kitchen I put on the coffee pot. 'Caf or decaf?' I asked with my back to them.

'Caf for me,' the DCI said. 'It's been a bastard of a night.'

I didn't answer as I fiddled with the coffee, but I knew I'd have to face them sooner or later. I turned to them as I put mugs on the worktop. I didn't say anything but gave them a look that said let's hear it. Wilson stood, hands in his trouser pockets, and sidekick Steve just looked as though he wished he wasn't there.

'So,' Wilson said, 'your car is clocked on CCTV in Glassford Street last night at the precise time this Turkish guy took a dive from the window of the flat.'

I didn't answer. I flicked a glance at Steve who averted his eyes. I knew he was reading my mind, knowing he could have given me a heads-up, even though I knew he wasn't the type of cop to do that. Too strait-laced, too much of a cop. I thought for a moment about Scanlon, wondering how much he knew from the door-to-door and CCTV reviewing that would be going on. I was pretty sure if he knew my car had been caught on camera he would have called me. Not that I would've been able to do much about it, except lie, which was what I was about to do.

'Yeah. I was in the street last night. I was hoping to meet someone, but he didn't turn up,' I said, making sure I looked both of them straight on. 'Then all this shit happened, the sound of gunfire, and the guy falling, or being pushed, through the smashed window. Looked like someone shotgunned him through it, to be honest. So I just got off my mark. I've seen enough of this kind of shit to know things can get a whole lot worse very quickly, and innocent people can get caught in the crossfire. So I left.'

The coffee and the milk frother bubbled and gurgled like someone choking. I poured the coffee, put in the warm milk and slid the mugs across the worktop to them. The big DCI lifted his to his lips, and sipped, then looked at me.

'That's two murders in the space of a week, Billie – one of the victims you actually interviewed the day before he was shot.' He paused for effect. 'And then there's also the shotgun death scene at the farmhouse you happened to be trampling all over before that.' He gave me the eyebrow arch that said whatever I was about to say he didn't believe me.

'I'm a private eye,' I said, folding my arms. 'So some days you just sit watching a front door of a building all day long, and other days, it all happens. I've no control over that.'

'Who were you meeting?'

'You know I can't tell you that.'

'Look, Billie, this is a murder investigation, the second one you've been at the scene of in a matter of days, so I'm not swallowing this crap about a client.'

I shrugged. 'What do you want me to say, Harry? I mean, are these murders, shootings, whatever went on, are they connected?'

I hoped my expression was convincing and curious, but I know how wily he is.

'We can't say at the moment.'

'So you know how it goes then.' I picked up a mug and sipped from it. 'So who's the Turk, as a matter of interest?' I thought I might as well ask, as I didn't have much to lose here. I wondered if it was Mehmet or one of his henchmen.

'Can't say at the moment.'

'So what is he? A drug dealer?'

He sighed. 'Well, there's a lot of stuff we're looking at. But don't bust our arses here. If you're involved in something then you'd be smart to tell us. Because if this investigation goes further down the line and we find you somewhere in the murky shit that surrounds it, then it's not going to look good. And even worse, if you're into something, looking at these guys, then you could be placing yourself in a lot of danger.'

I didn't reply, but nodded my head slowly to convey his point had been taken. I was still waiting for them to tell me whose flat it was, but not even a hint was coming, and

I didn't want to ask in case they thought I knew something. I knew that by this time they would be well aware that it was Hewitt's flat and that he was missing. Even if I'd wanted to say anything right now, I couldn't. If I'd truly believed they were in a position to wade in and find Jackie's kid in the short space of time that was required before it was too late, I might have considered telling them everything. But I didn't believe that. And in any case, I was now so far down the line with Harper and his way of doing it, it was a bit late to tell the cops. They were still looking at me, both of them, waiting for an answer which they probably knew wasn't coming, when suddenly I decided to throw out a little probe.

'So is this a terrorist thing or what?' I asked, with my best open face on. 'Newspapers are saying drug-turf wars, but what's the sketch? Whose flat is it?'

As soon as my last question was out, I saw them flinch, and I knew I'd hit a nerve. Wilson glared back at me in a way that said he knew that I knew more than I was letting on. Steve still had that guilty look like a dog who's ripped your sofa apart while you're at work and sits in the hall to greet you with an I-wish-this-could-be-different expression.

'We can't say that at the moment, Carlson. You know that,' Wilson managed to say, but I could see the rage simmering in his eyes. He slowly put down his mug. 'But if you're not levelling with us, then you are making a big mistake. Do you get my drift?'

I looked him in the eye, trying to work out if there was a double meaning to his threat. There was. He knew something.

'Loud and clear,' I said.

He gave Steve a look that said drink up, and he obeyed by gulping the remains of his coffee. Wilson turned on his heels to leave. As Steve followed him he flicked a little glance in my direction but I gave him the frostiest look I could come up with, and he left.

CHAPTER TWENTY-THREE

Millie was already in the office in front of her computer screen by the time I arrived, and she looked over the top of her glasses as I came in. By her expression I had the feeling she had something important to tell me.

'There was a weird bloke waiting in the corridor when I got in this morning,' she said.

I took off my coat and hung it on the stand.

'Weird in what way?' I asked. 'As in weird-looking, or dodgy . . . or dangerous?'

We get all kinds in here, so weird wasn't that unusual.

'Dodgy, I think.' She got up and moved across to the coffee machine. 'Maybe even dangerous. He gave me the creeps. Just standing there, hanging around. I asked him whether he was looking for someone, but he didn't answer – just looked blankly back at me.'

'Young, or older? What kind of age?' I asked, beginning to feel paranoid.

She flicked on the coffee switch and secured the water at the back.

'Don't know for sure. Maybe thirties or early forties. Big bloke, powerful-looking.'

My gut did a little tweak as my mind flashed back to the big Turk who'd dragged me out of my car.

'Did he look like, well, maybe Turkish or something?'

She raised her eyebrows. 'You know this guy?'

'Well. Not really. But I've had a bit of a problem with Turkish thugs recently.'

'Turkish thugs?'

She looked at me and rolled her eyes to the ceiling. Then she gave me that Millie look that was never less than a telling-off.

'You know, Billie, you're going to have to be careful.' She glanced at the bruise on the side of my eye from the Turkish beast who had tried to abduct me. 'Whoever knocked you about there is not messing. What are you doing, girl?'

I sighed. She'd never mentioned the bruise from the other night, and she must have seen it when I got into the office the following morning. But that was Millie. She respected my privacy, but she wouldn't shy from wading in if she thought I was in danger of doing something stupid. I touched my bruise.

'I know,' I said. 'But I think that's being dealt with.'

Another reproachful look.

'Are you involved with some very heavy people, Billie? Look, I know you keep me out of certain things, and that's all fine by me . . . but—'

I put my hands up.

'I know, Millie. I know.' I touched my bruise again. 'This is all about Jackie Foster. She's been involved with some truly heavy gangsters and it's, well, it's snowballed.'

She puffed. 'So is there actually a baby?'

'Yep. There sure is.'

'Jesus! Where is it?'

'Your guess is as good as mine. We had a real handle on it two days ago, and we were about to move in. But they've moved the baby.'

'Who?'

'The heavy gangsters she's involved with, and who she's running from.'

There was silence for a few moments and then the coffee gurgled. She held up a cup and I nodded. With her back to me she continued.

'You know, you really should talk to the police. Don't get in over your head, Billie. Seriously.' She turned around.

'I know,' I said. 'I think it will be over soon though.'

As she handed me the coffee, she looked me in the eye.

'Oh, and by the way, that Turkish guy who got thrown or fell out of the window down in Merchant City. Is that by any chance anything to do with these people?'

I couldn't help but smile as I moved towards my desk.

'You know, Millie. You should be a private eye. You're good at this!'

She took her cup of coffee, sipped it and shook her head as she sat back down at the desk.

'You are worrying me, you really are!'

My mobile rang and I could see Scanlon's name on the screen. I had to be ready for this.

'How's it going, Danny?' I tried to be chipper.

I heard him push out a sigh.

'You seen the news, Billie? The papers?'

'I have,' I said. 'You mean the stuff from last night in the Merchant City?'

I guessed he might think I was bluffing, pretending to be vaguely interested in something I knew more about than the cops.

'Come on, Billie. Cut the crap,' he said. 'You know exactly what I'm talking about. You free for a coffee?'

'This morning?'

'Yeah. If you can make it.'

'Sure. Give me an hour to get some calls done. Meet me in Starbucks on the Buchanan Street precinct. That's handy enough for me. You okay with that?'

'Great. I'll be there.' I half expected him to hang up, but I could sense he had something else to say. 'And, Billie? There's some heavy chat up at HQ about you.'

'Hmmm,' I said. 'I got a visit from the DCI.'

'I know you did. He's not happy you fobbed him off.'

'He's such a dick though, Scanlon – you know that.'

'I have to go,' he said. 'I'll meet you in an hour.' He hung up.

As I placed my mobile on the desk it shuddered and rang again. It was Harper.

'Billie,' he said before I had the chance to say hello. 'Two things. Barton had the snuff films. And we know where the kid is.'

'Jesus!' was all I could manage. 'That was quick work, Paddy.'

'Aye. We don't mess about when there's a kid. Hewitt made the call.'

'So what happens now?'

'We're going there. In twenty minutes. You want to come?'

It was a no-brainer for me. Even if it might get messy, which it no doubt would, I had to be there to make sure Jackie's little girl got out safely if there was a bloodbath. The consequences didn't come into it for me, because all I could think of was if someone was in a position to do the same for my Lucas, wherever he is, then I hoped they wouldn't shrink from it.

CHAPTER TWENTY-FOUR

I took my own car and followed behind Harper and his crew in a big Land Rover Discovery. I'd decided not to go along with them for a couple of reasons – one of them being that I didn't want to be sitting in the back seat with Hewitt, a kidnapped serving police officer, who was leading us to the house where an abducted child was being held. I could just imagine how that would look to the big DCI if this all went tits up and I was discovered in this kind of company. Harper said I might be safer with them, because he didn't know what was going to happen when he got there. But I told him of my vague plan – well, more of a hope than a plan – that if they did find Jackie's kid, then they could bring her to me pronto and I'd get off my mark. Whatever mopping up they'd be doing, I needed and wanted to be well out of it, not just for my own sake, but also for the baby's. All I wanted was to get the kid and get the hell out of there. As I drove behind them, out of the city centre and towards the Southside, there was a heavy feeling of dread that I was way out of my depth here, that anything could happen, and that niggling feeling that I really should have talked to Scanlon and got the cops involved even at this late stage. When my mobile rang on the passenger seat and his name came up on the screen I ignored it, and immediately felt that it might be a decision I'd come to regret.

We were driving out of the city centre and deep into Govanhill. It was once an area where hordes of shipyard workers lived in tenements, which later became rundown. But in recent years it had gone the full circle of rehabilitation to attract trendy first-time buyers. Some parts of it that hadn't been snapped up by developers were messed up, run by landlords who didn't give a damn about who they rented to. The houses were mostly sandstone and tenements. I hadn't been here for a very long time, but from what I knew it was home to a diverse group, from impoverished, homeless Glaswegians, to refugee families who had been housed here, some by landlords and some by the local council. Many of the houses were boarded up in this part, and only a few people hung around on street corners. They looked Middle Eastern. They'd probably come over here illegally in a crowded dinghy with dreams of a new life, but swiftly discovered it was not going to happen. I just couldn't figure why the thugs who were holding Jackie's kid would move her from Calton to here. I followed

Harper's car, assuming Hewitt was directing them. I couldn't help thinking how the hell he could sleep at night or get through his days as a cop knowing what he did, knowing the people he was involved with. Soon, we were slowing down in a deserted street outside a block of sandstone grimy flats that were mostly boarded up. Upstairs in a third-floor window I saw a bare light bulb behind a torn net curtain. My phone rang. It was Harper.

'You best sit tight outside, I'll get one of the boys to be with you. And if it works out, we'll bring the kid out. If that happens, it will be quick, so be ready to get away. If it doesn't work out within a few minutes, then get off your mark anyway. You understand?'

'Yeah,' I replied.

But I didn't really, and hearing his precise ordered voice made my stomach churn with fear. As they pulled up, Murdoch got out of the car and came to join me, slipping into the back seat.

'All right, Billie?' he asked, closing the door as though we were on a car share to work.

'Yeah,' I answered. 'As much as I can be, Jimmy.' I caught his eye in the rear-view mirror. 'To be honest, I'm shitting myself.'

'It'll be fine. No matter what happens. We'll be fine.'

His expression was flat and his demeanour concentrated. He wouldn't have been a stranger to any frontline confrontation. We sat in silence for a couple of minutes, my eyes flicking from the front doorway to the flats, to the window with the bare light bulb. It had to be in there, unless they were in one of the boarded-up houses. As a cop I'd been to houses with steel doors before and it was amazing what you might find when you got inside. Once, on a call-out with Scanlon and a couple of uniform cops, I burst through a door and there were at least ten junkies in various states lying on the floor spaced out, some unconscious, one of them actually dead – and had been for at least a day by the look of him.

There were no other big cars here so perhaps the Turk or Jackson hadn't got here yet, or they'd got word that Hewitt was double-crossing them. My palms sweated even though I was cold and a little shivery which I knew was pure anxiety. I took a breath and held it for a few seconds to get myself under control. This was not the time to let panic wash over me. My mouth was parched from nerves and I swigged from a bottle of water. Then it happened. The front door burst open and I could barely believe my eyes when one of Harper's boys came running out. Christ! He was carrying a little kid. He ran straight to my car, Murdoch opened the back door and jumped out. I switched my engine on.

'Go!' Jimmy said. 'Fucking go.'

But my engine cut out. Christ almighty! I turned my ignition again, fingers trembling on the key. It stalled again.

'Aw, for fuck's sake, Billie! What the actual fuck!'

'I don't know, Jimmy. It happens sometimes.' I glanced at the mirror. The girl looked filthy and flushed. Then she burst into tears.

The car sprang to life, and just as I was about to kick away, two cars came screeching around the corner, one from behind and one from the street in front.

'Fuck!' Murdoch said. 'Just go, Billie. I'll deal with it.'

'What about the baby, Jimmy?'

She was screaming blue murder now. But I couldn't see her. It was all happening so fast. I put my foot down.

'Where is she?'

'It's okay. She's in the footwell. Just move.'

'Fuck! The footwell?' I stepped on the accelerator and jolted off, swerving to avoid the car.

Then a shot was fired. It pinged off the metal and hit my side window. Then I heard a shot from the back. Jimmy leaned out of the window and was firing at the car behind.

I was driving in some kind of frantic stupor, racing out of the housing scheme and onto the road, checking in my mirror that we weren't being chased.

'Get the baby up, Jimmy. Strap her in, for Christ's sake. Is she all right?'

I could hear her wailing. My heart was in my mouth.

'Come on, sweetheart.' I saw Jimmy's gentle coaxing as he lifted the baby and held her to his chest. 'There now, baby. You're all right. Let's get you strapped in and take you to your mammy now.'

Something about the way this hard-ass was soothing the baby brought a surge of emotion to my throat, and I watched as he strapped the baby into a seat belt. I hoped to Christ we didn't get stopped by cops as we had no baby seat. Once we were out of Govanhill, I drove as fast as was legal towards the city centre. By the time I was there I knew we were safe and everything in me wanted to stop and hold the wee girl. I wanted to hug her and tell her it was okay, that she was going home. The thought that one day my Lucas might come back to me flashed in my head and I choked back tears. We were nearly there. As we got into the area, I called Jackie.

'I'm heading to the flat. Open the door.'

'What. You all right?'

'Just open the door. I'll be there in two minutes.'

We got there, and I looked up and caught a glimpse of Jackie at the window. For just a second I saw her face light up, then she disappeared from the window, and as I got to the door, the front entrance buzzed open and I ran in with the baby and Jimmy behind me. Jackie was running down the stairs to greet us, already sobbing.

'Elena! Elena! My baby!'

She put her arms out, and at first the baby looked reluctant, still wailing. Then there was a flash of recognition, perhaps from the scent of her mother or just the basic primal instinct that tells a baby where it belongs. She stopped crying as her mother held her and clutched her hair and buried her head in her shoulder. I wondered whether I would ever see such a perfect, joyous moment again as long as I lived.

I left Jimmy in the flat with Jackie and the baby and headed for the supermarket on the corner. I was carrying a list of essential items she needed for the baby, and as I walked into the shop, I stopped for a second and glanced down the list. Nappies, baby cream, bath bubbles, baby cereal, soft fruits ... It pulled me up short. How quickly we forget when our children were babies, when every minute of every day is centred around them, feeding, bathing, changing, and the way they fall asleep in your arms, their little cherub mouth parted in deep slumber. Had I really forgotten so much about those days? The early months go by so fast, and then the first two years. It all goes past in a flash. As I stood there in the aisle gazing at the shelves, a pang of regret surged through me for not making enough of those early days at the time. Had I not been there enough? Had I been so focused on work and the pressure of my job that I'd neglected to put everything into the most important person in my life? Now I could never get those moments back. A whole surge of emotions rose up inside me, from anger at Bob, to guilt and self-blame. If only I had been there more ... If only ...

I had tormented myself with these thoughts so much, and it always came back to the inescapable truth – it wouldn't have happened if I had been there. But I shook myself back to the present. I had a job to do. I shopped quickly, throwing things into the basket along with some other shopping for Jackie to see her through the day. Then I headed back to the flat, always looking over my shoulder, just in case.

Back upstairs, Jackie had run a bath for the baby, and Jimmy nodded me into the kitchen. I followed him in and he closed the door.

'A lot of shit went on down there, Billie,' he said in a low voice. 'Jackson and his mob turned up just after we left and all hell broke loose.'

'Jesus,' I said, glad we'd got out of it, even if I could still scarcely believe we'd made it.

'Jackson took a bullet to his chest in the mayhem. Two of his men went down, and one of ours.'

'You mean, dead?'

'Jackson is, or he looked that way by the time Paddy and the boys got out. Our man lost a lot of blood and he's in hospital. But I think at least two of Jackson's men are dead.'

'Christ. Were the cops there?'

'No, but they probably arrived not long after we left. I've just spoken to Paddy and he told me what happened. We took our man to the hospital – it wouldn't have been what we wanted to do as they ask too many questions, but he was losing too much blood.'

'So what will happen when the police come to ask questions? How is he going to explain gunshot wounds?'

'It's Glasgow, isn't it? That kind of shit happens from time to time. He'll think of something.'

'What about Hewitt?'

'We've still got him.' He shrugged.

'What will you do with him?'

He shrugged again. 'Don't know. It's up to Paddy. But Hewitt's a right bad one, that's for sure. And him a cop too.' His mouth turned down at the side with disgust. A bent cop was worse than the worst of criminals.

I didn't answer. But I wondered if they might just drop him into a very deep river. There were plenty of right bad ones in the criminal world and many of them got their comeuppance eventually. But a bad cop doing bad things to people like Jackie Foster and innocent people who had been trafficked? That was a different matter. The world would be no worse off if nobody ever saw Hewitt again.

I knew the cops would be all over this bloodbath by now, and the neighbours were bound to be telling them everything they saw, including, probably, that a man had run out of the flat with a baby in his arms. Or maybe they would say nothing. Areas like that sometimes looked upon cops as the enemy and knew it was better to keep their mouths shut.

'So what you going to do with Jackie now?' he asked. 'You going to keep her here? Is it safe enough?'

'It has been so far. But now that she's got her baby back, she'll want to get out of Glasgow, I suppose. She should get as far away from here as possible.'

Jimmy nodded. 'I think she'll be the least of their worries now. There will be a lot of pieces to pick up after what just happened, so they won't make any more trouble for her for the moment.'

'I hope not.' I shook my head. 'Jesus. That was some moment when she got her baby back.'

Jimmy looked at me, and I knew by his expression that he knew what I was thinking about. Paddy would have told him about Lucas. He suddenly reached across and squeezed my arm.

'You're a good kid, Billie. I mean that.'

The rest was left unsaid. It didn't need to be addressed. I knew he hoped that one day it would be my turn.

'Thanks.'

I went into the bathroom where the baby was splashing around in cloudy water.

'She was filthy,' Jackie said, lathering the soap on her blonde curls. 'My poor wee baby going through all that. How could they just leave her like that?'

'Lowlifes,' I said.

I watched as she eased the baby back and cupped her head in her hands, pouring fresh clean water from the spray onto her hair, her little legs splashing. They say children as young as that don't have any long-term memory but as they get a year or so older they can recall things. Lucas would be three and a half now and he would remember, he would remember every day that I wasn't there, until one time he would stop remembering.

'What are you going to do now, Jackie?' I ventured. 'I mean, you're safe enough here, I think, and I'm sure I can get Jimmy to find someone to keep an eye on you. But have you thought about what happens next?'

Jackie lifted the baby out and wrapped her in a towel. Then she sat on the toilet seat towelling her dry.

'I've thought about it so much over the past few weeks, where I'd go, all that stuff. But right now I'm not sure. I'm scared to even venture out of the door in case someone finds me . . .'

'Jimmy thinks they won't be after you any more. There was a bit of a bloody end to the scene after we got Elena out. We were gone by then, but by all accounts it was messy. So the cops will be all over the place.'

'I don't want to be involved with the cops, Billie.'

'I know,' I said. 'I understand that. But you have the baby back and they'd be able to make sure you were really safe. You have a lot of information that could put these men away for a very long time. You should maybe think about that.' I paused. 'Plus, there's the fact you saw Tracy, in that basement, and she's still missing. Maybe that is key information for the cops.'

She sat still for a long moment, holding her baby close.

'I've seen stuff on the telly about witness protection. Does that happen in real life?'

I smiled. 'It does. And it might be something for you to look at. But for the moment, just enjoy having your baby back. I'm so happy for you.'

'Thanks, Billie. You made this happen. I don't think I would ever have seen her again if it wasn't for you. This is the happiest day of my life.'

Her eyes filled with tears as she put her cheek to the baby's damp head and held her close. And in that moment I would have given everything I've ever had in the world to have a second like that with Lucas.

CHAPTER TWENTY-FIVE

I drove back to my flat, edgy all the way in case I was being followed. Jimmy had arranged for someone to guard Jackie, and Paddy had said his guys were happy to do it for as long as they were needed. You know something? You can shout down criminals for the thieving, the dealing and the murderous way some of them exist, but in my book there's a scrap of decency in a gangster who can give a young mother a reason to live. I'm not saying it's all rosy Robin Hood figures, but now and again there's an honesty about someone who knows what true suffering is. Paddy Harper was one of them, and so was Jimmy. They planted a watch outside Jackie's flat and would be in constant phone contact with her if she needed anything. I got out of my car and again looked around the square and the street before climbing the five steps to my front entrance, shoving the key in, and rushing to my flat on the ground floor. The paranoia followed me all through the hall and into every room as I made a cursory check that there wasn't anyone lying in wait. Then I came back into the kitchen, stuck the kettle on and filled a large glass with cold water from the fridge. I sat down heavily on the sofa in my living room and breathed out a huge sigh of relief. Peace, quiet, breathe. My mobile rang from the kitchen where I'd left it and I got up and picked it up after a few rings. I could see Scanlon's name on the screen, and I knew this would be a difficult conversation.

'Billie. Where the hell did you get to? I waited half an hour. Then all sorts of shit happened. Please tell me you weren't anywhere near it.'

I let out a sigh.

Sorry. I got . . . well, I got caught up.' I paused long enough to know what he was thinking.

'Christ, Billie. I knew it.'

'Where are you, Scanlon? I can meet now. I think we should talk.'

'Great. Can you meet me in that Willow place café we met the last time?'

'Sure. Now?'

'I'll be there in fifteen. I'm at Pitt Street.'

I spotted Scanlon way down the back of the café in the shadows, and by the look on his face when he clocked me, I could see he was annoyed. I knew it wasn't that I'd patched our coffee date, but he'd be pissed that I hadn't kept him in the loop. But the thing was, I had to be careful about how much I involved him in anything, and I'd told him that before. He was a youngish cop at the right age to move through the ranks swiftly as a detective and he was getting noticed by the top brass. He knew that his friendship with me, a cop who'd left under a cloud, might take the shine off him, and I loved him for the fact that he saw past that and remained my greatest supporter. But I didn't want to drag him too deep into all this.

'Howsit going, Danny?' I said, slinging my bag onto the back of the wooden chair and plonking myself on the sofa.

He sat forward and shook his head. He looked like he'd just stepped out of the shower, freshly shaved and handsome. Eventually he looked at me and smiled.

'I don't know what I'm going to do with you, Billie. I honestly don't. What the hell are you in this so deep for?' He paused. 'You know, there were three dead in some flat in Govanhill. Is that something you were involved in?'

The waitress came up and I asked for a flat white and Scanlon did the same. When she left, I let a moment pass for effect.

'We got Jackie's baby back, Danny,' I said, knowing that one line would blow him away.

His eyes popped wide open in surprise and disbelief. 'You kidding me?'

'Nope.' I smiled, shaking my head, conscious there was a

hint of smugness about my face. 'I just handed the kid over to her about two hours ago.'

'Holy fuck, Billie! I can't believe it. How the hell did you do that? Was the kid in that house in Govanhill? Were you in the house?' The questions tripped off his tongue.

I put up my hand. 'One at a time,' I said, smiling. 'She was in the house. We only found out about it this morning so that's why we had to move fast – hence ditching our coffee.'

'We?' he said, his eyes open. 'Who's we?'

I pushed out a sigh. 'Danny, I don't really want to put you in a position where you know something you feel you might have to pass on. You know what I mean, don't you?'

He puffed, a little irritated.

'Like you've not put me in that position before now? And have I passed anything on? No. I should have, but I didn't. I wouldn't, Billie. You know that.'

'I know, Danny. Look, I'm sorry. That didn't come out right. But okay. You want me to tell you what happened, I will. I trust you. But listen – I'm trying to get Jackie to talk to the cops.'

The waitress came and placed the mugs of coffee on the table and just the smell of the freshly brewed decent coffee was nectar.

'How is Jackie? That must have been some moment when she got her baby back. I can't believe you did that. Did she know anything?'

'No. I kept her in the dark throughout. Right until I appeared with the baby. I had to. If she'd had any idea that the kid was being held, she'd have been battering on the doors and got herself killed. That's why I had to go about it that way and involve the people I did.'

'Instead of coming to us.'

I let it hang for a moment, then I shrugged.

'You know how it is, Danny. My only priority was to get the kid out of whatever house she was being held in, and the cops wading in just wasn't an option.'

He puffed, indignant. 'Of course, it went really well with whoever you got to do it, did it not? A bloodbath. And three stiffs at the last count.'

'We got the kid. That's all that matters. The stiffs were scum. They're the ones who took her, and you already know what they are.'

He picked up his mug and sipped the coffee then sat back on the sofa.

'The boys are all over this, Billie. I'm not on the case, but the Serious Crime Squad are in mopping up at the moment, and they'll be talking to everyone. You know the drill, neighbours and stuff. Someone is bound to say something.'

'The place where it happened is mostly boarded up and the neighbours are immigrants; I don't think they'll want to get involved.'

'So were you in there?'

'No. I was outside in the car. Then one of the guys came

out with the kid and we got off our mark. Then a car arrived with some heavies and there was a bit of a shoot-out in the street. I'm lucky to have got out.'

'Christ. You could have been killed.'

'I know. It wasn't meant to turn out like this, Danny. When Jackie walked into my office I thought I was going to be doing an investigation that might not turn up anything. But the more she told me and the deeper I dug, the worse it got. You know everything I told you. About Hewitt's involvement.'

'He's been missing for three days. Since the Merchant City shooting.'

'I know.'

'Is he dead?'

'I don't know. It was him who gave us the address that led us to the kid, so he's working with the guys who are helping me.'

'Christ. This is a cop that's been kidnapped.'

'Scanlon. This is a cop making snuff movies, who's part of a gang who are butchering trafficked people for entertainment.'

He nodded. 'You're right. And don't think for a minute I'm on his side. He'll get what's coming to him, and if he gets bumped off then tough shit. But I'm concerned in case it gets out that you're involved in this. They will lock you up, when they should be locking up him and the rest of these hoodlums.'

We sat for a long moment saying nothing, sipping our coffee, reflecting on how the frenzy of the past couple of weeks had come to this.

'Billie, the reason I was trying to meet you was about the missing girl – this Tracy girl? We really need some help.'

I looked at him.

'That's what I want to talk to you about too, Danny. I've spoken to Jackie, and I've told her she really needs to go to the cops now that she's got her kid safe. I've told her they could protect her. What do you think? I don't want to find myself sitting opposite big Wilson reading me my rights – that's the problem I have with going to them. And I don't want you to be anywhere near it.'

He took a deep breath and let it out slowly, and I could see his cop mind turning over how he could work his way through this without all of us landing in the shit.

'Okay. We need to think about how we're going to do it. People know we were partners and that we're still friends, but they just won't know how much.'

'So you have to stand back from it.'

'I don't want to do that, though, Billie. I don't want to tell you to go to them and find you're hanging out to dry.'

I nodded. 'I know what you mean. But put it this way. Hewitt is missing, he's part of this web, he's the son of a chief super. And the body count is building up. I think if they're smart they might have more on their plate to consider than locking me up.'

He pursed his lips. 'It sounds good when you say it like that.'

I said nothing for a moment, then I looked at him.

'I'm going to make the call. To Wilson.'

He shook his head. 'I wish I could be a fly on the wall for that conversation.'

CHAPTER TWENTY-SIX

I had arranged with Jackie that I would bring a takeaway dinner from the local Indian restaurant, along with some other stuff she asked me to get from the supermarket. I could easily have left it to Jimmy to get someone to do it for her, but I guessed she needed the company as much as I did. The image of Jackie and her baby kept flooding my mind all afternoon, the picture of sheer love and contentment on her face and how she looked like a different person from the haunted woman who walked into my office that day. I wondered if I would ever get that look again, that relaxed serenity you have when you look at your child in bed asleep, or their first-thing-in-the-morning face when they're so glad to see you. Where did they go when they were asleep? I used to think. Did they dream when they drifted off, were we in their dreams? I was just glad to be going back there to the smells and the freshness of a baby. It was something for me to cling to when I got back to my flat later.

Jackie was preparing to set out the food in the kitchen and asked me to amuse Elena. I went to the window with her in my arms and pointed out the birds flying past and she seemed content to watch the outside world. Then Jackie and I sat and ate the meal together at the table in the living room and drank water.

'I'm going to talk to the police,' Jackie said, suddenly.

It took me by surprise. I was going to broach the subject when we'd finished eating, but she had clearly been giving it some thought.

'You are?' I said. 'Are you sure?'

'You think I shouldn't?'

'No. I think you definitely should. If you're sure. I really think it would be for the best.' I paused. 'I talked to a contact of mine today and he was saying there is a team of detectives now working on finding Tracy. Someone from the escort agency she worked for phoned the cops after they made an appeal and said that she'd worked there and said something about porn movies.'

'She did say she worked for the escort agency. I didn't ever know that at the time though. I mean, people who worked for them just did it through a phone call. I only did it a few times.'

'The police will be really keen to talk to you about that,' I said. 'They'll want you to take them to the basement where the filming took place. Do you remember where it was? Would you be able to take them there?'

She thought for a moment, then nodded.

'I think so. I know the direction. It's out of the city. I'd be able to direct them, I think.'

'Good. That'd be a good start. And they'll want you to identify some of those people. You know, the ones I showed you in the pictures?'

'Yes. I can do that.' She glanced at her baby. 'But will they not want to try to prosecute me? I mean, for not reporting it? Maybe they'll think I was part of it. I did some stupid things, especially letting Barton stash that stuff at my flat, but I didn't know at the time what it was. I don't want to open myself up for all of that.'

'I know. The way I would do this is that I would talk to them first. Tell them how it has to be.'

'But can you do that? Will you not get accused of withholding information?'

'I will.' I nodded. 'But I can deal with that. I'm an ex-cop, as you know. So I know the person I have to speak to.'

'Billie,' she said, 'I don't want to do this without you. Will you be with me all the time?'

I looked at her, again the haunted look.

'I'd have to see if that's going to be allowed. But I will do my best. I won't just walk away, Jackie.'

We sat for a while in silence, watching Elena roll around the floor playing with a soft toy.

'Do you have any children, Billie? You never said. I didn't like to ask.'

Her question startled me, even though it was a very simple and obvious question. I didn't answer straight away as I was thinking of how I could put it without pouring out all the shit in my life.

'I'm sorry,' she said. 'I didn't mean to pry. It's just ... you're so natural with Elena.'

I looked at her, then at the baby, and eventually I spoke.

'I have a son,' I said softly. 'Lucas.' I looked her in the eye, then glanced away. 'But he's ... he's not with me at the moment. It's hard to explain, Jackie. But I know what you've been through.'

She looked at me, her blue eyes full of understanding, and I felt like the victim now instead of her. I swallowed hard and pulled myself together.

'Anyway. I'll tell you about it some time. But not now.'

I picked up the empty plates and took them to the kitchen, aware that she was watching me, that she'd seen the hurt in my face and recognised that we have both been to the same dark place – and that I'm still there.

Millie looked up from her screen as I opened the door and came into the office the following morning. I'd slept better than I had for weeks and lay in bed for an extra half hour just enjoying the feeling of a job well done, and one that had meant so much to me.

'I was just about to call you, Billie,' Millie said. 'Did you see the police on the way in?'

I gave her a quizzical look.

'Police? No?'

She sat back, took her glasses off and held them in her hand a little theatrically.

'They were just in here looking for you.'

My eyes narrowed.

'You sure they were cops? There might be some dodgy people looking for me.'

'No. They were definitely police. A big guy, DCI Wilson, and a younger sidekick. McCartney, I think. They showed me their warrant cards.'

'What did they say?'

'Just that they were looking for you – as a matter of urgency.'

I shrugged and hung up my jacket. 'They could have phoned me.'

Millie got up and went to the coffee machine.

'I saw something on the news about Govanhill. Some shoot-out. Tell me you weren't there, Billie.'

I looked up at her and half smiled.

'I got Jackie's kid back, Millie.'

She turned around, open mouthed. 'You're not serious, are you?'

'I am. I just took her there yesterday. To the flat. Poor wee thing was filthy, but it was a bit of a moment, I can tell you. Brought tears to my eyes.'

Now she beamed. 'That . . . That's just amazing! I can't believe you did it. Jackie must be over the moon.'

'She was. She is. They're up in my flat and I've got someone watching over them. I think she's going to talk to the cops now. It's time to move this on. There's a lot more to these bastards who stole her baby.'

'Good. Does that mean you are out of it now and can get on with some other work? I've got two cases pending an answer, Billie, as well as that insurance company.'

'Great,' I said. 'We'll live to fight another week then. But not quite yet. Get back to the people and tell them I'll let them know in the next couple of days. I've got some things to tie up here, and Jackie said she won't talk to the cops unless I'm there.'

'They're not going to like your involvement, especially since you've sat on the information and didn't go to them in the first place.'

'I know,' I said. 'That's why I'd better get on the phone to the big DCI and set up a meeting.'

'He looks like a bit of a hard man, the DCI.'

'Yeah. He's all of that. But I'm not about to take any shit from him.'

I gave it five minutes while I drank a cup of coffee and filled Millie in with some more detail about Jackie and her baby and the scenes up at the flat when they were reunited. Millie was delighted, and I knew that although she had been deeply sceptical of Jackie in the beginning, she'd warmed to her because I had, and she knew how much it would mean to me on a personal level being able to get her baby back. She didn't need to say it, but I knew that she was wishing it could happen to me and my son.

I scrolled down my mobile for the DCI's extension at HQ and heard it ringing. I was about to hang up when it was picked up. But it wasn't DCI Wilson. It was Steve.

'Is he around?' I asked.

'Is that you, Billie?'

'Yes. Is Wilson around? I need to talk to him.'

'We were at your office.'

'I know. I was out.'

There was a two-beat silence, then he spoke.

'Billie, listen. I'm sorry about the other day. Really. But you know . . . well. Look. I can explain. Can we meet up? Maybe have some dinner?'

I let it hang.

'Just get me the DCI.'

He didn't answer and must have placed the phone back on the desk. It was almost a full minute until a big voice came on.

'Billie. I was looking for you.'

'Well here I am.'

'We need to talk.'

'That's why I'm calling you. I need to talk to you.'

'Come into the office then. Now?'

'Not a chance, Harry. I'm not coming near there. Meet me in café Bruno, bottom of Charing Cross.'

'Don't fuck me about, Billie.'

'Look. Just meet me in the café. It's important for you, believe me. I'll be there in fifteen minutes.'

He hung up.

CHAPTER TWENTY-SEVEN

Wilson was already in the café, standing at the counter surveying the menu on the blackboard. As I walked in he turned around, his face like fizz. I'd have to stand my ground, however grizzly he was. At the end of the day, I was in a position to help so he'd better be grateful.

'Harry,' I said brightly. 'You look like a wet weekend in Shotts.'

'Don't start with your pish, Billie. You're lucky you're not in the pokey.'

'I'll have a flat white,' I said, ignoring him and looking at the barista. 'Coffee, Harry?'

'Aye. Black.'

He turned away from me and headed to a table at the back of the room, and I followed him as I knew he'd be expecting me to. He sat down heavily on the wooden chair, shaking his head and sighing as I sat opposite him, slipping my coat off and draping it over the back of my chair.

'You were in Govanhill, Billie,' he said, frustrated. 'What the actual fuck is going on? Every time I bump into you there's somebody lying stiff.' He leaned across the table, his steely-blue eyes a little bloodshot from lack of sleep, or last night's whisky. 'You'd better start talking.'

I nodded, spread my hands but said nothing for a moment as the coffee arrived and was placed on the table. I took a sip and put the cup back down.

'It's a long story, Harry,' I said. 'But before I tell you anything, I need some promises from you.'

'Fuck that, Billie.'

'Listen, Harry, this is massive. And you need to get people moving now. Just listen to me for a bit. Can you do that without threats?'

He took a swig of his coffee and sat back.

'Right. On you go.'

I fished my mobile out of my bag and scrolled down to the photos and videos. I stopped at the picture of the big Turk.

'This guy,' I said, pulling up the pic. 'His name is Mehmet. He's behind people trafficking, porn movies, snuff movies, in Glasgow. He's in with Malky Jackson. They're all involved.' I paused, pointing to the Turk. 'Tell me. Is this the guy who took a dive from the window?'

He studied the picture.

'No,' he said. 'It wasn't him. It was a Turkish criminal, we've established. But who is this guy?' He pointed at

Mehmet. 'You got proof? I mean proper proof? Jackson's dead. In that Govanhill shithole. Good enough for him.'

'I've got more than that. But you need your people moving now to get the Turk in case he skips the country. You should do it now. Here's where you can find him.'

I told him the address and he scribbled it down on the back of his fag packet.

'You need to tell me more.' He looked up.

'Okay. Remember the girl in the car crash, who said her baby was stolen, then retracted her story?'

He looked furtive. I knew he would know because of the delay in the witness report.

'It was true. And this mob are behind it. The baby was taken because she has proof of what they did. Or she had, and that's why they were after her. That's why they took her baby.'

'She was a nutter, by all accounts.'

'She's not. She's as sane as you and me, and she's got her baby back. She came to my office and I took the case, and I initially thought there was something unhinged about her. But it's true. They took her baby. But now she's got her baby back.'

He looked at me. 'That was you in the car today, outside the house. One of the neighbours said someone came running out with a baby and handed it over, then a car screeched off. That was you?'

I nodded. 'Yes.'

'Why the fuck did you not tell us before? That was our job. Who the hell did you get involved with?'

'I can't help you with that.'

'Well, whoever it is bumped off three of them arseholes, including Jackson, so it's no great loss. But since we don't live in Dodge City, Billie, there are fucking laws against just shooting up some house and settling differences.'

'I know, Harry. But there was no option. It was happening so fast.'

'Listen to me. The moment you knew for sure it was a kidnapping, you should have come to us.'

I gave him a long look. An image of McPhee, mouth gaping open, shotgun in hand that day in the farmhouse, came to mind.

'But somebody already did come to you, Harry. And they're dead.'

'Who?'

'You know who,' I said. 'McPhee. That day when I saw you at the house, you maybe didn't know it then, but I know you worked it out later. McPhee was the guy who reported to Milngavie police station that he saw a baby being taken from the car. But Milngavie managed not to pass it on.'

I could see the recognition on his face and he blinked a few times.

'Yes, well, that was a pretty bad oversight on the part of some uniform dick over in Milngavie. These things happen.'

'Not just any uniform dick, Harry. You know that too.'

He looked at the table and we sat silent.

'Hewitt,' I said. 'He's Kenny Hewitt's son.'

'He's missing. Been missing since the Merchant City shooting. You were there too.'

I nodded. 'What does that tell you, Harry? You're the detective. Did you join the dots?'

He ran a hand over his forehead.

'Listen, Billie, we've got a missing cop here. Christ knows what's happened to him. I don't know what he's involved in.'

'But he didn't pass the information on about the witness to the baby being stolen. Did you never wonder why that was?'

'We just took him at his word. He got distracted and forgot to pass it on. And the Jackie character disappeared, so that was it.'

'You filed it in the "keep it quiet folder".'

'Fuck's sake. He's the chief super's son. What the hell could we do? And we couldn't find this Jackie bird.'

'Because she was on the run, hiding from the thugs who stole her kid from the back seat of her car that day.'

'So what are you getting at?'

I scrolled down the phone again, and brought up the video from inside the bar and froze the frame on Hewitt. I turned the phone to him and he screwed up his eyes, then I watched his face fall.

'Fuck's sake!'

'Yep. That's Hewitt. That's your missing cop. He's up to his arse in porn movies and people trafficking with these guys.'

'Jesus wept.'

'He's rotten, Harry.'

'Do you know where he is?'

'No, I don't.'

'Do you know who's got him?'

I shook my head, hoping he couldn't see my lie. 'But if I was you, I'd get all these guys rounded up and locked up because there's a bigger picture here. It's not just that a baby's been stolen. What about the missing teenager? That Tracy Logan? I heard from people that she worked with an agency and was making porn films – Jackie told me it was with this mob, but then she disappeared. So you need to find her. Get them and find her.'

'What about Jackie? Will she talk to us?'

'She said no all along. But now she's got her baby back, she might. But she needs protection. Big time. Can you guarantee that?'

'Yes. I can guarantee it. We need to talk to her ASAP. We need her to take us to the place where the films were made. Will she do that?'

'She doesn't know the address. But she knows where it is.'

'And you've known this for how long?'

'Just since she got in touch with me. Not long.'

'You should have come to us, Billie. You know that. You broke the law.'

I looked at him, the image of him planting evidence those years ago flashing into my mind. He never knew I saw him, and I wouldn't mention it now. But he was no stranger to breaking the law himself and he knew it.

'We all break the rules sometimes, Harry. You know that.'

He glared at me but said nothing. Then he took his phone from his jacket pocket and pushed a key.

'Steve, get the team organised. We have addresses to hit in the next twenty minutes. Take down these names.'

He hung up and puffed out a sigh, shaking his head.

'I need to see this Jackie pronto, Billie. Can you organise that?'

'I'll call her now.'

I was already in the flat with Jackie, who was pacing the floor, when I got the call from Wilson to say they were on their way. He said there would be a female detective with him.

'They're on their way,' I said. 'It'll be the DCI and a female detective. So, as I've told you, you just take your time and tell them the truth. You're not in any trouble here, so don't worry.'

I knew that wasn't entirely true, as she had witnessed a murder being filmed and hadn't reported it to the police, but I'd explained to her earlier that they would understand that she was petrified and on the run.

I watched as she picked up the baby who'd just woken up from a nap, and was struck how she was a completely different person when she had the child in her arms. It was as though she was complete now, and the woman who had walked into my office, the haunted figure she'd been, twitching and terrified, was gone. As long as she had her baby she was powerful and confident. I couldn't remember feeling like that when I had Lucas. I remember the love and the adoration every time I looked at his face waking or sleeping, but I don't know if it changed me as a woman. Maybe it should have, maybe if it had I wouldn't have taken my eye off the ball. I pushed away the negative thoughts. I looked out of the window and saw a car pull up in the car park, and went across to see Wilson and a young female detective getting out of their car.

'Here they come,' I said. 'Now just stay calm. Remember. You are helping them. They need you.'

She nodded, but didn't look convinced.

A few seconds later the doorbell rang and I answered the intercom and let them in. I opened the door and met big Wilson. The detective at his side was young, possibly around the same age as I was when I was breaking through. She smiled at me as I stood back and beckoned them in. Once they were in the living room, Wilson introduced me to the young officer, Laura Stirling, turning to her with something resembling a wry smile.

'Billie here, as I was telling you, Laura, was one of a kind, and if I'm honest it's a loss to the force that she's no longer with us.'

His accolade took me by surprise and made me feel I was at my own funeral with my old boss paying tribute.

'I'm still here, Harry, I've not died yet. Maybe keep that tribute for when I've gone.'

'It's true, though, Carlson. One of the best, you were.'

To my surprise his face broke into a smile, and I could see he was trying to lighten the mood. He'd probably noticed that Jackie was jittery. He was an old hand and knew that he had to relax the atmosphere if he was going to get this girl on his side. I quite admired him for the way he was operating and I found myself falling into line.

'Well,' I said. 'Changed days, but I've still got my conscience and want to do what's right.' I turned to Jackie. 'I'll leave it to you guys to ask the questions, but when Jackie came into my office that day, I could see that she was deeply disturbed, and I found out why when she actually opened up about what had happened – it really is a horrendous story. So everyone needs to bear in mind that she's vulnerable and frightened, but that she wants to do the right thing.'

Wilson put his hand up. 'Exactly. I can see all of that, Billie.' He turned to Jackie. 'Now, Jackie. You don't know me or

Detective Constable Stirling from Adam, but we are here for you to help us and also for us to help you. Whatever you tell us, I can assure you we will look after you.'

He was good at this, Wilson. I hadn't seen too much of his softer side before, as most of the people we were questioning were hardened villains, murderers, rapists or drug dealers. Then there had been no time for pleasantries, it had been bad cop all the way, and sometimes a punch in the ribs wouldn't have been considered out of order. I took this as the interview beginning and Stirling took her notebook and pen out of her pocket. I offered them tea and went into the kitchen as the chat began. As I was filling the kettle and getting mugs out of the cupboard I could hear Wilson gently saying, 'Okay, Jackie. Why don't you just start at the very beginning. Is that all right for you?'

CHAPTER TWENTY-EIGHT

It was already dark by the time I left Jackie's house and drove back to my flat. Wilson and the detective had taken two hours to get the full story from Jackie, and I'd watched as she told it slowly and deliberately, breaking down in the parts when she said she was so sorry and ashamed that she hadn't done anything when she saw the Vietnamese man being murdered. I had to take care of Elena from time to time during the interview and I made dinner for her. As I'd sat in the kitchen cajoling the kid with some fish fingers and mashed potato, it was like going back in time with the noises and the games you have to play to make sure a child clears its plate. When she was done she put her arms up for me to pick her up and she snuggled into me, and it struck me how easily a kid at this age just falls in with whoever feeds and takes care of them. I wondered if Lucas was being passed around friends or relatives of Bob, because I knew how derelict he could be with his own life, and I prayed that he was being vigilant with my son. The not knowing was the hardest part.

By the time Wilson left, I'd ordered a takeaway and sat with Jackie while we ate and then watched as she bathed the child and put her down. I was glad how well she'd coped with letting everything out to the police, and knew that when she talked about Barton and the coke and the money, Wilson and the detective would be forming an opinion of her, not all of it good, but they wouldn't let it show. I was caught by surprise when I overheard Wilson saying to Jackie that they had checked out births across the UK, explaining that it was important to establish everything about her, but that he could find no record of Elena. I considered interrupting and asking what this had to do with anything, but I let it go. I heard Jackie tell him exactly what she'd told me, about running away from Elena's father who was a drug dealer and a criminal. She said that was the reason she didn't register Elena even in the last year in Scotland, because she was afraid he would come after her. To my surprise she even gave Wilson his name on the promise that he would never be anywhere near her and her baby. As I was leaving, Jackie saw me to the door and pleaded with me to make sure I was with her tomorrow when she led the cops to the basement where the movies were made. I promised her I'd be there. Wilson said there would be a team of Forensics and uniforms in the convoy as we drove to the place because if there was anything to see there, then they would want to be on top of it straight away. He'd told me in the kitchen privately that they'd already rounded up some of the names and faces from the photos I'd given him, and the kebab shop was now closed, with officers taking it apart looking for information.

I was just pulling into Charing Cross to head up to Blythswood Square when my mobile rang in my pocket. I slowed down and pulled into the side when I saw Johnny's name on the screen.

'Johnny,' I said. 'You all right?'

The pause lasted several beats and I didn't like it.

'You okay, Johnny?' I said again.

Again there was silence. Then he spoke.

'Billie. I . . . I need your help.'

My gut tightened. 'What's wrong, Johnny? Where are you?'

He was taking too long to answer. Either he'd taken a bad hit of something and was ill – there were plenty of stories of rogue batches of heroin on the streets from time to time and the dead junkies piled up – or maybe he'd been rumbled. I hadn't heard from him in a few days, and he hadn't answered any of my calls. But he was a drug addict and their chaotic lives had only one purpose – to get their next hit – so I'd left it at that as so many other things were going on.

'Billie. Can you come and meet me? I need your help.'

'What's wrong? Are you hurt?'

Silence.

'Johnny?'

'I . . . I'm not well. I don't know what to do.'

'Are you sick? Have you taken something?'

'Aye. Maybe.'

'Do you want me to phone an ambulance? I can call 999.'

'No. Can you come and see me?'

I didn't like the sound of it, but there was a desperation to his voice, and that disturbed me more. I wondered if someone was sitting with a knife to his throat or a gun to his head. But what was I supposed to do? Just tell him, No, I'm too busy, I'll get back to you? Whatever was going on here, I couldn't just abandon him. I thought of calling Wilson, telling him what I was going to do, then I worried that I was dragging Johnny to the cops and he didn't want anywhere near them.

'Are you in the city? Where are you?'

After two beats he spoke.

'I'm down near the Sheriff Court by the river on the other side of the bridge.'

'Where exactly by the river? You on the walkway or on the street?'

'On the walkway.'

'Can you walk up onto the street? So I can see you as I drive past?'

There was no way I was prepared to go off the street onto the walkway which I knew would be deserted and dangerous at this time of the night. The street would be easier and at least there would be passing traffic. It took him a while to answer, then he did.

'I can try.'

'Are you injured or something?'

'I . . . I got a doing earlier and I'm struggling.'

Christ. What was I supposed to do here? He sounded like he needed an ambulance more than a friend. But there was something about his voice that made me feel I couldn't just run out on him.

'Okay, but I'm not local at the moment,' I lied, playing for time. 'Give me about fifteen or twenty minutes. Get out onto the main road, though, where I can see you.'

'Aye. Okay.'

He hung up. Alarm bells were going off all over in my head. I couldn't go down there on my own in case this was some kind of trap, and I couldn't just walk away from him, because if it hadn't been for Johnny, I wouldn't have got Jackie's kid back. Simple as that. Before I could stop myself I had pushed the key for Harper's mobile.

'Billie,' he answered after a few rings. 'You all right? Was going to phone you later. About Hewitt.'

'Hewitt?'

For some reason the name threw me, as though the last few hours had been such a blur, I'd almost forgotten that Hewitt was still being held by them.

'Aye. We're going to chuck him.'

'Chuck him?'

That could mean anything.

'Aye. We don't need him any more. And I don't think, the level of shit he's in, that he'll be telling his polis pals all about the boys he's spent the last few days with.'

'Oh, right,' I said, somewhat relieved that 'chucking' him didn't mean throwing him in the river.

'So what's happening?'

'I've got a bit of a situation,' I said. 'I might need a bit of help. Maybe back-up. I'm not sure.'

He interrupted. 'What's wrong? Where are you?'

'I'm at the bottom of Charing Cross, heading for my house, but I just got a call from that Johnny guy, you know, the junkie who helped us get the kid? The one who dropped us the info all the time on her whereabouts?'

'Yeah. I know who you mean.'

'Well he's just called and he sounds like he's in some kind of trouble. Said he needs to see me. Wants me to meet him now. Down at the riverside near the Sheriff Court.'

I heard him blow out a puff.

'Not on your own you don't, Billie. That's well dodgy. Do you think it could be a trap?'

'I don't know. He sounded ill.'

'Listen, Billie. He should get himself an ambulance then. I know you care about people, and that's why I like you, but this is not your problem. Leave it. Don't go near it.'

I was silent for a moment.

'I'd hoped maybe you could get someone to be with me maybe?' I realised I was pushing it. I couldn't be using a guy like this for everything.

He sighed. 'He's a junkie, Billie. He was useful, and I'm sure you paid him well. But you can't be taking on all the problems in the world or you'll never get any peace.'

I didn't answer because I didn't know what to say. Maybe he was absolutely right. I get too close to people like Johnny and have done in the past even as a cop. There was a touch of the bleeding heart to me and it didn't always end well.

Eventually, Harper spoke. 'Right. Okay. I'll get someone down there. Where, exactly? I'll get a couple of the boys on the street. They'll be in a car.'

'I don't know specifically but I said to him to get off the walkway and come to the main road so I can see him. I was just going to drive down there in a few minutes and see what I can see.'

'Okay. Give me fifteen minutes to organise someone. Then head down.'

'Thanks, Paddy.'

'Let me know how it goes.'

He hung up.

I felt stupid and naive, like having to pull in help from a villain because I was maybe just afraid of the dark. I told myself this was the last time I'd do this for Johnny. I indicated and got back on the road.

I waited a few minutes then drove slowly through the

town and down along the Broomielaw so I didn't arrive too early. I kept checking in my mirrors to see if any of Harper's men were following, but I didn't know what kind of car to look out for. The Jamaica Bridge was quiet and I drove slowly across it. The further I went this side of town the quieter and more eerie it became. I took the road behind the Sheriff Court. There were mostly old deserted buildings here, some of them boarded up. I knew the walkway was close by, but I would have to park my car if I wanted to get close to it. I drove around the block again slowly, and this time as I came around the back of the court I saw a figure standing in the shadows. I eased my car along the road for a closer look, then I saw an almost hesitant hand come up, not quite a wave, but an acknowledgement. It was Johnny. I pulled my car over to the kerb, but kept the doors locked, glancing around to see if there were any other cars. I'd seen none as I drove around the block, and there was nothing to see on the street, not one car. I kept my lights on and in the glare I could see Johnny's pale, gaunt face, and his skinny frame. He looked a little bent over as though he was in pain, nursing sore ribs or something. I lowered my window halfway down.

'Johnny. You all right?'

He didn't answer, but there was a terrified look in his eyes as he shook his head very slowly, and I knew immediately that it was a trap. I was still staring at him looking for answers when suddenly I was blinded by a car coming straight at me. Before I could even get my car into gear to get away, the car screeched and did a turn so that it was sideways in front of me and I couldn't move. Two big thugs jumped out and came straight at me with baseball bats. I braced myself as the windscreen dented in the first hit, then as they rained blows, it shattered, and the last thing I saw before I closed my eyes was an arm going around Johnny's neck and a gun pointed at his head as he was dragged backwards. I heard him shouting, 'I'm sorry, Billie. I'm sorry.' But by now the guy who was smashing my windscreen was trying to rip my door open, and when he found it was locked, he smashed the side window. I immediately felt blood on my face. Then two big arms reached in and grabbed me by the throat.

'Open the fucking door or I'll pull you out the window, bitch.'

I struggled and thrashed my head, but the more I did the tighter his grip on my throat became and I couldn't breathe. I put my hand up in submission. Then I pushed the central lock button and the doors popped open. In a flash I was dragged out and punched hard in the face. Dazed, legs buckling, I fell against the car. He pushed my face onto it and the splinters of glass were pressed in even further.

'The bird!' he spat. 'Where's the bird and her fucking wean?'

'Please!' I heard myself whimper. 'Please.'

He drove my face further onto the metal and I felt my teeth burst through the skin inside my lip. The agony, the pain. Jesus Christ. I'm going to die here. I thought of Lucas, how would he ever know, who would tell him that I never stopped looking for him, that I never stopped loving him?

'Where is she? Take us there right fucking now.'

I caught my breath enough to attempt to speak.

'I can't. She's with the police.'

There was a stiff punch to my kidneys and I thought they were going to come up into my mouth. I buckled.

'Fuck's sake,' a voice I hadn't heard. 'Just throw her in the fucking river. She's no use to us now.'

As soon as his words were out there was the sound of a gunshot and the guy who was hurting me let me go and I fell limp to the ground. Then there was another shot, and I saw a car screeching to a halt, blocking off the exit from the attackers. I lay on the ground as bullets whizzed past. I knew it would be Paddy's men. But there was so much shooting going on that anything could be happening. I wriggled underneath the car until the shooting stopped. Then I heard the voice.

'Billie. It's okay, darlin'. It's over.'

I turned my head as much as I could to see the face of Jimmy Murdoch shining the torch from his mobile.

'Fuckin' hell. You're in a right mess. Don't worry. You're all right now.' He reached under and touched my hand.

'Can you move, just a bit, to get yourself out from under there?'

'I'll try,' I croaked.

I twisted my body, aching with every inch, and managed to get myself out from beneath the car. I could feel the rain on my face and the glare of street lights. Then I felt the strong arms of Jimmy underneath me, trying to ease me to a sitting position. I was dizzy, warm blood trickling down my face and I could feel my lip puffing up. At least my teeth were still intact. Jimmy wiped my face with a handkerchief.

'There. It looks worse with the blood. But you'll be okay. I've seen worse at the karaoke nights up in Possil.' He grinned, and put his arms around my shoulders. 'Can you stand up?'

He gently eased me to my feet on shaky legs but a searing pain jolted through my back.

'My back,' I winced. 'He punched me in the kidneys. Jesus!'

'You'll be okay. You might be pissing blood for a couple of days,' he said as though I'd just fallen off my bike. Then he looked at me. 'Do you want to go to the hospital?' He glanced around. 'We need to get out of here fast before the cops come.'

'No. Yes. Aw. I don't know, Jimmy.'

'Listen. I'll call Paddy. We'll get a doctor up to see you at his place. He'll patch you up and if you need an X-ray then we'll get you to hospital.'

I nodded, barely able to breathe for the pain. He helped me into the back of the Land Rover, almost carrying me, and a guy in the front handed me a can of juice, telling me to drink it for the shock. I took it. My neck was throbbing and my face hurt. Then they drove off, and as they did I scanned the area for any sight of Johnny, but there was none. The Land Rover bumped as it went over one of the bodies in the street, and I caught Jimmy and the driver exchanging a little chuckle.

CHAPTER TWENTY-NINE

Jimmy dropped me off at my flat, and despite my protests that I was fine, he made sure I was inside my house before he left. There was something gallant about that, even though he and his boys had just popped at least two thugs to save my bacon. I stood in the hallway with my back to the door in the darkness and silence, and took a moment to let what just happened to me sink in. I took as long a breath as I could before the pain in my ribs stabbed me. Then I let it out slowly to try and relax myself a little. I could feel my face was wet and when I gently touched it with my fingertips I could feel there was blood. I slipped off my coat and let it fall to the floor then walked slowly to the bathroom, flicking on the lights as I went. In the bathroom I pushed on the light switch and my swollen mouth dropped open when I saw my face. Jesus almighty! It was peppered with blood from the impact of dozens of splinters of glass from the windscreen. Jimmy had picked out some glass, he'd told me, and said it was just small cuts. I ran a soft wash-cloth under warm water, wrung it out and dabbed at the cuts, scrutinising for bits of glass shining in the light. There were none to see, so maybe Jimmy was right. My face was beginning to swell just below my eye where I'd been hit the first time, and now my lip was puffed and bleeding from being bashed onto the metal of my car. I rinsed the cloth and applied it again, and the more I did it, the less blood there was. The cuts were visible and angry, though not deep. I'd live, I decided. This time. I sat on the toilet but found it hard to pee, but when I did, I could see there was blood in my urine. Not good. But I didn't feel ill, just shocked, and a bit bewildered as it had all happened so fast. In the five years that I'd been a police officer I'd never been hit once, and as a private eye I'd had a few scrapes, but the last few days had been crazy. I toyed briefly with the idea of calling Scanlon, as I knew he'd be here like a shot just to be with me. But I couldn't face explaining it all to him, especially the fact that I'd been rescued by criminals. I dried my face off and applied some iodine which stung like a bitch and made my face a light brownish colour. I sighed and gingerly walked into the kitchen and stuck the kettle on for some tea. While it was boiling I poured myself a glass of red wine, something I rarely did these days, mostly because if I had nobody to share a drink with I couldn't really see the point, but also because these days I wanted and needed to be in control at all times. I took a decent drink of the wine and relished the taste as it slipped down my throat. The house was so still it somehow added to the desolation of the moment, standing here totally alone, drinking a glass of wine with my face like something from a butcher's window. I was thinking of running a bath and considering whether that was wise, given the pain in my kidneys, but then another thought suddenly dawned on me. My car. Jesus. I'd left my car at the scene of a crime and any minute now the police would be at my door, because by now they'd be down at the riverside picking up the bodies. The last thing I needed right now was to be grilled by the cops. Just then my mobile rang and I nearly jumped out of my skin. I went into the hall and picked it out of my jacket pocket on the floor.

'Billie. I hear you've been in the wars. Bastards.'

It was Paddy Harper. I let out a sigh of relief. At least it wasn't DCI Harry Wilson.

'Yeah, just a bit, Paddy. But thanks to Jimmy and your boys, I'm still alive.'

'You sure you don't need a doctor? Hospital?'

'No. Thanks, Paddy. I'm fine. I'll take a couple of painkillers and lie down. My face is a bit of a mess, but I'm okay.' I paused. 'But listen, Paddy . . . My car—'

'Don't worry,' he interrupted. 'Been taken care of. I had one of the boys drive it up out of the way, so we'll get the windows fixed and drop it back to you in a couple of days.'

I was astonished and touched at the efficiency of this well-oiled hoodlum enterprise.

'Thanks, Paddy. That's what I was just about to say to you. In all the drama I completely forgot about it.'

'Don't worry about it.'

I wanted to ask about Hewitt, but I bit my tongue. I didn't need to know. If I didn't know then I couldn't be accused later by cops of holding back information. But I did wonder if they'd bumped him off.

'Paddy,' I said, swallowing, 'thanks for today. For Jackie's kid. What you did by getting her baby back gave Jackie a reason to live, because I honestly think she was running out of reasons fast.'

Part of me wished I could somehow magic Paddy Harper and his gang onto the hunt for my son and give me back my reason to live. But I knew that could never happen.

'Glad to be of help, Billie. Now get yourself a drink and go to bed. Any problems, phone me. I'm here for you.'

He hung up, and I swallowed hard because the kindness and the sheer shock of the last couple of hours suddenly washed over me. But there was no time for tears right now. There had been enough of those.

I didn't sleep much. I was in pain every time I moved a muscle, and I couldn't lie on my side because the cuts on my face were too raw to touch the pillow. When I did sleep, it was full of fitful dreams and angry faces, and once or twice I woke up convinced there was someone standing at the foot of my bed with a baseball bat. It was one of those nightmares where you think you are awake, but you are unable to move because your limbs are lead weights. Eventually the sound of traffic in the street stirred me awake and I got myself up out of bed and organised. After breakfast I called Jackie and told her there had been a problem, that I was coming in a taxi, and when the police escort arrived at her house that we would transfer and go with them in their cars. She asked what had happened, and I told her and warned her that my face was a mess. I decided not to tell Wilson yet, because I couldn't face any awkward questions this early in the day. He'd see me soon enough. Having a shower and getting dressed was an ordeal, and I popped a couple of paracetamol for the pain. But I was relieved to see there was no blood in my urine, and so far it didn't look like I was headed for the renal unit.

When I got into the taxi outside my flat I was wearing dark glasses and a high-neck sweater with the collar of my coat pulled up to cover most of my face. But as we drove up towards Maryhill, I caught the driver stealing little suspicious glances at me. Given the address I'd come from, I wouldn't have been surprised if he thought I was a working girl who'd had the misfortune of picking up the wrong kind of client. But he said nothing. When he dropped me off at the flat, there was an unmarked police car already there, and I could see Wilson in the passenger seat and

Steve in the driving seat of the big grey Audi. I paid the driver and climbed out of the black hackney. Wilson got out of the car at the same time and stopped in his tracks when he saw me.

'What the fuck, Carlson?'

I looked at him through my shades but didn't answer.

'Let me see,' he said, stepping closer to me.

I raised my glasses and saw his eyes widen, at the same time as Steve got out of the car and looked shocked.

'Jesus, Billie. What the fuck happened?' Wilson said, shaking his head.

I attempted an indifferent shrug.

'Would you believe me if I said I fell downstairs?'

He tutted. 'I'd believe you if you said you went through a windscreen.' He peered at my face, my swollen lip and eye. 'Who the hell did this to you?'

I sighed. 'Very bad people, Harry.' I really didn't want to get into this here. 'I'll tell you once this is over.' He glanced at Steve, who was staring at me, his face a mix of anger and sympathy. He knew me well enough to know that I'd have been struggling last night after this happened, and the look on his face told me that he was thinking that I should have called him. Fat chance.

'Did you see a doctor?'

'No,' I said. 'It's painful. But superficial, I think.' I turned to go upstairs. 'Let's get this part over with. I'll live, Harry. Don't be fretting.'

'The way you're going, Billie, you're not going to live long. For fuck's sake. You should have phoned us last night.' He walked beside me up the steps. 'I don't need to ask you, but I know this is something to do with the dead bodies the boys were sweeping up last night down at the back of the Sheriff Court.'

I attempted as much of a smile as I could, and pressed the buzzer.

'You're good at this, Harry.'

He shook his head and didn't reply. As the door opened, we walked into the hall with Steve behind us, and I gritted my teeth through the pain as we climbed to the second floor.

CHAPTER THIRTY

Nobody spoke much on the way out of the city. I sat with Jackie and the baby, strapped into a child's seat, in the back. Steve was driving and Wilson was in the passenger seat, taking phone calls but saying very little. Jackie turned to me a couple of times and shook her head, looking at my face and whispering that she was so sorry. At one time she filled up, and I took hold of her hand and told her not to get upset, that these things happened and she just needed to concentrate on where we were going.

We left the motorway and took the road out that would eventually take us in the Clydebank direction, but Jackie was sitting forward, looking out as though she was checking for landmarks to show her the way. As we drove down the road on the outskirts she said, 'Here. At this junction. I remember this. Turn right and keep going.'

Steve pulled the car right at the lights and we were now

going away from the city and further into a quiet road leading to an industrial estate with various units.

'Up here,' Jackie said. 'It's near here.' She lowered her window so she could concentrate on the area.

We drove along three or four roads within the industrial estate, only passing the occasional delivery van and one small car, but there was little sign of life anywhere around here. At the end of one of the roads was a long, low, grey corrugated roof, a windowless building apart from one glass entrance at the front.

'That's it!' she said. 'Here. That building. That's where I was.'

'In there?' Wilson said. 'Is there a basement in that building?'

'Yes. It's at the back.'

As we pulled up outside, there were no cars and no sign that it had been occupied recently. A big, chunky metal chain and padlock was on the double doors. There was no sign on the building indicating what it was, but there was a dark space to show where one had been taken down at some stage. Behind us were two police cars and a van, which I presumed was Forensics with searching equipment. Officers piled out, including two with German shepherds on leads. The dogs were excited, leaping around as though they were on an outing.

'Wait in the car until we get the doors opened,' Wilson said as he got out of the passenger seat.

As we sat watching the officers with their cutting

equipment and a heavy metal battering ram, Jackie was silent, her face taut.

'You okay?' I said.

She nodded. 'Just being here brings it all back. Everything. My stomach is going like an engine.'

'Are you going to be all right about going inside?'

She took a nervous breath and puffed out her cheeks.

'Yes. I have to be.'

We sat for a few moments, then I asked, 'When Barton told you all about it, did he say where they put the body of the Vietnamese guy, or anything else?'

She shook her head. 'I suppose they will have disposed of them, burned them or thrown them in the river. Who knows. Evil.'

The sound of the cutting equipment on metal, the battering down of the door and the sound of shattering glass sharply brought back the image of last night's attack. I touched my swollen lip.

'Are you all right, Billie?' she asked. 'I mean, after last night. That must have been terrifying.'

'It was.' I forced a half smile. 'But I'm here. I'm alive. You've got your wee pal there, sound asleep. Things could be worse.' She didn't know it, but things were already a lot worse for me and they had been for a long time.

We watched as the doors were kicked in and the dogs yelped at the side of their handlers. Wilson came over to the car.

'Can you come out now, Jackie, and I'll talk you through what we want to do.'

'Okay.' She glanced at the sleeping baby.

'Don't worry,' Wilson said. 'We'll get an officer to sit in the car with her.'

She glanced at me and I gestured for her to go out – I knew she was looking for reassurance that I'd be going too. We both got out and stood for a moment in the cold. An icy wind had got up, and I wrapped my scarf around my neck, pulling it up high, conscious of the uniformed officers glancing at my injuries.

Wilson beckoned us towards the building, turning to Jackie as we walked across.

'Right, Jackie. What I want you to do here is go inside along with us, take it nice and slowly, and talk to us every step of the way,' Wilson said, then continued as she nodded in agreement. 'You have nothing to fear here. The building is empty. What we need you to do is talk us through exactly what your movements would have been on any of the days you visited here for filming.'

'You mean where we got dressed and stuff, and where we sat and all that?'

'Everything, Jackie. Every single thing you saw. Take your time as you go in and think back to where everyone and everything was, from the reception area to wherever the basement is. We will be filming this, but don't worry.

It's just so we can be absolutely clear of what went on. You understand?'

'Yes.'

'Okay. Right. In we go then.' He gestured to the female detective who had accompanied him to the flat to join them.

Jackie glanced at me, and Wilson nodded his approval for me to go ahead with her. We walked through the door first, the two of us. Behind us were Wilson and the female officer, then officers with filming equipment. All wearing zoot suits. It was the weirdest sight, like we had arrived from some sort of space age. Inside there was what looked like a reception area for whatever this building had been before. Officers went behind the desk but it looked as though everything had been cleared away, even the telephones, and everything was pristine. It was like walking into a brand new building for the first time. There was a faint whiff of cleaning fluid.

'Normally there would be one guy behind the desk here,' Jackie said. 'But he wasn't a receptionist or anything. He must have been part of their mob, because he looked more like a bouncer than a receptionist.'

'Did you ever speak to him? Did you know his name?' Wilson asked. 'Can you remember what he looked like?'

'I didn't know his name. He never said much. He was a skinny guy with greasy hair, and grubby-looking. He had tattoos on the back of his hands. I remember that. But I would just tell him my name and that I was here for the filming.'

Wilson nodded, and we moved along the corridor. There were a couple of doors off the hall that could have been offices or storage.

'What about these?' He pointed to the doors and the cameraman filmed. 'Did you ever go in there? Are they offices?'

'No. They were always closed when I was in. I never went in there so I don't know what they were. I was only ever in the basement. It's a big area.'

Wilson gestured to his officers with the metal ram and they promptly battered the doors in. He stepped back and glanced inside as we stood.

'Empty,' he said. 'Not even a desk or chair.' He turned to Jackie. 'So is it along this way?'

'Yes,' she said, pointing to the end of the corridor. 'If you go to the end, there's a door and that leads to a metal staircase. That's where the basement is.'

We followed her and as we got nearer to the closed door at the end, she stopped and appeared to freeze.

'You all right?' Wilson said.

Her mouth tightened.

'I . . . I'm just nervous. My legs are like jelly.'

'You'll be okay,' I reassured her, touching her arm.

An officer went in front and tried the door at the end of

the corridor but it was closed. Wilson beckoned to his men, and it was promptly booted open, splinters flying around. At the other side of the door was a red metal staircase, a tight spiral of a few stairs going down. We all stood in the tiny space in the stairwell. The smell of cleaning fluid was stronger now.

'Can you take us down there, Jackie?' Wilson said. 'Just talk to us as you go down, tell us how it was each day, you know, you would walk in this door and down the stairs. I see there's another door at the bottom of the stairs.'

'Yes. That's the place.'

She walked slowly down the stairs, me at her back, wincing with the pain of moving any muscles. At the bottom, the officer squeezed past us and battered the door in as we stood back. Once the door was off we stepped forward and into a large basement room, with a couple of anterooms off it, including a kitchen. Inside the basement it was empty, eerie, sparkling as though it had been deep cleaned in every area. There was nothing to see. All we could do was imagine what had gone on in this windowless basement where innocent immigrants met their death and young women were exploited. Jackie stood gazing around her, shaking her head.

'Everything's gone,' she said, seeming surprised. 'Everything. This room was full of props.' She gestured across the room with her arm. 'There was a bed, there were chairs and a couch, and some more chairs over there that the bosses who ran the show sat on. The room over there that looks like the kitchen is where we changed into ... into ...' She stopped. 'I'm sorry.'

'Take your time,' Wilson said softly. 'You're doing great.'

She sniffed. 'Over there, where the bed was, that's where the porn films were made. I would come in from the kitchen dressed in whatever outfit I was told to wear, and then there would be some guy waiting. And the cameras – they were over there.' She pointed to an area. 'There was one cameraman, Barton, and he would film the whole thing.'

She stopped again, transported to the darkness.

'And what about the day you said you saw the Vietnamese man?'

She shuddered. 'He was brought in, and then he was tied up. He wasn't saying anything, but I think he must have been told it was part of a film or for some form of entertainment. He looked a bit confused. Not terrified though. Not until ... Until ...' She stopped.

She then described what happened, struggling to get through it towards the end.

'Just take a minute or two, Jackie. You're doing fantastic, really you are.'

Jackie composed herself and then went on. 'I was standing in the kitchen area. I think they thought I had gone at this point, but I was still there and I saw everything. I saw them push him onto the chair and slap him in the face a few times. He was so frightened. I'll never forget the terror in his eyes. They kept filming all the while, and then they started to hit him harder and there was blood. I was gasping back in the kitchen and crouching down, but it wouldn't have mattered because they were all there and watching, involved. Nobody was even stopping them. And ... And then they hit him with some heavy thing. I think it was like a small sledgehammer. They slammed it across his face and I heard the crack and saw the blood go everywhere. When I stuck my head up, his face was bloodied, a total mess and they kept hitting him, and there were bits of flesh and skin flying everywhere. They hit him so hard I could see what I think was his brain. It wasn't recognisable as a head or a face any more, just a mound of blood and flesh. He wasn't moving by this time, I'm sure he was dead. They kept filming though. It was dark and quiet and the smell of blood made me retch. While they were all watching I slipped quietly out of the door and ran all the way to the reception. The guy wasn't there so I just got into my car and drove away like hell.' She paused, gazing at the spot as though she could still see it. 'They murdered him. He was just a poor immigrant.'

She took a moment again, and then told about the missing girl, Tracy, describing her, how she had been lovely and hadn't really seemed scared at all. While she was doing that, I saw the dogs being given a T-shirt to sniff, and

I assumed it was something they'd obtained from the children's home for their investigation. The dogs were going wild, pulling the handler to the door, and we all looked at each other and followed. Once outside, the officer let the dogs off the leash and they barked and ran around sniffing, until they got to the back of the building, with everyone following them. Then the dogs went completely crazy at one area, where it looked like the earth had been freshly dug. Wilson stepped away and waved across to the cops hanging around the minibus smoking. They came across with spades, three of them, and started digging. It didn't take long – the dogs were desperate to dig too, but they were trained not to do that in case they disturbed evidence. We all stood watching in dread, the way you do when you know there is a dark inevitability about the ending. Then the digging stopped, and an officer stooped and scraped some earth away. Everyone visibly froze when we saw the pale hand and a scrawny forearm exposed. The dogs were sniffing and yelping. They had found what they were looking for. I turned away and motioned to Jackie to step back too. I thought of poor Tracy, of what had brought her to this, who she'd been, who was waiting for her. And I thought of Lucas, of my own frantic search, and of all the people whose searches never had a happy ending. I steeled myself, because Jackie was in tears, so I guided her gently towards the car.

'It's her, isn't it, Billie? The girl. Tracy.'

I nodded, puffing, my breath steaming in the coldness. 'I think so.'

In the back of the car, Elena stirred and cried out for her mama, and I watched as Jackie climbed in beside her, grateful that her baby was here and safe and loved.

CHAPTER THIRTY-ONE

I stood at the side of the car watching as the hive of police forensic activity swung into action. I had seen it many times before as a uniformed cop and as a detective. Once the body was found, a well-practised protocol was let loose. Officers cordoned off the area with plastic sheeting so there was a gazebo-style tunnel for them to walk through to the area where they would be carefully digging and sifting the earth until they uncovered the entire body. I shivered in the cold, gazing around the deserted industrial estate, rows of empty units, a depressing landscape, an anonymous row of buildings that looked like any other at the edge of any town or city. Yet this was a chamber of horrors, where a murderous terror show had gone on – maybe even on a daily basis – and nobody knew. How could nobody know? How could this be hidden in plain sight? I thought of Tracy, who she'd been, where she came from, and how at some stage before this day was out, the police would be knocking on the door of whatever family she had, to break the news that their daughter was dead and had been murdered. I wondered who they were and would they feel the guilt that they could have done better by her, or were they hopeless addicts who had long since given up the girl they'd brought into the world? So many children were born and unwanted, abandoned to the system, which almost always failed them. What were Tracy's thoughts when she realised what was happening? Did she scream for her mummy, had she begged for mercy, bewildered and confused as to why this was happening to her? What a way for anyone's life to come to an end. I saw Wilson emerge from the tunnel and come towards me.

'Christ, Billie! The bastards cut her throat.' He shook his head. 'She's just a fucking wee lassie.'

I'd never seen him look as shaken as this.

'God almighty!' was all I could say.

He took a packet of cigarettes out of his pocket and offered me one. I declined, even though I would have loved a long drag on a cigarette at that moment and the light-headedness that a first fag in months would have given me.

'What's the thinking?' I asked. 'I mean, does Marion think she's been there long?'

He drew the smoke deep into his lungs, held it, then finally let it out through his nostrils.

'First impression is not long. Less than a few weeks is the

best guess. There's work to do.' He took another long drag then said, 'But vermin have already been at her. Fucking hell! What kind of people would murder a kid like that?'

'Monsters,' I said. 'They'll pay though, Harry.'

'You bet they will.'

We stood for a while not saying anything, just listening to the crackling noise of the police radios, and watching the shadowy activity behind the plastic cordon. Part of me, the part that had gone rogue since I began looking for Jackie's kid, wanted Wilson to hand over the monsters to Paddy Harper, because then they would get the justice they deserved. But I knew that could never happen. They would go to court. They would use their own dirty money to get themselves top briefs, and who knows, they might even get off, walk away. That's the system, all right, but it's not justice. I'd seen it too often. Eventually, Wilson turned to me.

'Do you think Jackie would be up to identifying her?' he asked. 'Obviously not as the official identification as we'll get the family for that when we can track them down. But just so we can be sure before we go to them?'

'I don't know,' I said. 'She only saw her a couple of times, and if she's been there a few weeks, then she might not be recognisable as the girl she was. But if you want, I can ask her.'

'It would only be a look. Just her face. That's all we would show.'

I was surprised that Jackie agreed to the request, but she

seemed eager to help the police as much as she could. She said she regretted not going to them before, but her only priority at the time had been to get her baby back, and it somehow hadn't occurred to her that they would murder the girl as they had done the Vietnamese man.

I walked down the tunnel with her and Wilson, and when we got to the area Forensics were working on, they looked up, and silently stepped back. There was a cloth over the girl's face and we couldn't see any of her body as it was covered by a plastic sheet. The pathologist looked at Wilson, then at me, then at Jackie. Then she beckoned Jackie a little closer. She gestured to her assistant who stepped forward and slipped off the face covering so that all that could be seen was Tracy's face from her chin up. I stood looking at her, the face of this thin bluish dead child. Because that's all she was, a child, even if she'd been working the drag. A poor, murdered little girl, who had seen so little of the world. I saw Jackie look at the pathologist, and heard her sniffing.

'That's her. As I remember her. She was beautiful.'

Wilson touched her arm, and she turned around, and then the three of us walked back down the tunnel in silence.

Wilson arranged for a uniformed officer to take Jackie and me to the flat, while he stayed on at the murder scene along with Steve. When we arrived, I went into the kitchen to put the kettle on as Jackie put the baby on the floor to play with some toys. We'd barely spoken during the journey, and Jackie had sat staring out of the side window, the same haunted look in her eyes I'd seen the day I met her. There was nothing to say, really, to make any of these moments better, and I'd learned that a long time ago as a young police officer on my first murder scene and death knock. You would never get the image out of your head, and there was nothing you could do about it. I'd told Jackie that when we first got into the car, but I knew deep down she was feeling guilty. Most of us are haunted by something, and most of the time it's because we feel we could have done more. For me, the guilt was there long before anything happened to Lucas. It was a teenage memory from growing up in Sweden, and one reckless, drunken evening with the gang of friends that ended in tragedy. It was long buried in the annals of my mind, and I'd be lying if I said I felt guilt on a daily basis. I just didn't go there any more, hadn't for a very long time, because I was always haunted by the 'what if' of that night. I toyed with the idea of bringing it up to help soothe Jackie, but I couldn't in all honesty take myself back there right now, not with where I was with Lucas, and how I walked a very thin line every day between barely coping and falling off the edge.

We drank tea and sat for a while with Jackie asking about what I thought would be the next move for the police. I told her that Wilson had said they would be in touch with her today and look at either moving her from the flat or keeping her there for a few more days until they were able to interview the suspects they had rounded up. They told her there would be a police presence outside the house and they would install a panic button. As far as I could see, it was over for the murdering thugs who had butchered the Vietnamese man and killed the missing girl – and who knew how many more victims. Wilson said they were going to dig all around the grassy area in case there were more bodies. The problem with illegal immigrants and trafficked people is that you can't keep track of them. While some get jobs in restaurants or construction or anywhere on the black market, others simply disappear. The refugee council really has no idea how many illegal immigrants there are in the country at any given time.

Eventually, I looked at my watch and told her I had to get back to my office. I didn't have to really, but I needed to get out and take a breath from the misery of this morning and take some time out to rest and get over the attack on me last night. I called a taxi to take me back down to the city centre.

Millie wasn't in the office when I arrived, and I guessed she must have popped out for a sandwich, so I hung my coat up and sat on my desk. It was a funny, weird feeling, that way when life goes on, the daily grind, when you've just spent your morning watching police sniffer dogs uncover the body of a teenager. I let out a long sigh. I had to shake myself out of this. I got up and switched on the coffee machine and stood watching it for a minute as it bubbled and gurgled then dripped coffee into a mug. When the door opened, Millie came through, carrying a paper bag from the bakery.

'Oh, you're here,' she said automatically, without looking at me. Then when I turned to her she stopped in her tracks. 'Jesus, Mary and Joseph! What the hell happened, Billie?'

It had slipped my mind that my face was a mess, and I should have phoned to warn her.

'I got attacked last night. In my car. Windscreen battered in. Glass everywhere.'

'Christ. Did you go to hospital?'

'No,' I said. 'It's okay. Looks worse than it is. Sore though.'

She placed her sandwich bag on the desk.

'Sit down. Let me have a closer look.'

'I'm fine. Honest.'

'Sit down, Billie. I want to examine it.'

I did as I was told and she took her coat off and came across, hovering over me, bending to scrutinise the dozens of tiny cuts in my face.

'Christ. It's like a pizza.'

'Thanks.' I tried to smile through my tight, swollen lip. 'Don't make me laugh. It hurts.'

She examined the cut on my eye and the swelling from the punch and my lip.

'So what happened?'

I told her about the call from Johnny, and how I got Paddy Harper's men to help, but how the guys attacked me just before they came. I told her that they were history now and she didn't ask for any details but rolled her eyes to the ceiling.

'This is beyond playing with fire, Billie. It has to stop. Really. It has.'

She crossed the room and fixed me some coffee then placed it on my desk.

'I think it's over now,' I said, the image of Tracy flashing up in my mind.

I told her where I'd been and described how Jackie led the police to the basement near Clydebank where they made the snuff films, and how the sniffer dogs uncovered the girl. She listened, shaking her head, perplexed.

'My God, that poor girl. It's unthinkable. Her parents.'

'Don't know what the sketch is with that as she was in care. No doubt I'll hear about it. But it's been a tough morning.'

Millie fixed herself a coffee and sat at her desk, but didn't open the bag with her lunch.

'You should maybe go home, Billie. Have a day of complete rest, you know, a long bath and just relax.'

I thought about it. She was right, but I didn't want to be alone today in that big empty flat with all the demons chasing me in every room. My mobile rang and I recognised the number as an extension inside police HQ.

'Hello,' the male voice said. 'I'm trying to find Billie Carlson?'

'You found her,' I replied.

'Billie, this is Detective Inspector James Walsh. Do you know an individual called John Reilly?'

My heart sank. I knew what the next line would be because I know how these things work. I cursed myself because I didn't even know Johnny's second name, but I didn't know any other John that would cause a police inspector to be calling me on my mobile.

'Yes. Well, I don't know his second name. But I do know a boy called Johnny. An addict.'

'Yes.' He paused two beats. 'We found your number on his mobile, Billie.'

'Where is he? Is he in trouble?' I asked, coldness flooding through me.

'John is . . . I'm afraid he's dead.' The officer let it hang there for a long moment and I saw the pictures in my head of what the scene would be. 'His body was found on the walkway this morning. He's been murdered. We found that the last number he phoned was your mobile. Last night.'

I took too long to answer, as I was thinking of his face in the shadows last night, how pale and terrified he'd looked, how he had been forced into luring me to what these bastards had hoped would be my death. I knew how awful he must have been feeling at that moment when our eyes met, when he knew he had done this to me, betrayed me. They probably told him if he enticed me there, that they would let him live, and his instinct, despite the nick he was in from drugs, was to survive. Poor bastard. They were never ever going to let him live.

'Billie?'

'Yeah. I'm here.'

'We would like to speak to you as soon as possible. Can we come and see you? Or can you come to Pitt Street?'

I took a breath. This could be tricky and I needed to know I wasn't going to be banged up before the day was out.

'I'll come to the office,' I said. 'If you give me an hour, if that's okay.'

'Okay. If you come to the main entrance and ask for me.'

'I will,' I said politely, and hung up.

I keyed in Wilson's mobile and he answered immediately.

'Harry. You still at the murder scene?'

'Aye. Will be another half hour or so, I think. They're just about ready to get the kid into the wagon. What's the problem?'

'I need your help.' Saying it kind of stuck in my throat, but right now I had no option.

CHAPTER THIRTY-TWO

I was leaving the office to head to the police headquarters when Scanlon called me. He said he was just coming off shift but the place was buzzing with the news that they'd discovered the body of the missing girl.

'You know what it's like, Billie. A kid in the system, murdered like this. There will be all sorts of shit flying for the social work department. They're all in a meeting just now, as they'll have to release the news before the night's out.'

I listened to him and pictured the buzz of activity as police and social services worked out how and when to break this news, and also to make sure they had answers, because in a case like this, the media would be looking to blame somebody. This time, it probably wouldn't be the police. And social workers, faced with media outrage, would be wringing their hands, their only defence being that they are damned if they do and damned if they don't.

'You there, Billie?'

'Yeah. I'm here.'

'I heard you were with Jackie and the troops when they found the body.'

'Yeah,' I said. 'It was grim.' I took a breath. 'You know they murdered Johnny? The heroin addict who helped me?'

'Yeah. I heard. Jesus. Poor bastard. Listen. You free for a quick coffee?'

'Sure.'

He knew me well enough to know that I'd be feeling guilt over Johnny and for not going to the police earlier, even though it was clear from forensics that the girl had been lying in that shallow grave for weeks. I couldn't have helped her even if I tried. But Johnny? He was a different matter.

'By the way,' I said, 'I got a bit of a beating last night, so I'm not as attractive as I usually am.'

'Christ,' he said. 'I'll brace myself.'

I sat down on the faux leather sofa at the far end of the busy Starbucks in Buchanan Street precinct, aware that Scanlon was gaping at me in shock.

'Christ almighty, Billie!' he said. 'Did you go through the windscreen?'

I self-consciously fingered my face.

'More of a case of the windscreen came through to me.'

'Shit! Last night?' he said. 'That shooting down behind the Sheriff Court.'

I knew it wasn't a question. He pushed a flat white across to me. I grimaced as much as my swollen lip would let me.

'Afraid so,' I said. 'They killed Johnny. Not in front of me. But they would have killed me too if help hadn't arrived.'

'Help?' he said, the look on his face knowing that it wasn't the cops. 'Jesus. Close to the wind, Carlson. Too close.' He sucked his breath in through gritted teeth.

'I know. But hopefully it's coming to an end.'

'Did you know they fished two bodies out of the river this morning? They'd been shot.'

'It must have been them,' I said. 'The guys who did Johnny. Good enough for them.' I shook my head. 'They must have just shot him right there and then. Poor guy. You know, Scanlon, there was a decency about him, even though his life was a total mess.'

He leaned across the table for a closer look at my face.

'Did you see a doctor with this?'

'No. I think it's okay. It's just a lot of little splintery cuts. And my teeth went through flesh on the inside of my top lip a little.'

We sat for a long moment not speaking and I could see him watching me as I lifted my coffee to my lips and tried to sip it from the side of the cup.

'You should have called me last night, Billie. When you got home. I'd have come to see you, made sure you were all right.' He glanced over his shoulder and lowered his voice. 'I don't care who got you out of it. I'd have been there for you.'

I looked at him and sighed.

'I know, Scanlon, and you know I love you for that. But in the middle of the shit last night, the last thing I wanted to do was drag you into it. Imagine how that would look if anyone had found out.'

'I know. But I'd have come around to your flat. I wish you hadn't been alone after all that crap.'

I shrugged. 'I'm getting used to shit happening.' I looked at my watch. 'Okay. I'd better go up there and face the music. I called Wilson after I got the phone call from the DI asking to talk to me. I didn't want to go up to Pitt Street and be grilled by some smartass who might think about locking me up. So I'm hoping Wilson will be there.'

Scanlon grinned and I was glad to see it.

'Must have choked you having to phone Wilson for help.'

I chuckled. 'It did. But what the hell. I'm helping him more right now than he probably deserves. He owes me.'

I stood up, and Scanlon got to his feet too and we walked towards the door.

'Listen,' he said, 'once this all dies down, let's go for a bite to eat. It's been frantic lately.'

'I know. Sure. We'll do it soon.' I turned and left, knowing that he was standing watching me as I walked briskly up the precinct and disappeared into the crowd of afternoon shoppers.

*

I'd only ever been in the Pitt Street headquarters a handful of times since I'd left the force. I purposely stayed away from it, not that I'd have been particularly welcomed by some of the people in there anyway. I did still have some serious allies at lots of levels in the force, but most of them were out in divisions of the CID across the city. Walking down St Vincent Street towards the huge building, the watery sun reflected on the mirrored windows of the six-storey-high building that was one of the iconic landmarks of the city. The reflective glass was like the kind you see inside an interview room where cops can look in on the suspects being interviewed but they don't know who's watching them. This was the same. The building was the hub, the nerve centre of crime fighting in the city, and so much went on in there, from administration for the whole force to serious crime, drugs squads, and on the top level was where the top brass lived, the uniformed bosses with enough scrambled egg on their hats and pips on their lapels to mark them out for special respect. A very small part of me tugged for the days when I'd been in here learning the ropes as a rookie cop. But it wasn't enough of a tug to make me ever want to go back . . . not that I'd ever be invited. But the famous building was headed for demolition to make way for flats, and staff would soon be moving across to the new HQ in the city's East End.

Inside the reception area, I told the woman behind the desk that I had arranged to speak to DCI James Walsh. She gave me a look that told me she'd formed an opinion of me from my face – I could be a battered wife or maybe even a hooker who'd had a hard night. She told me to take a seat, but I stayed standing, looking at the photos on the walls, the Chief Constables down the years, the city fathers – all that spin that made you think that Glasgow was protected, safe and thriving. I suppose it was, but not for everyone, not for people like Johnny. It was only a couple of minutes later that the lift doors opened and a female officer in a blue trouser suit emerged with a friendly smile. I felt as though I knew the face but couldn't quite place it.

'Billie,' she said. 'I'll take you upstairs.'

I followed her into the lift and she hit the button for the seventh floor. We stood in awkward silence, then she spoke to me.

'You don't remember me, Billie, do you?'

I scanned her face, her black hair scraped back into a short ponytail. She would be older than me, I guessed, by a few years.

'I'm not sure, to be honest.'

'I was at your house a couple of times. When ...' She hesitated. 'Your son ... there was a lot going on.'

I was a little startled even by the mentioning of it, but didn't judge her for it. I couldn't place her face – everything in those early days was such a blur.

'Yeah,' I said. 'Sorry. It was all overwhelming for me at

the time.' I looked at my feet. I didn't want to have this conversation. 'Still is.'

'I'm sure,' she said softly.

I probably should have been touched by her concern, and I wondered if she even knew if there had been any progress on my missing Lucas, or if the case file had just been stuffed in a drawer somewhere because technically it was out of their jurisdiction. I wondered if she felt the police had failed me in the beginning. We stayed silent until the lift pinged and the doors opened onto a long corridor of cream-coloured walls on the seventh floor where the big shots lived. I walked beside her past open office doors, and in fleeting glances I could see officers at computers or some sitting back in their work stations or on the phones. We got to a closed door and she knocked it gently and stuck her head round. She opened it wide and I walked in. Wilson was on a padded chair below the window, and DCI Walsh got up from behind his desk. We looked at each other and I recognised him.

'Billie,' he said, stretching out a hand. 'It's been a long time.'

'Yeah,' I said, glancing at Wilson who was looking back, his face impassive. 'It has.'

He'd been a sergeant in the CID based out at London Road when I was a cop and our paths had crossed a few times in cases. Most I didn't remember, but one I did, and that was Paddy Harper's son's case. He was one of the officers who hadn't been happy that I'd told the truth in the witness box that day, and he'd told me so. But he'd defended me when his inspector told me to my face that day that I would never make it, that my card was marked among the troops. The DCI had done well, by the looks of things, so his card had clearly not been tainted, unlike mine.

'You remember me, Billie?'

He had an open face and from the first few moments I somehow didn't get the feeling that he was going to heavy-duty grill me. I hoped not, anyway.

'Of course,' I said, glancing at Wilson who rolled his eyes a little as though he was hoping we weren't going to have a little reminiscing over the good old days.

Walsh motioned me to sit down.

'You want tea? Coffee?'

'Yeah, okay,' I said. 'I'll have tea.'

He was either trying to soft soap me, or he was just a genuinely decent cop. He got up and went to the door, put his head round, and asked for some tea for the three of us. Then he sat back down.

He leaned forward, tugging his grey suit trousers a little at the thighs in that way some men did when they sat down. I could see his black socks and shiny black leather shoes gleaming in the ceiling light. Wilson looked unkempt next to him in his crumpled navy trousers, with his shirt collar open and his tie askew, a day-old stubble on his chin and cheeks.

The DCI spread his hands. 'So, Billie.' He raised his eyebrows. 'You want to tell me what's going on?' He flicked a glance at Wilson. 'Harry's filled me in a bit on this morning, and on recent events. And we're very grateful for your help, as I'm sure you know.'

I didn't answer but met his eyes briefly then looked away.

'We fished a couple of guys out of the river today,' he said, matter-of-factly. 'Looks like they're the ones who might have killed the drug addict ... this John fella.' He paused, looked at me. 'You knew him?'

I nodded. 'I did. Met him recently during my investigation into Jackie Foster's kidnapped baby. He helped me. He helped me a lot. In fact, if it wasn't for him, she wouldn't have her baby right now.'

'Harry told me about this guy's role. And I do understand that you wanted to keep things tight for the sake of the child.' He took a breath and pushed out a sigh. 'But, Billie, you should have come to us long before it got to this. There are bodies all over the shop.' He paused again, glanced at Wilson. 'And a missing officer. PC Hewitt.'

I didn't reply because I wasn't sure just how much he knew, and I didn't want to open any new lines of enquiry here. But I knew he was waiting for an answer so after a while I spoke.

'So, what do you really want with me? I don't know who the guys were you fished out of the water. But they had it coming to them.' I looked him in the eye. 'You know that as well as I do.'

'Aye, well, probably not many people would disagree with you there. But we live with rules in our society. We're not some Wild West town where people can routinely go shooting the place up, even though on some weekends it looks like that.' He gave me a righteous look, waiting for me to react. I didn't. 'You're here because we need to know who did this.'

'What?' I asked, feeling a little irked. 'Who did what?' I pointed to my face and my lip. 'Who did this to me? Who murdered poor Johnny? Who slit the throat of the little girl? Who stole Jackie Foster's baby?' I paused, knowing it was having an effect. Wilson rolled his eyes to the ceiling. 'You tell me.'

The DCI sat back, folded his arms, glanced at Wilson and sighed. I wasn't sure how much he had known of the bigger picture, but I was pretty certain he would know most of it by now.

'You should have come to us in the very beginning.'

I took a breath because I could feel anger rising in my chest and felt my cheeks burn.

'I did come here, Detective Chief Inspector. A long time ago. You know that.'

He glanced again at Wilson.

'I know. And I'm sorry if you feel we fai—' He couldn't say the words 'failed you', but I knew that's what he wanted to say.

'Failed me?'

He shook his head. 'Look, Billie. Let's not go down that road. You know there are a lot of people in here and across the force who are shattered by what happened to you, and that was long before your son disappeared. I mean, from the shooting. There are a lot of people here who live with regrets. But we have a job to do. We have to get on with it. If we just let people run wild all over the place how would that be for anyone?'

I said nothing and we sat in a long, heavy silence. Then Wilson spoke.

'To be fair,' he said, 'as I was saying to the DCI, there is a much bigger picture here. Because of Billie a little kid-napped girl is back home with her mother now. And because of Billie we know the place where this kid Tracy Logan lay murdered. We have a huge case here and we have people in custody – a Turkish gangster who is a big player in smuggling, along with a couple of his sidekicks. And we have two members of a notorious Glasgow gang. They're not getting away with this. We'll get convictions. And that's down to Billie.' He paused, glancing at the DCI. 'But I've tried to explain to her, that you cannot enlist the help of gangsters.'

'Who said I did?'

'The word on the street is that a well-known Glasgow mob is responsible for the latest spree of killings.'

I spread my hands. 'I can't help you with that.'

'We have bodies piling up in recent weeks, and DCI Wilson tells me the common denominator is that you were at nearly every crime scene.'

I glared at Wilson with my thanks-for-that-mate face. I didn't answer. Anything I said would have been sarcastic and right now I knew that wouldn't go down well.

'Is Paddy Harper involved in any of this?'

I shrugged. 'I've no idea.'

We sat for an age. I picked up my tea and drank a good gulp, waiting for the next line I knew was coming.

'You know you'll be in trouble if we find you are withholding any information about a crime.'

I didn't answer, but looked at Wilson, who said nothing.

'Billie. You can just give us a name. Or just tell us whether you got help from people? How did you get your face like that from the other night?'

'Accident. My car.'

'Where's your car?'

'In some garage somewhere. Can't remember. It's been a difficult few days.'

He sighed. He knew he was getting nowhere, and I wondered if he was just going through the motions, and whether Wilson had told him this was the kind of reception he would get from me. Maybe I was fortunate that it was him rather than another DCI, who might have locked me up by now.

'Hewitt,' he eventually said. 'Do you have any idea where he is? You know who he is, don't you?'

I nodded but said nothing. I looked down at the back of my hands for a moment, knowing where this was going.

'He's been missing for days now. We need to find him.'

I turned to him. 'I take it Wilson has told you what he's been involved in and that there's proof.'

He blinked an acknowledgement.

'That's for the investigation, Billie. Due process. You know that. We need to find him. If there is proof then there will be due process and he will face court. But right now we have a missing cop who is the son of a chief superintendent.'

We sat for a moment. I was angry that his main priority was to find Hewitt. That was the only reason I was here. They didn't give a damn about the stiffs they fished out of the water, or the junkie found with a hole in the back of his head, or even a kidnapped baby and a sad, tragic teenager lying in the mortuary with her throat cut. All they cared about at the end of the day was the son of a missing high-ranking cop. I put my cup down.

'Are we done here, Detective Chief Inspector?' I looked at my watch. 'I have some place to be.'

His open friendly face was gone, but he wasn't angry, he was controlled. He was never going to win this round, or any battle, and somewhere behind his expression he knew I was right. But the police were about protecting themselves. That's why I was hauled over the coals when I shot that pervert. It was never about the truth, it was about how you managed it. I knew that no matter what happened, they would make sure the evidence against Hewitt somehow disappeared. He would at best be kicked off the force but he wouldn't be in jail where he deserved to be. He knew it and I knew it. I stood up.

'I'm sorry, Detective Chief Inspector. It's been good to see you. But I can't help you.'

I wondered if he would even bother with the threat that I could be locked up, because he could see that it wouldn't even make me flinch. He didn't. He glanced at Wilson, who made a defeated face.

'I'll see myself out,' I said, as I turned towards the door feeling their eyes burning my back with every step.

CHAPTER THIRTY-THREE

Outside the church, the giant white sculpted image of the crucifixion dwarfed the very basic red-brick building. Jesus was outstretched on the cross and the women of sorrow had their hands raised in agony. It was a stark image, a reminder from the Catholic Church that bigger sacrifices than the ones any of us might have thought we were making were nothing compared to this. It was all about guilt, and the Catholic Church were masters of it. St Paul the Apostle chapel was deep in the East End of Glasgow – in Shettleston, a deprived, rundown area a couple of miles outside the city, where life expectancy was the lowest in the whole of the UK. If you made it past sixty-three, the data said, you were doing well. I worked in the police station there as a rookie uniformed cop when I finished training, and although it had been a baptism of fire with drug deaths on an almost daily basis, I grew to love the place and the warmth, resilience and humour of the people. Sometimes

I used to come back to some of the old cafés on Shettleston Road just to sit there and wonder where all the time had gone.

Scanlon had managed to get me the details of Johnny's funeral arrangements, and I felt I had to go and pay my respects. I didn't know Johnny's family situation, only that he had a mother, because he'd told me that he was planning to get clean so he could go and see her again. He'd never got the chance. Scanlon had said that it was his sister who did the formal identification of his body at the morgue, so I figured his mother hadn't been able to face it.

The church smelled of candles and incense and took me back to childhood days when my Irish mother had taken me to Sunday mass. My father had no religion at all, and I used to sit there bored, watching all the people, and half listening to the priest preaching about how to live a better life with God. I believed it then, and the truth is sometimes I still believe it. But if you were to question me closely on the subject I would say I go to church and pray because sometimes in my heart I have nowhere else to go.

I slipped into a seat near the back of the church and shivered. It was so cold I could see my breath. There was nobody there apart from a couple of passkeepers and two old ladies who were probably regulars at the ten o'clock morning mass. The coffin was at the front, light oak with gilt handles. I was a few minutes early, so I went forward to the front of the chapel and lit a candle below the statue of the Sacred Heart. Old habits die hard. Then I went past and paused for a few seconds at the coffin. I could see the brass plate with 'John Francis Reilly' and his date of birth below. Christ. He was only twenty-three. There was a colour picture in a white frame on top. It was of Johnny as a little boy, hands joined with rosary beads draped over his fingers on his first communion. There was another photo of him in a football strip aged around thirteen, I guessed, with his mother, proudly clutching a trophy in his hands. I swallowed hard and turned away, then sat at the back again. I checked my watch. Then, there was a blast of cold air, the sound of heavy doors opening, and I could hear the shuffle of people arriving. As they filed past where I sat, I saw a young girl with a mop of black curly hair, dressed in a warm navy coat, her arm linked in support of a tiny woman who I presumed was Johnny's mother. The older woman had papery skin and she was dabbing at her red eyes with a handkerchief. Behind them were a couple of women around the same age as his mother, and three young men in their twenties who were in denim bomber jackets or fleeces. Funeral attire would not be on their agenda at this age. And that was it. Desolate. Empty. I don't know whether the tears in my eyes were for Johnny who died so young, or just the sheer lack of people who were there to see him off. In years of drug abuse you lose everyone around you, and eventually it's just you and your family, if they are still there somewhere waiting for you.

The priest was at the front of the altar and greeted them with handshakes. An older man did the altar server duties. I listened as the mass got started. Halfway through, the priest spoke of Johnny, a promising young footballer who had lost his way. He said his love for his mother and sister had been the cornerstone of his life. He said that people in this area, and across the city, had problems but they were all children of God and today Johnny would be welcomed into the kingdom where he would at last have peace. I kept seeing images of Johnny that day when he tried to monster me at my office corridor, then of him in the café that night and how hungry he'd been. I remembered his phone calls and the help he gave me – the help that brought about his death. I wanted to go forward and say to them that I knew him and that he was kind, and that he'd been trying to get clean. But I knew I couldn't go anywhere near them because only I knew why he was dead, and I felt responsible for that. My GP friend had told me he'd look at trying to place Johnny at a rehab centre, but it was all too late now. Again with the guilt. Once a Catholic . . . I watched at the end as the undertakers instructed four boys to carry his coffin. The funeral directors had to help. Not even enough friends to bear Johnny on their shoulders. How sad is that. Outside, the mother came out supported by her daughter and climbed into the car. I wondered how long it had been since she'd seen her son; she probably knew that one night the knock on her door would come and it'd be her turn to mourn, to suffer, to ask God why this had to happen. I watched as the car whispered past me, and as it did, the woman looked at me and our eyes met. I looked away because somewhere inside I was ashamed that I hadn't done more, even though I don't know what I could have done. I should have told him to stay away and not to get in touch. But saving little Elena was all I could think of, and Johnny was the only possible inside track I had. I'd used him, and I hated myself for it.

I saw Scanlon's name on my mobile screen as I drove back to the office. The ringtone blared through the speakers, and I was in two minds about whether I should answer it. I was in that place where you need silence and solitude, even though I knew that continuing to beat myself up was hurting nobody but me. By the fifth ring I answered.

'How you doing?' Scanlon said. 'Did you go to the funeral?'

'I did. Was grim enough. Only a handful of people. Not even enough to carry the coffin. I'm just driving back to the office.'

I could hear Scanlon's breathing and knew he'd be trying to pick the right words to say. Eventually, he spoke.

'Listen, how about we go out and have a bowl of pasta or something tonight. A glass of wine. It'll do you good.'

'With this face? People will think you've been beating me.'

'I know,' Scanlon said. 'I'll get some funny looks, but

what the hell. It'll be good for you to go out for a couple of hours and unwind. It's been a helluva few days.'

I didn't answer while I considered the idea. I had spent plenty of nights eating and drinking with Scanlon, and not all of them for him to hold my hand and support me through the bad times. Sometimes we just hung out together, had a laugh, talked about the gym, work, what we were binge-watching on TV. And sometimes we went out because he was passing me information to help me on a case. No matter what we did, I always came home feeling better, more relaxed, and not so alone.

'What the hell, Scanlon,' I said. 'You're right. It would be good to go out and break bread with my favourite cop. But I'm going to have to do some heavy duty repair work on my face before I'm seen in a restaurant.'

'You'll look just fine. What time?'

'About half six maybe? Early. I can't handle a late night, I'm shattered,' I said, but then cursed myself for sounding boring.

'Okay. Why don't I meet you at your flat, and we'll walk down to that Italian place off George Square.'

'Perfect,' I said. 'See you then.' I hung up, feeling buoyed that I wasn't going to be alone in my flat all evening.

Back in the office, Millie had put some papers on my desk with the most recent possible cases I might want to handle. She made me some coffee while I flicked through them, glad that most of them looked straightforward, involving no more than a couple of days' work and some photographs. Standard stuff that could be done, dusted and paid for in no more than three days. Sleazy as it was, it would be some light relief from getting my face panned in against my car.

'So how was that poor boy's funeral?' Millie asked from behind her computer as she sipped her coffee.

'Grim,' I said. 'Cold and empty. I felt so bad for his old mum, heartbroken like that.'

'Well,' Millie said. 'I'm sure her heart's been sore for a very long time.'

'Yep. For sure.'

'How's your face?' she asked. 'And your ribs. Still in pain?'

'Yeah. Feels a bit easier today though.'

'Get a hot bath and an early night. That's what you need.'

I glanced at her. 'Actually, I'm going out with Scanlon tonight for some pasta. He just phoned me.'

She raised her eyebrows in that knowing way.

'You know,' she said, 'you and that man should get together. Solid, he is. And handsome too.'

I smiled, indulging her attempts at cupid.

'We're just good friends. That's all. He makes me laugh.'

She pursed her lips. 'Well. All I'm saying is that a man like that who cares about you and understands you is worth his weight in gold . . . Some of the losers that are out there . . .'

I knew she was having a dig at Steve, my on-off, but

mostly off, relationship – if you could even call it that. No. You couldn't call it a relationship. She'd never met him, but she disliked him anyway. And she was probably right.

'Yep,' I said. 'I haven't got a great track record in the men stakes, but Scanlon is off limits. Too much of a good friendship to lose.'

'Hmmm,' she said, undeterred. 'Well. You know what's best for you, I suppose.'

I drank my coffee and smiled at her, and just at that moment an email pinged on my computer. I took my feet off the desk quickly and put my mug down when I saw Dan Harris's name. I opened it and read it, once quickly, then again slowly, scarcely breathing.

Morning Billie. I have a quick update. That line of enquiry in Cleveland is looking good. I've tracked down the guy who saw Bob recently, so he's going to meet me later and take me to the place where he last saw him. It's a trailer park. He might not be there any more, but it's a good start. Will keep you posted. Keep the faith. Dan.

Cleveland, I thought. A trailer park. I should really be there. What if he actually found Bob? What if Dan found him and could actually be standing right next to him and Lucas, telling Bob who he was and why he was there? What if . . . I should be there. But I knew it wasn't the thing to do. Dan would tell me when it was wise to come. But my gut was in knots with the possibility that this might be a promising lead.

I sifted through the documents Millie had left and made a few notes on them. I told her I would get back to all of these people in the next couple of days and tell them I'd take their cases. Then I told her I was going home early to fix my face up so I could be seen in a restaurant. She gave me a wry smile as I left, and I knew she was thinking that I was making the effort for Scanlon, even if I wouldn't admit it to her, or to myself. Millie was no fool.

CHAPTER THIRTY-FOUR

I watched from my living room window as the rush hour traffic thinned out and the darkness crept into every corner of the square. The rain had turned to sleet and it fell onto my windows in short-lived icy blobs that quickly melted. I'd taken a call from Wilson while I was getting dressed, and he'd told me they were planning to move Jackie and her kid tomorrow to more permanent accommodation – a house, he said, with a garden, away from here, where they could be looked after and totally secure. They'd rounded up half a dozen so far of the snuff film and trafficking gang, and Forensics were still digging around the area behind the basement in case there were more bodies. He said they were looking at murder charges and conspiracy to murder as well as a raft of other serious charges. The gang wouldn't see daylight, he told me, for a very long time, if at all. I listened to him, shocked that they might find more bodies. I'd rather the gang went up against a firing squad led by Paddy

Harper's men than just be sent to jail. I wouldn't say that out loud any time soon though. Wilson said they were going to tell Jackie early in the morning – they didn't give people notice and time to think about moving – and someone would help her get her things organised. But he said if I wanted to go up and say goodbye to her then that was fine by him. It was out of my hands, was what he was saying. Stand back, and let the grown-ups take over from here. I wasn't bothered by that, but there was a twinge of something like dejection that Jackie and her whole world of chaos and problems would be out of my life by lunchtime tomorrow. Sure, it was for the best, but I would miss her. I'd thrown myself wholeheartedly into the hunt for her baby and the rescue, and somehow my life would feel a little emptier when they were gone. I don't know why I felt like that because I didn't even know her that well. It wasn't as though we'd formed a deep friendship, and I had told her very little of my own loss and heartache. But perhaps the happy ending of her story only helped to underline the failure of mine, of my succession of blind alleys. I don't know if that's what it was, but I knew that by this time tomorrow I'd be missing them.

I was glad to see the tall figure of Scanlon emerge from the rise of the hill onto the square and walk briskly towards my house. I watched him for a moment, in his faded jeans, boots, a leather jacket, and a rust-coloured scarf bulked up at his neck. He waved when he saw me at the window and

I smiled at him. I went into the hall and pressed the entry button and opened the door to my flat.

'Hey,' he called, appearing at the open door. 'Will I come in or are you ready?'

'Come in. I'll be two minutes.'

I had one last check of my face in the bedroom mirror as I pulled on my leather jacket. I was wearing tight jeans and a black V-neck sweater. I looked fine, but there were still angry shards of redness across my cheeks and forehead. And although the swelling on my lip had gone down a little, it was still noticeable and lipstick would not have improved it. I'd finally decided there wasn't much point in covering my injuries with make-up as I might pay for that with infection by tomorrow, so this was as good as it was going to get.

'Here I am,' I called as I came out of my bedroom down the hall, my ankle boots clicking on the polished oak floor. 'Carlson in the raw.' I touched my face. 'I can't believe I'm going out for the evening like this.'

Scanlon was standing with his back to the window, the street lamplight throwing a shadow onto one side of his lean face as he smiled.

'Nonsense.' He stepped towards me. 'You look great.' He leaned in, his lips brushed my cheek and I caught the whiff of wax from his hair and his aftershave. 'I feel as though we haven't been out on the town for ages.'

'I know,' I said. 'Been a while.' I gave him a stern look.

'But we're not actually going out on the town, remember. Don't be dragging me around your late-night haunts like the last time.'

We both smiled, remembering how we'd ended up smashed after going out for tapas, when I was the woman I used to be. Nights like that had been few and far between over the last eighteen months. For the first six months I had barely been able to leave the flat. But in time, I rationed myself to the occasional night out with food, as everything these days with me was about staying focused, never hungover, always ready to move at the drop of a hat.

'Of course not. My body is a temple these days. I'm in the gym first thing in the morning.'

We headed into the hall and out of the front door.

Inside the restaurant we were ushered to a booth. I was glad as it was more secluded than the open restaurant, which was surprisingly busy this early in the evening.

'Do you think the waiter took one look at my face and shoved us in here so as not to frighten other diners?' I joked.

Scanlon chuckled. 'It's not as bad as you think,' he said. 'In fact, it's quite fetching in the candlelight.'

'Yeah, if it was Hallowe'en.'

We both laughed, relaxed in each other's company. The waiter handed us menus and asked if we wanted a drink. Scanlon looked at me to decide.

'We could manage a bottle of wine maybe?'

I sucked in a breath.

'Don't know about a whole bottle. I wouldn't want to be enjoying myself or anything.'

Scanlon puffed and ordered a bottle of house red.

'We don't have to drink it all.'

'Famous last words. Remember you have the gym first thing.'

He shrugged. 'I'm hardcore.'

I poured us a glass of iced water from the jug on the table and drank a good glug.

'They're taking Jackie and her kid away tomorrow,' I said. 'Wilson phoned me earlier to let me know. Going somewhere away from here so they can be looked after.'

Scanlon nodded, nibbling on a breadstick.

'Not surprised. Word is they've arrested a few of the gang. Big charges are on the way.'

'That's what he told me,' I said. 'Hanging's too good for them.'

We sat for a moment, then when the waiter came we ordered a shared starter to pick through followed by seafood linguine for both of us. When the wine came I only allowed half a glass to be poured for me, and Scanlon poured his own. I wanted to tell him about the call from the private eye, but I didn't want it to overshadow the whole evening's conversation. Scanlon had been patient with me for a long time as I obsessed and worried and offloaded all my shit on him in recent months.

'You've gone quiet,' he said, sipping his wine.

I smiled. 'I was thinking,' I said. Then I couldn't hold it any more. 'I've got some news. From the States.'

His eyebrows went up in anticipation. 'You have?'

'Yes. Well. I'm trying not to get too excited. In fact I'm definitely not getting too excited. But the private investigator phoned and said the contact he's been talking to recently told him Bob was in Ohio – Cleveland. The guy actually saw him with Lucas. And the private eye, Dan, is going down there in the morning.'

He pursed his lips. 'That could be big news, Billie.'

'Yeah,' I said. 'But I've been there before, with a sighting, and it turned out to be nothing.'

He nodded. 'Maybe this will be different.'

'I thought of going there. You know, just jumping on the first plane. But I decided against it. I don't know if I could face another disappointment like the last time.'

'I know,' he said. 'I think you're right. If your man out there is good then he'll get on top of it quickly.'

'Yeah. I just hate having no control of it though. I mean, I've been totally throwing myself into looking for Jackie's missing baby, and it gave me this feeling that I was winning. And when we were able to get Elena back, that was such a moment. But when it comes to my own child, I'm far away and hoping for the best. I don't like it.'

'Sure. I know what you mean. But the only alternative is to up sticks and go there for a couple of months and really try to work with your guy. But it's always so tricky. You know, paying all the money out to a private eye, and waiting and hoping.' He looked me in the eye. 'I feel for you, Carlson. I really do.'

'I know you do,' I said.

His mobile buzzed in his jacket pocket and he took it out. As he read the text message his eyes widened. Then he looked at me.

'Christ!' he said. 'They just found Hewitt.'

'Shit. Really? Where? How?' I was thinking of his body washing up on some beach.

'Wandering around farmland near Busby, apparently.'

'Busby?'

Scanlon was texting back, then a second later his phone pinged another message.

'He was dazed and badly beaten, his hands tied with rope. He's in the Queen Elizabeth.'

'Is he talking?'

No doubt he'd be selling everyone out to save his skin. Scanlon messaged back, then another text came in.

'Not saying much so far. Only that he was kidnapped and dumped there.'

I took a drink of my wine as the waiter put down a starter to share.

'I wish I could be there for the police interview when Wilson and Co. tell him he's nicked.'

Scanlon snorted. 'Yeah. I'll believe that when I see it.'

'Seriously?' I said, surprised. 'You think that too? That they'll just cover up his involvement? Surely to Christ not?'

He shrugged. 'It's entirely possible. If they have enough bodies to stick away, then Hewitt might just get away with it.'

'He bloody shouldn't get away with it. He's as guilty as every last one of them. If this ever got out that one of their own was involved and they'd brushed it under the carpet . . .'

'For sure.'

We sat for a long moment, picking at the food and saying nothing.

'I'm so glad I'm not a cop any more, Scanlon.'

He nodded slowly, and looked at me then into his glass. He would get my drift: if Hewitt got away with it, then as a decent policeman, he shouldn't be able to stomach it. But Scanlon was a cop. He always would be.

The pasta arrived, and I changed the subject because I didn't want to start a conversation on the morality of being a cop. It wouldn't have been the first time I'd bent the rules a little to give some guy a break who'd fallen on the wrong side of the law. And I'd done a lot more than that since becoming a private eye. That's what I liked about the job. You make your own rules, and depending on your morality threshold and what you were faced with, you could lower or raise the bar. That suited me, especially in recent days, with the dodgy people I'd been working with.

'So do you really think this mob that Wilson has rounded up will swing?' I asked.

He shrugged, twisting a forkful of pasta and fish.

'I think so. From what I hear the Turkish connection will quickly fall apart. And the others are part of Jackson's mob, so even if they're not big players, they'll know they're facing huge jail time unless they can cut a deal by talking. Word is they might all fold. Jackson's mob will know where the trafficked people are, and there's a team already working on that.'

'Good. I hope they find the immigrants – alive.'

After we ate, we sat for a while, sipping more of the wine and drinking decaf coffee. Scanlon was telling me amusing stories about a couple of rookies he'd been mentoring lately, and we laughed, remembering our early days when we came out of training together, wet behind the ears. Then, out of the blue, he looked at me, and asked me a straight question.

'Billie. Are you involved with Steve . . .? McCartney? I mean, like, in a relationship?'

The question jolted me and I looked back at him, feeling my cheeks burn. I saw him scanning my face and he raised his eyebrows.

'Oh,' he said. 'Sorry. I shouldn't be . . .'

I tried to make light of it, blowing out my lips, and gave him a curious look.

'I'm just surprised. That's all. You never ask me things like that, Scanlon. And I never ask you.'

I didn't know what else to say. I was a bit stunned, but eager to know why he was asking.

'I know, I know,' he said quickly, as if trying to forget the whole thing. 'It's just that . . . Well, I was in the mess room the other day and somebody made a remark about you, and they said something about you and Steve.'

I could feel a little bit of anger at the idea that I was fodder for mess-room banter – and maybe a bit of shame, too, that I might be being used by Steve – though the bottom line was that the using went both ways.

'Who? What did they say?'

He put a hand up. 'Nothing. I mean, it wasn't insulting or anything. Just that . . . Well . . . He said Steve had been doing a line with you.'

Doing a line, I thought. Is that what it was? Or was it just locker room chat, because I'd heard all of that kind of shit before. Most of it was guys making wildly inaccurate claims that they knew stuff about certain women. There was no reason for me to feel I owed Scanlon an explanation here, but I just did, and the more he fixed me with his stare the more I felt I had to say something.

'Why do you ask? What's it to you?' I didn't say it aggressively, at least, I hoped he wouldn't think so.

He narrowed his eyes a little, drained his glass, and I could see he was a little tipsy. He'd had more of the wine than me, and I still had some in my first glass.

'It's just that . . . Well . . . You know, Billie. I like you a lot.

You know that. And I just don't want you getting hurt or messed around with a dick like Steve.'

We sat in awkward silence for a while, and I felt I had to say something to break the tension.

'It's nothing to worry about,' I said. 'And in any case, I'm not seeing him any more. It was never anything really.' I paused and looked him in the eye. 'I know you care about me, Scanlon. And don't think I ever take it for granted.'

His hand stretched across the table to mine and our fingers touched, and we both looked at them and then at each other. I felt a little stab of electricity between us that I had never paid too much attention before. I grinned to take the heat out of it.

'Come on. You're getting pissed. Let's get the bill and get out of here.'

He smiled and waved the waiter over, and we split the bill, then left the restaurant.

We walked up the street towards the square and although we chatted as though that brief moment in the restaurant hadn't happened, I knew it was on both of our minds. But I swiftly pushed it away. When we got to the steps of my house, I knew Scanlon wouldn't expect me to invite him in, so I turned to him.

'Thanks for making me go out tonight, Scanlon. I really needed it, even though I didn't think I did. It was good fun.'

'Yeah. Me too. We'll do it again soon.'

There was a second where I didn't know how to end the

moment – whether I should turn away and go up the steps to my house, or whether I should say something else. Then, suddenly, Scanlon took a step closer to me and moved in for a hug. He held me tight and his embrace was warm and loving and we stayed that way for a long time. Then he eased away and we stood, our faces close together, our breaths warm, and the moment had passed for a peck on the cheek. He kissed me on the lips. It wasn't long, but it was soft and gentle, and I didn't stop him. Then I drew back.

'Go home, crazy cop,' I said, brushing him away, 'you've got an early gym class.'

He shrugged, and didn't seem at all fazed by the moment.

'True,' he said. 'You sure you're okay? I mean about everything. About the USA and stuff. If you hear anything tomorrow, good or bad, just call me. Immediately. You got that?' He pointed a finger.

'I got it.'

He made a gesture with his two hands like a gunslinger pointing fingers.

'I love you, Carlson, you know that.' He grinned.

I smiled, shook my head. 'I know,' I said. Then I turned away and put my key in the door.

CHAPTER THIRTY-FIVE

There were a couple of cars parked at Jackie's place, and I pulled up across the road from them. I assumed they would be the hand-picked officers who would whisk her away to a new life out of reach of the lowlifes who had brought this nightmare to her. I recognised the female detective in the driving seat of one of the cars, and she lowered the window as I got out of my car and crossed the road.

'Wilson's upstairs. He said for you to go up,' she said, nodding towards the building.

'Cheers,' I said, and went to the entrance.

Inside the flat, there was a female officer keeping Elena amused with a cuddly toy, while Jackie buzzed around packing things into a couple of brand new suitcases. I noticed that most of the clothes still had labels on them and there were enough to keep her and her baby going for a while until they got established. She looked up at me and smiled, but it was more of a nervous stretching of her lips than an actual smile. I could see she was jittery.

'You okay, Jackie?' I asked.

'Yeah,' she said. 'Just nervous. I want this to be over. You know what I mean? I want to feel safe.'

'You will,' I said. 'I promise you.'

Wilson was standing with his back to the window surveying the scene. I looked across at him and he jerked his head towards the kitchen and walked in that direction and I followed him. He stood at the sink and turned to me.

'They've got Hewitt,' he said.

'I know. I heard.'

I decided that there was no way I could muster a convincing look of surprise.

'You heard already?'

'Yeah,' I said. 'Some people still talk to me. I didn't hear much detail though.'

He eyed me a little suspiciously, but he wasn't naive enough to expect nobody to keep in touch with me after I'd left the force. I'd had a lot of close friends back then. Some stayed with me, others patched me.

'So are you going to charge him?' I asked, looking him in the eye.

He gave me a look that said keep out of it, but I knew he'd feel compelled to answer.

'He's in hospital,' he said. 'He was found wandering

around out in some farmland in the Southside – Busby. Badly beaten and dumped. So we're waiting to talk to him.'

'To talk to him?' I raised my eyebrows and my tone of indignation.

'Look, Carlson,' he glared, 'you're not on the force any more, so you can butt out any time you want.'

I let that hang there a moment, because I knew he was actually grateful I'd handed him an open and shut case for the gang he was about to lock up. I wasn't one of his own any more, but on this occasion I was near it.

'Don't take it the wrong way,' he softened. 'There's a lot to get to the bottom of here, and we want to know what Hewitt's involvement was in this whole shit. If we can prove he was part of it then he'll get the book thrown at him.'

'What about his father?'

'What about him?'

I shrugged. 'You don't think that will come into play when decisions are being made?'

'Of course not.' Even as he said it I could tell he didn't believe it.

'Yeah, well. We'll see.' I didn't feel like arguing, and anyway I was out of this now. 'I don't have a dog in this fight any more,' I said. 'So good luck with it.' I looked at my watch. 'What time you leaving? And, not that you'll tell me, but are you going far?'

He took a breath. 'As soon as she's ready we're off. We've got a place for her an hour or so away. Bungalow all set up.

Nobody will know her. Completely new life. And when she gives evidence, it will be in camera, so nothing will come out about her in the papers during the trial. It's up to her to keep her profile low now.'

'Good. I'm sure she will.'

Wilson's mobile rang and he fished it out of his trouser pocket, turning away from me. I stood where I was. He seemed to be listening intently, but not speaking. Then he hung up and turned to me.

'The boys have found another body. It's looking like it might be the poor Vietnamese bastard. Face and head caved in. Fuck me!'

'Christ. That's awful. Poor guy.'

'Forensics are working on it,' he said. 'They found a mobile phone in his jacket pocket. Our language boys have translated a message from it. Says something like, "Arrived safe. In Scotland. Going to start work today." Fucking heart-breaking.' He shook his head. 'I'll need to move and get out there as soon as I can.'

'Christ almighty,' I said. 'Monsters.'

Once the cases had been packed and taken downstairs by the officers, Wilson followed them, leaving just Jackie and me in the flat, while her baby played on the floor.

'So this is it. This is really happening,' Jackie said, as she stood a little awkwardly glancing around the room. 'I'll never be able to thank you enough, Billie. Honestly.'

I made to shrug it off.

'It was a bit of a job all right,' I joked. 'But you know what, Jackie, when you came into my office that day, and told me what had happened, I knew I wouldn't be able to walk away.' I sighed. 'So I'm just hugely relieved it worked out for you and for everyone.'

She smiled. 'I'll miss this place. I-I'll miss you, Billie.'

I shook my head. 'Soon you'll have a completely new life, and you will be able to put this behind you for ever. You're very lucky to be able to do that.'

'I know,' she said, 'I am.' And the way she looked at me, it made me think that she knew something about my story. I brushed the idea away and changed the subject. This was her day, her happiness, her new life, her happy ending. All I could do was hope that one day it would be mine.

'You best be going,' I said. 'Don't keep the troops waiting.'

She nodded. 'Will I be able to keep in touch with you, maybe, just chat or something? I … I don't have any friends, I don't have anyone.' Her voice trailed off.

I grimaced a little.

'Probably best not to, Jackie,' I said. I could see this was hard for her. 'You'll make friends. And soon. The people around you will make sure of that, and before you know it you'll have a whole circle of friends. And Elena – she will take up so much of your time now. It's going to be great.'

She nodded and tightened her lips, then stepped forward and threw her arms around me. I could hear her sniffing on my shoulder and I held her tight because I didn't want to break away in case she saw the tears in my eyes. When we parted, I was able to put on a brave face.

'Go on then,' I said. 'Go and have a great life, Jackie.'

'I will,' she said. 'I'll never forget you. Never.'

And with that she picked up her baby, and turned towards the door. I watched her back as she went down the hall and the steps. Then I watched from the window as she climbed into the rear of the car with her child and sat as an officer buckled the kid into the seat. I watched as the car pulled away from the kerb and onto the street followed by the car behind, and as they began to get smaller in the distant gloom, my heart sank a little more.

I'd used much of the rest of the day keeping my head busy because I had to draw a line under Jackie Foster and move on. She was a client, that's all, I told myself. I'd managed to convince myself that by throwing everything at my next cases I'd feel better. By lunchtime back at the office, I'd had a conversation with the wife of the missing husband and arranged to meet her tomorrow. She told me she didn't want to come into the office and that she wanted to be more or less invisible. I didn't ask why. But I'd be asking a lot more questions once I got to see her. For the other couple of cases Millie had put on my desk, I contacted the people and said I'd take them on, but it would have to be in a few days. I knew a lot of them involved research that could be done on the internet and background checks, so

I'd gladly pass that to Tom Brodie to chase up. I made a mental note to call him tomorrow. By the time the mid-afternoon winter darkness crept across the sky, I told Millie to take an early cut and head home, and that I was going to do the same. She was glad of the break, she said, and when she left I sat in the office just listening to the silence. I wasn't ready to go home yet, I wanted to kind of debrief myself of the last couple of weeks. But more than anything I knew I was just killing time until the USA would be awake and alert enough for me to phone Dan Harris. I'd managed to get through my day without my gut churning too much in a mixture of dread and anticipation. The clock on my mobile screen said four, and I was about to pick it up and scroll down for Dan's name when it jangled to life. It was him. I answered immediately.

'Dan. I was just about to call.'

The silence on the other end was too long.

'You there?'

'Yes. I'm here, Billie. Listen. I . . . I need to tell you some news, but I want you to stay calm.'

'Dan. I don't do calm. Just tell me. Did you go? Did you find anything? Come on, man, I'm dying here.'

'Okay. But I need you to just hear me out. Okay?'

'I'm ready. I'm listening.'

'Okay. Well here's what happened. I got a call last night, after I talked to you, from the contact and he said he saw him again – Bob and your kid. I was on my way down from the airport in a hired car and all that shit, so I was driving. Then the line went dead. I tried to phone him back, but there was nothing. So I'm stuck in limbo, heading roughly in the direction of the area he told me about, but no idea of an address or whatever. I had a motel booked in the vicinity, but I needed this guy to meet me and actually take me to this trailer park. You with me?'

'Yes. Yes. Go on.'

'So I waited at the motel, kept calling the mobile and nothing. Then at about four this morning, just as I'd dropped off to sleep, the mobile rings and it's him. He asked me where I was and I told him I was at the motel I'd said I'd be in, and he said he was heading to get me right now. I asked him why, and he said he would tell me when he got there. He sounded a bit frantic. Then he hung up.'

He paused more for a breath than for me to talk. I was close to hyperventilating with stress, trying to picture where he was and how fast the scene was moving.

'Go on,' I said.

'Then he turns up in the parking lot at the motel and by this time I'm outside. He comes up to me and said we should go in his car, that it's not far. Then he says, "There's been a fire." '

My stomach dropped to the ground. I didn't know if I could actually stand to hear the rest of this, because I just knew that if he was telling me this in these staccato instalments it was because he didn't want to get to the end. I said nothing, barely breathing.

'You okay?'

'Go on.'

'By the time we get to the trailer park there's fire engines, cops, ambulances, the whole works, but we managed to get inside a little closer, and finally to the trailer.'

He stopped. I was holding the phone so tightly my knuckles were white and my hand was stiff. Then he went on.

'Billie, listen, kid. I don't know how to tell you this, but the trailer was in ruins. Burnt out. I don't know how it happened, but firemen were there, and … and … they brought a body out of the trailer.'

'A body?' My voice croaked. 'A body? Who? Who was it? Jesus, Dan! Whose body was it? Did you see?'

There was a silence so long I thought I was going to pass out. Then he spoke.

'I saw,' he said softly. 'Billie. It was Bob. I'm so sorry.'

The words bounced off my ears and my brain and echoed somewhere in my head and I could see the man on the stretcher, the man I'd fallen for, the man who betrayed me and stole my baby. My chest was bursting and I could barely breathe.

'Dan. What … what about Lucas?' I could hardly get the words out. I was afraid to ask.

'He wasn't there, Billie.'

'What do you mean he wasn't there? How?'

'I talked to the fire chief and they'd been through the place or what was left of it, but there was no sign of a kid, they said. Nothing.'

'So where is he? Where's my son?'

After a long pause, Dan spoke. 'I don't know, Billie. But Lucas wasn't in the fire. So he's out there.'

'Where? What do you mean he's out there? Where?'

'I don't know, Billie. I'm sorry.'

I sat looking at the phone, waiting for the next part, for some kind of answer, some kind of hope that my Lucas was not out there all alone in a trailer park or on a highway, or taken by some stranger. But the answer didn't come. My throat was so tight I couldn't get the words out. But Lucas was out there.

'Billie, listen to me, kid. We'll find him. I promise.'

I nodded as though we were sitting in the same room, and then tears of relief came. Lucas was alive.

ACKNOWLEDGEMENTS

If the last two years have taught us anything it is to make every moment count and cherish everyone around us.

There are so many people I want to thank who truly enrich my life. Firstly, my sister Sadie, my greatest friend and the most generous person I know. Also her family, Katrina, Matthew and Christopher, who listen to my ideas, and often that's where my novels begin. And their spouses, Iain, Katie and Laura.

Also their beautiful children, the bright future that is Jude and Max, Cillian and Ruairi. And Maisie Islay, the latest delightful addition who has brought such joy to all our lives after losing her sister Eilidh.

I also want to thank the friends who have been there for me since the start of this journey. Mags, Eileen, Annie, Mary, Phil, Liz, cousins Annmarie, Anne, and Alice and Debbie in London. And my cousins Helen and Irene.

My old journalist pals from back in the good days – Simon

and Lynn, Mark, Annie, Keith and Maureen. And the cherished veteran hacks, Brian, Gordon, Ian, David, Jimmy, Tom, Bill and Brian. And to Tom Brown and Marie who have always had such faith in me.

Thanks also to my cousins the mighty Motherwell Smiths, and the Timmons family for their support.

And my good friends back in the wild west – Mary and Paud, Sioban and Martin, Sean Brendain. I'm grateful and blessed to have such wonderful people around me.

At Quercus, thanks to my editor Jane Wood, for being the brilliant inspiration she is and Florence Hare for such a good edit and advice on this novel. And all the team at Quercus who push and promote my books.

And last, but not least, the growing army of readers who enjoy my books and take the time to tell me. Thank you. Without you, I wouldn't be writing this.